A green-and-white t... of the diagonal parki... garishly off the grinnin... blue and white on the fr... ...ened the door and stood up. I hu...ied around the hybrid to greet him.

"Is something wrong? Somebody didn't break into the store, did they?"

"I need to know where you were at this afternoon and evening, Ms. Jordan."

"Why?"

Jim strode up. "What's going on? Was there an accident?"

"You might say that. Robbie?"

"I was cleaning here from the end of the lunch crowd pretty much until Jim picked me up for dinner at seven."

"What time did the last customer leave?" Buc...

"Around two-thirty. I sent Adele and Phil h... three."

Buck turned to Jim. "You can vouch for her wh... abouts from seven o'clock until now?"

"I can." Jim frowned. "Tell us what happened."

Buck let out a mournful sigh. "Stella Rogers's son Roy found her dead in her house tonight."

"What does her death have to do with me?" I heard my voice rise and swallowed hard.

"She did not die of natural causes," Buck said.

"Oh, no. That's awful," I said.

"Do you mean she was murdered?" Jim's voice came out low and slow.

"Yup. And then somebody stuffed a cheesy biscuit in her mouth."

Buck stared at me.

A cheesy biscuit. One of *my* cheesy biscuits . . .

Flipped
for Murder

Maddie Day

KENSINGTON PUBLISHING CORP.
http://www.kensingtonbooks.com

KENSINGTON BOOKS are published by

Kensington Publishing Corp.
119 West 40th Street
New York, NY 10018

All Kensington Titles, Imprints, and Distributed Lines are available at special quantity discounts for bulk purchases for sales promotions, premiums, fund-raising, and educational or institutional use. Special book excerpts or customized printings can also be created to fit specific needs. For details, write or phone the office of the Kensington special sales manager: Kensington Publishing Corp., 119 West 40th Street, New York, NY 10018, attn: Special Sales Department, Phone: 1-800-221-2647.

Kensington and the K logo Reg. U.S. Pat & TM Off.

ISBN-13: 978-1-61773-925-5
ISBN-10: 1-61773-925-5
First Kensington Mass Market Edition: November 2015

eISBN-13: 978-1-61773-926-2
eISBN-10: 1-61773-926-X
First Kensington Electronic Edition: November 2015

10 9 8 7 6 5 4 3 2 1

Printed in the United States of America

For my Bloomington partners in crime, 1977–1981:
Bobbi, Cindi, Janet, Jennifer, Katherine, Marios.
What a stimulating and glorious time it was.

Acknowledgments

Many thanks to John Talbot for getting excited about a series set in southern Indiana, and to the Kensington Publishing crew for sending me on this new cozy mystery venture. To Cindy Shultz and Benjamin for renovating the store in Story, Indiana, so long ago and giving me not only the idea seed for this series but also the practice of making whole wheat banana walnut pancakes. To Rick Hofstetter and Jane Ammeson for talking with me about the current Story Inn, on which I roughly modeled the interior of Pans 'N Pancakes, letting me take as many pictures as I wanted, and for their book, *Images of America: Brown County.*

I'm much indebted to Indiana University linguists Robert Botne, Dan Dinnsen, Judy Gierut, Diane Kewley-Port, and Robert Port, friends all, for help with matters of southern Indiana dialect. Any going overboard with colorful phrases is entirely of my own doing. My sister Barbara Bergendorf, a more northern Hoosier, was wonderful company and a source of much local information on my Midwestern research trip during the writing of this book. Officer Garnet Watson helped out with a few questions of police procedure, which I might not always have followed, and Dave DeCaro allowed me to use his blog detail and photograph of the Elite Club mosaic and alarm button.

I cite Maryann Kovalski's vivid and wonderful tale of a dream gone bad, *Frank and Zelda*. My friend, author, and investigative reporter Hank Phillippi Ryan unknowingly gave me the idea for the awful Sunday morning discovery near the end of the book. My son JD Hutchison-Maxwell helped out with cycling knowledge in this book. Thanks, all.

Books like this do not get done without the help of writer friends. Sherry Harris once again ably gave me editorial feedback before I turned in the manuscript. Sherry and the other Wicked Cozy Authors—Jessie Crockett (aka Jessica Estevao), Julie Hennrikus (aka Julianne Holmes), Liz Mugavero (aka Cate Conte), and Barbara Ross—are my lifeboat. Thanks, dears. Longtime mentor and author friend Kate Flora allowed me to spend four glorious solitary days in her Maine cottage as I revised the story. And Sisters in Crime—national, New England chapter, and Guppies—you're the best.

As always, my deep love and grateful thanks to my family. You know who you are.

Readers: a positive review of a book you read goes a long way to helping the author. Please consider posting your opinion on Amazon, Goodreads, Facebook, and elsewhere if you liked my story (and check out my other author names: Edith Maxwell and Tace Baker).

Chapter 1

My heart beat something fierce as the bell on the door jangled. It was make-or-break time. I'd been preparing for this day for weeks. I thought I was ready, but if I slipped up, I'd be in major hot water. Or financial ruin, as the case may be.

My first customer at Pans 'N Pancakes turned out to be Corrine Beedle, the new mayor of South Lick, Indiana, all five foot eleven and layered flaming hair of her. She sailed through the door like she owned the store. My country store and restaurant, that is. I'd seen her around town during the last month since she'd won the September election, but we hadn't actually met, and paying attention to a local race had been below the bottom of my infinitely long to-do list.

Her unpleasant assistant, whom I had met many times, followed, looking slightly disgusted with the world as usual. Stella Rogers's puffy upper eyelids and upturned nose gave her an unfortunate resemblance to the porcine genus.

"Welcome to Pans 'N Pancakes." Striding toward them, smoothing my blue-and-white striped apron, I hoped my smile wasn't slipping from nervousness. I pulled out a chair at a table for two. "Thank you for coming to our grand opening."

"Co-rrine Beedle." The mayor, emphasizing the *"Co"* as much as the *"reen,"* gave me a direct look and a wide smile as she pumped my hand. "Mayor of South Lick."

I extricated my hand while I still had feeling in it. "Robbie Jordan. Owner, proprietor, and head cook. Well, the only cook, normally." I gestured to the eight-burner industrial stove and griddle behind the counter, where my aunt Adele was aproned up and tending a dozen sizzling sausages.

"Glad to have a woman business owner in town," the mayor said, beaming.

"I'm happy to be here. And it's very nice to meet you, Madam Mayor."

"Oh, hogwash." She slid into the seat, her bony knee slipping out of the slit in the skirt of her red suit as she crossed one leg over the other. Her black-and-white heels looked about four inches high and a red-shellacked big toenail peeked out of the cutout in each shoe. "Just call me Corrine, honey."

I'd lived in the hill country of southern Indiana for more than three years now, and I still wasn't used to nearly every female older than my twenty-seven years calling me "honey."

"Got it, Corrine." I glanced at her aide, whose position as mayor's assistant seemed to be permanent. Corrine must have inherited Stella, because I'd had to work with her over the past six months when I was applying for my building permit and other permissions so I could fix up the 150-year-old store. I greeted her, too.

"Congratulations on finally getting open, Robbie. It's very quaint." Stella did not look like she meant any of it—except the dig about how long it had taken me to renovate the place.

Sure, it was quaint. I'd been aiming for an amalgam of what I hoped was everybody's dream, because it sure was mine: a warm, welcoming country store, a cozy breakfast-and-lunch place, and a treasure trove of antique cookware. The last was my particular passion, the vintage cookware lining the walls and several rows of shelves. I'd even hired a guy to restore the pot-bellied stove, fantasizing that a core group of locals might make this their meeting place, drinking coffee, exchanging yarns, offering advice. I'd worked my fingers off, and my butt, too, to get the place ready for today. My mom hadn't taught me fine cabinetry for nothing. I'd sawed and sanded, measured and nailed, painted and polished, until I could turn the sign on my dream to OPEN.

My friend Phil—short for Philostrate—sauntered up, also clad in a store apron, and laid two menus on Corrine and Stella's table. A bright blue shirt set off his deep brown skin and startling blue eyes. He'd volunteered to help today, which I'd gratefully accepted. I'd hired a waitperson, but she'd quit on me last week before we even opened, so Phil was saving my bacon today, quite literally.

"My name's Phil and I'll be your server this morning," he announced with a flash of a smile. "Coffee?"

"Good to see you again, Phil. I'd love some." Corrine smiled right back.

"Hot tea for me," Stella said with a sniff.

Phil winked at her and whipped a camera out of his

apron pocket. *Who winks at Stella?* I'd have to ask him how he knew her.

"Picture of the new proprietor with the new mayor?" he asked.

"Of course." Corrine stood again and put her arm around my shoulders.

I stood up as tall as I could and the top of my head still didn't even reach the mayor's chin. I slapped a confident smile on my face before he shot us.

"One more in case you blinked," he said, so we held our pose a little longer.

"You can start one of those series of framed pictures on the wall, Robbie. You with all the celebrities who are sure to pass through," Corrine said.

"Great idea," Phil said, heading back toward the kitchen area.

Adele waved at me. "Ready for bacon," she called.

"Enjoy your meal, ladies. Excuse me." I hurried to my refurbished walk-in cooler and brought two pounds of bacon to the stove. "How's it going?"

"Fine, of course. Don't you be worrying, Roberta. Everything's running like a well-oiled tractor." My mom's eldest sister, the only person I allowed to call me by my legal name, wore a blue baseball cap with the store's logo over her short gray pageboy. The logo, which the ever-talented Phil had designed, showed a cast-iron griddle held by a grinning stack of pancakes.

Of course I was worried. I had a lot riding on this venture, which was the result of both saving my chef's salary for three years and inheriting the proceeds from Mom's business after her sudden death last winter at her shop in California. To soothe my nerves,

I inhaled the tantalizing aromas of warm maple syrup, savory sausages, cheesy biscuits, and my two kinds of gravy: meat, and vegetarian, made with a secret ingredient.

The cowbell on the door rang again, a bell I'd hung from a little cast-iron hand and muscled forearm. I turned to see a crowd of older women bustle in. Four of them wore hair either snow white or salt-and-pepper, with the rest dyed shades of brownish red. Instead of turning into the restaurant area to their left, they beelined it for the cookware section. They exclaimed and pointed and nudged each other. As two men came in and seated themselves for breakfast, I smiled and moved toward the ladies.

"Good morning. I'm Robbie Jordan, and this is my store. You've found us on our grand-opening day. It looks like you're interested in cookware."

"Oh, yes," one of the white-haired women said, nodding. "We're an antiquing club from Indy, but what we really like is cookware."

"Then we have something in common," I said. "Browse as much as you'd like."

"I'm Vera, Vera Skinner," the woman said. The skin of her lined face looked as soft as brown sugar and her light brown eyes smiled at me. She wore a green-and-blue embroidered jacket with little inset mirrors, which looked like it came straight out of India or Morocco or somewhere. Not that I'd been anywhere near that part of the world myself, but a girl could dream.

"Happy to meet you, Vera. Everything except the top row on the wall is for sale. And we serve a delicious breakfast, too, if you're hungry."

"We came for cookware and breakfast after we saw the notice in the paper. Plus looking at the leaves, of course."

"They're pretty spectacular this fall, aren't they?"

Vera agreed as she extended her hand. "So nice to make your acquaintance, Robbie. Hmm. Jordan. I used to know a . . ." Her eyes strayed beyond me. "Bless my soul. Is that Adele? Yoo-hoo, Addie!" she called, waving.

Addie? I'd never heard my aunt called anything but Adele, Ms. Jordan, Madam Mayor, or Chief. She'd held a couple of influential positions in town, including head of the on-call firefighters.

Adele stuck both hands on her hips and let out a cry that sounded something like, "Sue-EE."

Vera snorted and headed toward Adele. "We called pigs together as girls," she added over her shoulder. "Haven't seen her in a couple-three decades."

Adele had never mentioned Vera, but I liked what I saw of her. *So many older women to learn from, so little time.*

I left the ladies to shop and headed toward the door to resume my meet and greet. The place hummed. A middle-aged man with a pained expression on his face and an unsuccessful comb-over pushed through the doorway, followed by a ruddy-complexioned guy of about the same age. The first one looked vaguely familiar.

"Don, just relax." The second man reached for his friend's arm. "She was elected fair and square. You gotta let it go."

The other man shrugged off the arm. "It wasn't neither fair or square."

I opened my mouth to greet them when the one called Don got his eyeballs on Corrine and about blew a gasket. He turned on his heel.

"I don't have to sit here and look at that bi . . . that woman lording it over this town like she was some kind of queen bee," he sputtered.

"Yes, you do. Peace among us, that's what the Bible says." The ruddy-faced man nudged Don back toward an open table.

"She cheated me of the election, and you know it. And that Stella helped her." He spit out Stella's name like it was an insult.

That's where I recognized Don from. I'd seen his face on campaign signs around town, although his thin dark hair had been better arranged in the pictures. I cleared my throat. Ruddy Face whipped his head over to look at me so fast I thought it would go sailing across the room. He cast me the narrow-eyed gaze a tennis champ gives while waiting for a serve from a worthy opponent. Then he plastered on a crooked-tooth smile.

"Ah, Ms. Jordan, the younger. Ed Kowalski, of Kowalski's Country Store." He tipped his Colts cap, but didn't proffer a hand.

"Welcome to Pans 'N Pancakes, Ed." I smiled at the man I now realized was my biggest competitor. I knew Kowalski's did a busy breakfast-and-lunch trade. But it was five miles away in the county seat of Nashville— Nashville, Indiana, that is—and I knew my store and restaurant projected a far different image than his.

"And this is?" I gestured at his companion, who still scowled in Corrine's general direction.

The man tore his gaze away from Corrine and Stella. "Don O'Neill. The once and almost mayor of this fair town." Looking at me, his brown eyes were kind, but they held a worried look around their edges. He surveyed the store and looked back at me with new interest. "Looks nice in here. You did a good job."

"Thank you. Nice to meet you, Don."

"I saw all the work going on. Should have stopped in. Who was your carpenter?" he asked.

"Me." I gave a little laugh. "My mom taught me all I know."

"Jordan." Don peered at me, and it turned into a long stare. "Hold on. Are you saying you're Jeanine's girl?"

"I am, her one and only." I didn't add, *"And she was my only parent."*

"Boy, howdy." He kept gazing at me with an odd look on his face. "You don't look much like her, except for how short you are."

I shrugged. "Genes are a funny thing, aren't they?"

"Jeannie and I used to . . . Well, we were friends. How is she, anyway?" Don cocked his head.

I swallowed. No way to sugarcoat it. "My mom passed away last January."

"I am so sorry to hear that. I truly am." He reached out and patted my arm. "I run Shamrock Hardware here in town. You need anything, you ask for me personally."

"Thanks. I've shopped there a number of times. The store is well stocked." I led them to an empty table and waited until they sat. "Now, what can I get you gentlemen for breakfast today?" I poised my pen above the Pans 'N Pancakes order pad I held in my other hand.

After I took their order—a stack of whole wheat banana walnut pancakes for Don; biscuits, gravy, and two eggs over easy for Ed—I wove through busy tables to the grill area, passing Corrine's table. Chin in the air, she gave a parade princess wave in Don's direction. I could almost smell the smoke coming out of his ears.

Chapter 2

By ten-thirty the breakfast rush was easing up. Only two older gentlemen remained, nursing their coffees and playing chess on the board I'd painted on one of the square tables. It was exactly the kind of scene I'd hoped would take place in my little establishment.

Adele and I pulled up chairs at a table near the grill area and nibbled at a few odds and ends of cooked ham, a misshapen biscuit, a couple of twice-warmed pancakes. Phil belted out a gospel tune from the sink, where he cleaned up pots and pans. I needed to get lunch prep going soon, but it was good to get off my feet for a few minutes.

"Stella was as unpleasant as always," I said, "but she did buy a sack of biscuits to take home." I leaned back and resecured my ponytail with a hair tie in the store blue. Owning a mass of curly hair was a pain sometimes, but I loved the feeling of it loose on my bare shoulders at night, so I kept it long.

"No telling with her. She might even have a heart under all that armor."

"Thanks for all your help, Adele. I'll owe you for all eternity."

She lifted her right eyebrow. "Don't be silly. You know I want this place to be a big success. Anything I can do."

My owning the store was Adele's doing. My mom's elder sister and only sibling knew about my passion for all manner of old cooking implements and had brought me to look at the store's vintage cookware collection to help ease the pain of my mom's death. When we discovered the place was for sale—lock, stock, and barrel—I took the plunge, with her blessing.

The bell on the door rang as Buck Bird, second in command in our local police force, ambled in, followed by Jim Shermer, my real estate lawyer. A cute one, too.

"Jim, Officer Bird. Join us?" I waved at them.

Buck Bird slid into the chair opposite us and laid his uniform hat in his lap. The guy had the skinniest, longest fingers I'd ever seen. They matched the rest of him, from his elongated face to feet that just kept on giving. His sandy hair stuck up like he'd just gotten out of bed before he used those serpentine fingers to snake it back into place. Jim was of a more normal height. His dark red hair curled around his ears and set off brilliant green eyes that could pass as jewels. His Saturday attire of a crisp white shirt tucked into faded jeans made him look as good to eat as one of my pancakes. He sat between Buck and me and I could smell his clean rainwater scent waft through the lingering aroma of bacon and flapjacks.

"Sure smells good in here," Buck drawled in the local way, sounding like his tongue was glued to the bottom of his mouth. "How'd the grand op'nin' go?"

"It's still going. All day long, in fact. We had a busy breakfast rush and are hoping for the same at lunchtime. What can we get you?" I figured he had a serious hollow leg, being so skinny and all.

"Oh, it don't matter. One of everything?" He raised his eyebrows in a hopeful look.

"You got it. How about you, Jim?"

"I'll take a couple biscuits with the miso gravy, and hot herbal tea, please."

"Side of bacon with that?" I snickered at his alarmed look and headed for the grill. Jim was a vegetarian and had convinced me to offer a nonmeat gravy for the likes of him. Plus the herbal tea, which mostly tasted like warmed-up grass, in my opinion.

I brought their orders back a few minutes later, unloading a stack of cakes, with biscuits, ham, and an apple muffin on the side for Buck, plus Jim's order.

"Her Honor, the mayor, was in earlier, and then Don O'Neill. He seemed to think he should have been elected instead of her. What's up with that?" I leaned against the edge of the next table and folded my arms.

Adele and Buck exchanged a look. "It was all fair and square," Adele said. "I worked as a poll watcher. Corrine won by only three votes. Don demanded a recount and that resulted in her getting two more votes. A close result, but a real one."

"They have some kind of past. Not quite sure what went on, but . . ." Buck shrugged and forked up a huge mouthful of pancakes. A slice of banana dropped off into the golden brown pool of syrup on his plate.

"He was mayor for three terms before. Town elected him right after I decided not to run again. He kinda figures the position belongs to him." Adele stood. "I've got to go let the sheep out, Roberta. Left the house too early this morning. But I'll come back in an hour to help with lunch. You're doing great so far." She patted me on the shoulder, tossed her apron on the chair, and aimed her no-nonsense stride for the door.

"I'll say you're doing great." Jim wiped his plate with a last piece of biscuit and popped it in his mouth. When a spot of gravy marred the pristine white of his shirt, he swiped at it with his blue cloth napkin.

"Was Stella here with Mayor Corrine?" Buck asked.

"She was. Why would she be working on a Saturday?" I cocked my head.

"Could be Corrine said this was an official event. Could be Stella wanted to come along. Stella pretty much gets what she wants."

"Not here, she didn't." I slid into Adele's seat.

"What do you mean?" Buck asked.

"She tried to stymie Robbie at every turn in the permitting process," Jim chimed in. "I heard she wanted her son to take over the store. We really had to fight her just to follow legal procedure."

Buck pursed his lips and nodded like he was filing the information for future use.

"Stella was part of the reason I didn't go ahead with developing the upstairs at the same time as this space." I frowned. "I want to create bed-and-breakfast rooms up there, but Stella made it so hard just to get the permits for the restaurant that I gave up. For now, anyway."

Jim finished his tea. "Best breakfast I've eaten in years. You're going to draw all Ed's customers away."

I wrinkled my nose. "I don't mean to do that.

Although when he was in earlier, he gave me some kind of look, like we were in a high-stakes tennis match or something. Maybe losing business is what he's afraid of."

"Wouldn't be surprised. He's been the only country store in Brown County for twenty-odd years, and only a few other places serve breakfast in Nashville," Buck said.

"I wonder how I never met him before today, since I worked in Nashville for three years. I guess because I didn't eat at his restaurant," I said.

"I bet he buys his hash browns frozen, and his meat patties, too." Jim sat back in his chair.

"I sure don't. But that reminds me I need to get started on making up my own patties for lunch. Don't worry," I said, glancing at Jim, "veggie burgers are on the menu."

Buck opened his mouth, but I held up a hand. "And beef and turkey burgers from Kiss My Grass Farm, Buck, so you'll have something to eat, too." Jim wasn't the only one who had cleaned his plate, but Buck still sported a somehow hungry look as he smiled at me. "Plus organic hot dogs, house-made sauerkraut and coleslaw, and fresh hand-cut fries, of course. Phil signed on as cookie and brownie chef, and you'll definitely want to sample those."

"Good to know. Good to know," Buck said. "Guess I'll be back in a couple hours for lunch, then."

I dug both their checks out of my pocket and handed them over.

As Buck unfolded himself from his chair, Jim looked up at me with somewhat more color than usual in his freckled cheeks. "If you're not too tired, can I take you out for dinner tonight? To celebrate all this?"

Whoa. A date? With Jim? I hadn't dated in nearly four years, since my rotten now-ex-husband had thrown me over for a curvy air force fighter pilot. I looked into those green eyes, whose gorgeous color was not dimmed by the black-rimmed glasses he wore. Could be interesting.

Buck cleared his throat and steered the brim of his hat through his fingers. "Sorry to interrupt your social arrangements. Just wanted to say thanks, and let you know I'm glad you're here in town, Robbie. This place will be good for all of us." He plopped several bills on the table and his hat on his head before he ambled back to the door.

I called a rather stunned "thanks" after him as I nodded at Jim. "Dinner sounds fun. Do I need to dress up?"

He laughed, a husky sound that came from his throat, the sexiest noise I'd heard in a long time. "You might want to ditch the apron. But no, we'll head out to the roadhouse. Pretty informal. They have line dancing if you like that kind of thing, too."

A dancing date. I never got enough dancing. This evening was sounding better and better.

I surveyed the platter the waiter set in front of me at the Hickory Hoosier roadhouse. "This is enormous." A dozen ribs oozing with sauce vied for space with corn bread, baked beans, and a little dish of coleslaw. "I'll never be able to finish it." I picked up a rib with both hands and nibbled off a few bites of the most tender meat I'd ever eaten, leaning over my plate in hopes I could keep the reddish brown sauce off my white top.

Jim laughed. "And I'm not helping you, either." He gestured to his own large serving of fish and chips. He raised his pint glass of beer. "Here's to a successful country store."

"Absolutely. Thanks." I hastily wiped my hands on the stack of paper napkins the waiter had kindly left and picked up my own glass of Cutters Half Court IPA. After we clinked drinks, I took a sip.

"This is good," I said, licking the foam off my lip. "Great hops. What did you get?"

"The Lost River summer ale. Glad they still have it halfway into October."

I drank again, and then dove back into the ribs. *Maybe the chef would share his recipe? Unlikely.* I rolled the sauce around on my tongue, tasting a hint of maple, maybe a bit of hot pepper, certainly tomato, possibly balsamic vinegar. I'd have to see if I could re-create it. I glanced up to see Jim smiling at me.

"You enjoy your food." He set his chin on his right hand and slowly stroked the moisture on his ale glass with one finger of his left as he watched me.

I swallowed to push down the lust he ignited. "I'd be a lot slimmer if I didn't, but hey." I tended toward the pleasantly plump end of the scale. I knew I was healthy and fit, though, and accepted that at five foot three, food didn't have too far to travel before it settled onto my hearty hips. I got out on my bike and rode a few dozen hilly miles regularly, and the hundred sit-ups I did every morning meant at least I had a waist.

"Who needs slim?" He raised one eyebrow and put his attention back on his fish.

"You're slim. What do you do to stay that way? Run marathons or something?"

"I go dancing every chance I get." He swirled a French fry in a little paper tub of ketchup.

"Really?" This was getting interesting. "What kind of dancing?"

"Everything. Line dancing, contra, West Coast swing, ballroom, Latin. Used to even go to international folk dancing over in Bloomington."

"At IU?" The huge flagship campus of the state university was only fifteen miles away.

"Correct." He lifted his glass and sat back. "So congratulations again on the store being up and running. You're going to be a big success."

I clinked my glass with his and took a sip. "Thank you. I have a pretty good feeling about the whole thing. Never could have pulled it all together without your help, though."

He air-batted away the compliment. "Just did my job. Stella was quite the opponent for a while there, wasn't she?" He pushed his glasses up from where they'd slid down his nose.

"I'll say. You'd think somebody who works in government might pay more attention to process."

"She's held that job way too long. Nobody dares give her the boot, though." Jim glanced at the stage, where two men in cowboy shirts and hats were picking up guitars. A woman in a hot pink denim skirt lifted a fiddle to her chin, and another one in black jeans with a matching cowboy hat settled into the drum set. "Here comes the music."

"I don't know how good I am at following. I love to dance, but mostly it's just been, you know, moving around kind of free style."

"I'll show you, Robbie. Don't worry."

After we finished eating, we joined the line dance, making me glad I'd worn a flared skirt and my turquoise cowgirl boots. And when the dance turned to West Coast swing, Jim led me through the moves in the most delightful of ways.

Chapter 3

I yawned as Jim piloted us back to my apartment behind the store. His Prius dashboard readout put the time close to eleven-thirty. He glanced over at me.

"Boring you, am I?"

"Of course not!"

He snorted. "I'm kidding you, Robbie." His voice quieted. "But I only kid people I like."

I let his comment hang in the air. I was too tired to see it and raise it one. And I wasn't quite sure of my feelings yet, anyway. We'd had a friendly business relationship until now, but this evening had upped the ante. I settled for: "Tonight was really fun. But I had a pretty long day, as you know. And I get to wake up bright and early tomorrow and do it all over again."

"I don't envy you your schedule," Jim said with a chuckle. "Me, I like to sleep in on Sundays."

I watched as we turned onto South Lick Road and rolled quietly through town, past Shamrock Hardware and First Savings Bank, both housed in Art Deco–era buildings from almost a hundred years earlier with symmetrical stacks of geometric forms. We passed the ornate gazebo labeled JUPITER, which had been a sulfur spring in the 1800s. The town had been famous for its spas, and Adele had told me Jupiter Water was sold as a laxative nationwide up until about 1950. When we turned onto Walnut, I saw Bill's Barbershop and Play It Again Consignment, where I'd purchased the very boots I now wore, and hadn't paid much at all for them.

"I live upstairs, right there," Jim said, pointing at the consignment store, which was also in an Art Deco–style building, with a rounded limestone corner and a pyramid-shaped cap in the middle.

"Really?"

"Third-floor condo. It's nice. Mine faces the back, so it's quiet, and I have a view of the creek, which runs right behind. Perfect for a bachelor gentleman." He grinned.

"If it's perfect for you, then that's all that counts. You know, I was thinking," I said, turning in my seat to face him, "getting to today was really just a big puzzle, and I love puzzles. Figuring out what I needed to do and putting it together. I worked hard, but I enjoyed the process." I tucked one foot under me. "I won a state crossword puzzle championship when I was in high school in Santa Barbara."

"I'm not surprised." Keeping his eyes on the road, he turned right onto Main Street, then reached over and laid his smooth, slender hand on top of mine. "You're a remarkable woman, Robbie," he said with a voice turned husky.

His touch sent a zing through me like the most pleasant of electric shocks and I wanted to hear that husky voice a lot closer. I'd opened my mouth to reply when he pulled up to my store.

"Uh-oh," I whispered instead. A green-and-white town police car sat idling in one of the diagonal parking spots, its lights reflecting garishly off the grinning stack of pancakes painted in blue and white on the front window. Buck's hair brushed the illuminated dome light inside the vehicle. He opened the door and stood up, up, up. I got out, too, and hurried around the hybrid to greet him.

"Is something wrong? Somebody didn't break into the store, did they?" My heart thudded like the bass drum in the band at the roadhouse.

"I need to know where you were at this afternoon and evening, Ms. Jordan." Buck hooked his thumbs through the front of his wide belt sporting all kinds of attachments.

I'm Ms. Jordan all of a sudden? "Why?" I craned my neck to span the foot-long distance between my eyes and his.

"Please answer me."

Jim strode up. "What's going on? Was there an accident?"

"You might say that. Robbie?"

"I was cleaning here from the end of the lunch crowd pretty much until Jim picked me up for dinner at seven." I shivered. My little black sweater wasn't enough to keep off the chill of the fall night, but I pulled it together at my throat for a bit more warmth. And comfort.

"What time did the last customer leave?" Buck asked.

"Around two-thirty. I sent Adele and Phil home at three."

Buck turned to Jim. "You can vouch for her whereabouts from seven o'clock until now?"

"I can." Jim frowned. "Tell us what happened. And your reason for asking Robbie where she was." He moved closer until his arm touched mine.

Buck let out a mournful sigh. "Stella Rogers's son, Roy, found his mother dead in her house tonight."

"Poor Stella. But what does her death have to do with me?" I heard my voice rise and swallowed hard.

"She did not die of natural causes," Buck said.

"Oh, no. That's awful," I said.

"Do you mean she was murdered?" Jim's voice came out low and slow.

"Yup. And then somebody stuffed a cheesy biscuit in her mouth." Buck stared at me.

A cheesy biscuit? One of my *cheesy biscuits? Damn. Double damn.*

Chapter 4

I busied myself making a pot of coffee a few minutes later, keeping my back to Buck and Jim at the table behind me. I'd insisted we talk inside. The image of Stella, dead with a biscuit in her mouth, filled my brain until I thought it would explode. Me, I didn't want coffee. My bottle of Four Roses Kentucky bourbon was calling out like an across-the-border siren. I slid it out of my private cabinet and measured a shot into a mug before I poured coffee for Buck.

"Tea, Jim?" I asked, setting Buck's mug down in front of him, managing not to trip on his stretched-out legs.

Jim shook his head. "Got anything stronger?"

Those green eyes were going to be my undoing, I could tell. Even took my mind off murder for a second.

"Sure. You can have what I'm having." I set the bottle and the shot glass on the table with another thick blue mug and joined the men, collapsing into a chair. "All right, Buck. Now I'm ready." I sipped the bourbon, which went down like a silky ribbon of warmth.

Buck rubbed the top of his head, which only made his hair resemble the locks of a cartoon character who had just stuck his finger in an electric socket. That is, more than it already had. A tablet device lay on the table in front of him.

"I know you had several disagreements with Stella," he began. "And I have to look at anybody who might coulda killed her."

Jim hoisted the bourbon bottle and poured a bit into his mug. I sampled my own drink again.

Jim gazed at Buck. "Do you have any evidence to link Robbie with the killing?"

"How could he?" I heard my voice rising.

"I'm a lawyer, Robbie. Let me ask the questions, okay?" Jim looked encouragingly at me and nodded in that way people did when they wanted you to nod back.

"No evidence to speak of. So far, anyway." Buck stared at the ceiling. "But it appears Robbie did have motive. You know, a reason to do away with Stella."

"I know what 'motive' means." I took another sip, set the mug down, and folded my arms. "Why in blazes would I want to jeopardize all this"—I opened my arms to encompass my store—"when I just this week finished the renovations and opened my new restaurant? Sure, Stella was difficult over the last year, but I'm looking forward, not back."

Buck looked straight at me and used his serious police voice. "I'm going to ask you again. Where were you at between three o'clock and seven o'clock tonight, Roberta Jordan?"

I swallowed. "I told you. I was here in the store, and

then in my apartment in the back." I'd watched enough TV shows to know the drill. "I didn't leave. I was alone. I didn't talk to anyone." I was innocent. They had to figure that out sooner or later. The former, I hoped.

Buck used his left index finger to type laboriously onto the virtual keyboard of the device.

"How was Stella killed?" Jim asked.

"Just a sec." Buck held up his right hand until he finished typing what was presumably my answer, then looked at Jim. "I can't share the method of death at this time," he said in a sorrowful tone, as if he would share if only he could. He stared at me for a beat. "Did you kill Stella Rogers?"

"No! There's gotta be other people in town who'd just as soon Stella disappeared," I said. "Right? She wasn't a very nice person. God rest her soul," I hastily added, even though I was about as unreligious as they came.

Jim took a sip of his drink. He set the mug down and folded his forearms on the table, narrowing his eyes. "What about Ed Kowalski? Robbie's his newest and only competitor."

"But why kill Stella to get at me?" I copied his arms and attentive gaze until I realized what I'd done, then unfolded my arms and sat back in my chair. "That seems crazy."

"If it was staged to make Buck here think you killed Stella, you'd be out of business," Jim said. "Hard to make pancakes from jail."

Buck let out a low whistle and nodded his head so slowly I wondered if he was falling asleep.

"Coulda happ'ned. Coulda indeed."

He kept his gaze somewhere near the ceiling so

long I looked, too. Had I missed painting a section, or was a bat roosting up there? I didn't see anything out of place.

I thought of something. "Where's Stella's house? My Dodge van was here all day, parked around the side like always. Somebody must have seen it, walking or driving by."

Buck shook his head real slow. "She lived three blocks down and one over. On Beanblossom Road. You coulda walked. Or ridden that bicycle of yours."

"Rats." I glanced at Jim, who raised his eyebrows and shrugged as if to say, *"Good try."*

When something started buzzing, Buck retrieved a big old cell phone out of a case clipped onto his wide belt and flipped it open with all the flair of the pre-smartphone days.

"Yup." Buck listened and sat up straight. "Yes, sir." He flipped it shut and stood. "Gotta go. Chief says to ask you to stick around town, Robbie. If you'd be so kind."

I rolled my eyes. "Like I'm going anywhere." I watched Buck amble out; the bell on the door tolled his departure. I turned back to Jim, who stared at me, chin in hand, looking a little bit inscrutable.

"What?" I asked. I took another sip of bourbon.

"I was just thinking this changes the picture."

"What picture?" Was he talking about him and me, that picture?

"I hope being a person of interest in a murder investigation doesn't jeopardize your brand-new business here."

Oh. "Ya think?" I shook my head. "I had such a good first day, too. Now folks might not want to eat breakfast cooked by a killer. Well, I didn't murder anybody. And they're going to figure that out sooner or later." I stretched my arms to the ceiling, and then let them collapse at my sides. I was out of fuel, as drained as a gas tank running on fumes. I closed my eyes for a second, then opened them when I heard Jim's chair scrape the floor.

"I'll let you get your beauty sleep," he said as he stood.

"Ha," I said, also rising. "All six hours of it." I walked him to the door. The electricity of the moment in the car had vanished with the pronouncement of murder, and I wondered if it would ever come back.

With his hand on the door handle, he looked at me with a somber face. "Thanks for coming out with me."

"I should thank you. I enjoyed getting to know you beyond the world of real estate law, and the dancing . . . well, that was great."

A smile spread across his face. "It was, wasn't it?"

On an impulse, I stretched up and planted a kiss on his cheek. "Let's do it again sometime." I stepped back before things got carried away.

Despite how tired I was, I took the time to clean out the coffeepot, set up the regular coffee and the decaf for the morning, and make sure all was clean and ready for what I hoped would be another breakfast rush. My brain was rushing along like the *Wabash Cannonball* and I knew I wouldn't be able to sleep yet. Instead, I pulled out butter, milk, cheese, and eggs. I could prep the biscuit dough now to save time in the predawn hours. It would hold fine in the walk-in overnight.

After I scrubbed my hands and put on an apron, I

measured out the flour, half whole wheat and half
unbleached white, into the big stainless bowl, mixing
in baking powder and salt. The image of Stella Rogers
with my biscuit in her mouth rose up as if I was looking at her in full color on the big screen at the Starlite
Drive-In in Bloomington. Who would have done a
thing like that? Was somebody really trying to frame
me? I didn't hate anybody. Well, besides Will, my
ex. But you'd have to hate someone to kill them.
Wouldn't you? Or to even frame them for murder.

I cut the butter into small cubes and used my big
vintage pastry cutter to slice it into the flour, pressing
the U-shaped wires down again and again until the
flour was the texture of coarse meal. What other rea-
sons would drive a man or a woman to take a life?
Rage at losing something valuable, like a spouse or a
treasure, I supposed, or at feeling unfairly treated.
Fear of being exposed could be another motivation,
exposed for having committed a crime or done something shameful.

Making a little well in the flour, I cracked in the
eggs and stirred them up with a fork, then added the
milk and the grated cheddar from the industrial-sized
bag. Buying already grated cheese might have been
cheating, but it saved so much time I'd decided to
give it a try. I stirred the dough until it just came together. Who in this small town felt that kind of rage at
Stella, or that type of fear?

I floured the big marble pastry slab I'd installed at
hip height—which for me was only thirty inches off
the floor—and turned out the dough. I kneaded it
only enough to bring it all together, then slid it into a
clean plastic bag, sealed it, and set it in the walk-in
along with the other perishables. After I cleaned up,

still wearing my apron I sank into the chair next to the bourbon. One more little splash wouldn't hurt, and it might help me sleep.

My gaze wandered to the framed picture on the front wall. My mom and me, each with an arm slung over the shoulder of the other, laughed into the camera. I lifted the mug toward the image.

"Hey, Mommy. How'd I do?" Adele had taken that picture the last time she'd been out to visit before I moved to Indiana. Mom and I had taken her to the Wild Pelican, a high-end restaurant perched above an unspoiled beach outside Santa Barbara, its wall of windows showcasing the sparkling Pacific that stretched out all the way to Japan. My mom's wavy blond hair was cut in a no-fuss short do and her blue eyes were brilliant in a face tanned from walking on the beach. I'd gotten my dark curly locks and Mediterranean skin tones from my long-disappeared father, but my body matched Mom's. We'd often talked about how we came from good peasant stock.

"You would have loved this place," I told her, taking a sip of bourbon, another taste we'd shared. My throat thickened, as it still did frequently, when I thought about her. She'd been my best friend. She'd taught me carpentry, giving me projects in high school to keep me busy and off the streets. Every summer she'd sent me out to stay with Adele for a month so I'd get to know my Midwestern roots. She'd fostered my love of puzzles of all kinds, and encouraged me to attend the engineering program at Cal Poly a hundred miles up the coast in San Luis Obispo. She'd even given me her blessing when I wanted to marry Will the day after I graduated, even though I could tell she didn't like him much. I should have trusted her judgment over my own.

"But I have the feeling you'd think this was the right move. This store, this restaurant. Right?" I didn't have much of a belief in the afterlife, but I hoped her essence was out there watching, listening, and giving me the thumbs-up with a great big old grin.

Chapter 5

Boy, howdy. Six hours of sleep was not enough, no way. Sleep had come at last, but not before about one o'clock. Thoughts of murder weren't exactly conducive to a good night's sleep. Or morning's, as the case may be.

I rubbed my eyes and then pocketed the key to my small apartment at the back of the store. I didn't want anybody wandering in there looking for the store restrooms, which were the next two doors to the right, even though I'd mounted a sign on my apartment door that read PRIVATE, just in case. The restrooms were clearly labeled, of course, with SHE ALL and HE ALL, the almost-too-silly suggestion of Phil. I'd let him paint those words because, so far, he'd demonstrated a pretty good design sense of what worked visually and what was just too country cute. I'd installed the restrooms and constructed them to ADA code, with doors wide enough for a wheelchair, levers on the sinks, grab bars, and more. The previous owner would have made do with an outhouse behind the store if he'd been able to. As it was, the single dingy bathroom had made you feel dirty before you even walked in.

For now, though, I had breakfast to make. Since it was Sunday, I'd decided we didn't have to open until eight. Two hours should be long enough to prep and get started cooking. Adele and Phil, who were the extent of my crew until I hired paid help, were coming in at seven-thirty. I donned a fresh apron, extracted the biscuit dough along with bacon, eggs, milk, and butter, and got to work.

But when I flipped on the coffeemaker, I froze. What if Buck came back? What if he'd been serious about me being a suspect? I had nobody to vouch for me, no alibi for those hours he'd asked about. Even the fact that my old Dodge van had been here didn't mean diddly-squat, since Buck had said Stella's house was an easy stroll from here.

I shook off the worry. My business would definitely fail if I got paralyzed by anticipating something that wouldn't happen. I hadn't killed Stella. I wouldn't be arrested. Period.

A bell dinged over and over. I strode to the wall near the door where a vintage phone in a wooden case hung on the wall. I'd had modern innards installed, but the heavy black receiver hanging from a hook on the side worked, as did the rotary dial on the front.

"Pans 'N Pancakes. This is Robbie." I listened to Phil croak out he was sick, and then grimaced before saying, "Just get better, dude. We'll be fine. Adele's coming in." But after I hung up, I hoped I was right. I was still getting used to the pace of the breakfast rush, and things could get tricky with only two of us.

By the time Adele walked in, the pancake batter

was made, the first batch of biscuits was in the oven, and I'd made a fresh batch of miso gravy. I was about to greet her when another woman followed her in. It was Vera from the day before.

I greeted her and then said, "But I'm sorry, we're not open yet."

Adele laughed. "She's with me, honey." She clapped Vera on the back. "We realized we needed a chance to catch up, so—"

"So I left the tour and spent the night with Addie. Hard to believe how long it's been since we sat down with a beer and shot the shi . . ." She caught herself with a grin. "And got reacquainted."

"She's going to help out this morning. Okay by you?" Adele cocked her head.

I nodded as I thanked Vera. "Happens to be perfect timing. Phil called. He's sick. Stomach flu. No way he's coming in." I tapped the countertop. "Vera, can you bake?"

"Can I bake? Addie, can I bake?" Vera set hands on hips.

"She used to run Vee's Bakery. Of course she can bake." Adele laughed loud and hearty.

"Whew. Phil makes the desserts for lunch. I'll need brownies and anything else. Can you do that by eleven-thirty?"

"Of course. You want me to bake here or at Addie's?"

"Here's fine."

"I make a pretty mean apple pie. You got apples?"

"You bet. There's a whole bushel of local Spartans in the cooler. It's apple season, after all. But start after the breakfast rush is over, okay?"

"What can I do now?" she asked.

"Adele knows where the aprons are. Tables need setting, and then you could make sure salt and pepper shakers and the ketchup squeeze bottles are full. Of course that's assuming we get a breakfast rush. I should tell you both what happened last night."

"About Stella coming up dead?" Adele asked as she tied an apron on after handing one to Vera.

"Of course you would already know. But it's more than that." I told them about coming home with Jim last night and about Buck here waiting for me, getting grilled about where I'd been, me with no witnesses to my whereabouts.

Adele whistled. "No fun. Don't you worry your head; they'll find the person who shot her."

"You already know how she was killed? Last night Buck wouldn't tell us." I turned my attention back to my cooking and began laying sausage links on the grill.

"I got my sources, sugar." She laid blue-and-white striped paper place mats on the table next to her. "She was shot, all right, and in the back, as I heard it. The biscuit in the mouth was a nasty touch, wasn't it? For her—although, of course, she was gone by then—but mainly for you."

"I'll say." I tried to focus on the now-sizzling sausage. "Shot in the back. That means it was somebody she knew? Who she let into her house, I guess." I jumped back when a drop of hot grease landed on my hand. *Damn.* Thinking about murder was Buck's job, not mine.

I wiped my forehead with a corner of my apron as the old clock on the wall chimed nine. My fears about people staying away because of the murder were unfounded. The breakfast rush was in full force. I'd been flipping pancakes, cooking short-order eggs, serving up gravy on biscuits, and frying bacon and sausage as fast as I could. Vera and Adele both waited tables and bussed after we'd decided to rotate jobs. The three of us were like a machine oiled and tuned to its exact specs.

"Any more apple butter?" Vera asked.

I pointed to the shelves above the cutlery station. Quarts and quarts of locally made apple butter sat at the ready, another popular topping for the biscuits. We served a dollop in little paper cups when customers requested it.

After I slid another tray of biscuits into the oven and set the timer, grateful I'd made up the dough last night, I took a breath and looked around. Two men and two women about my age wearing matching brightly colored stretchy shirts and biking shorts sat around one table, all of them lean and tanned, with platters of breakfast in various stages of decimation in front of them. One texted on a phone while the others examined a map. Maybe I should try to join a cycling group, myself. I'd been so busy I hadn't had any time for socializing. Until last night.

Several townspeople I recognized walked in and waited until Adele showed them to a table. She clearly knew them, and stood chatting for a moment before turning to clear the dishes for a couple who'd finished eating. The newcomers looked like they'd dressed for church, the man in slacks, a white short-sleeved shirt, and a green tie. The older woman wore a pink pantsuit, and the younger one, who appeared to be their daughter, was dressed in a conservatively tailored dark sweater and skirt.

I beckoned Adele over. "Trade jobs for a bit? I really should get out there and welcome my guests." At her nod, I swapped out my greasy batter-stained apron for a clean one, washed my hands, and headed for the breakfasting public.

First I stopped at the bicyclists' table and greeted them, introducing myself. "I ride, too. What's your route today?"

One of the women smiled and said her name was Lou. "Cycling is a workout around here, isn't it?"

"True words." I smiled back.

"Every time we go down a hill, there's another one to go up. We're grad students at IU, so that's fifteen miles to get here. We plan to loop around through Beanblossom and Nashville. Total about fifty miles."

"Unless we pop in on the Brown County Cyclefest down in the park," one of her companions said.

I raised my eyebrows.

"Road bikers weekend," Lou explained. "Bluegrass music and bunches of cycling folks."

"Sounds fun," I said. "Wish I owned a few free hours."

"You oughta ride with us some time," said the guy sitting next to her.

"I'd love to. I won't be taking weekends off for a while, though." I gestured around the store. "We only opened yesterday. But thanks."

"We have pretty flexible schedules," Lou said.

I dug my card out of my back pocket and handed it to her. "Text me next time you're going out and I'll see if I can join you midride. Nice meeting you all."

A woman waved her arm at me from the shelves of cookware on the opposite wall, so I headed in her direction. "Can I help you?"

She held up a two-handled chopping knife with a dark curved blade. "What do you use this for?"

I reached up and grabbed a wide, shallow wooden bowl with lines on the inside pointing all which way. "It's for chopping nuts or herbs. Anything, really, but I like it for chopping nuts."

"I see. So they don't spray all over the place?"

"Exactly. You kind of rock the knife. Works great." I gave her a price, and when she said she wanted it, I took it over to the cash register. Money in, cookware out, exactly how I liked it. I wrapped the knife carefully in paper and slid both items into a blue-and-white paper sack with handles.

I then moved on to the table of churchgoing breakfasters and repeated my welcome and introduction. The older woman, her puffy blond hair styled to a shellacked perfection, sniffed instead of speaking. Her husband, whose black toupee wouldn't have fooled even the most naive observer, leaned back in his chair and folded his arms.

"Heard you're a person of interest in a murder." He narrowed his eyes. "Wadn't shooting Stella enough? Why'd you have to stuff that biscuit in her mouth?"

Oh, boy. Out of the corner of my eye, I saw heads perk up at the nearby tables.

"Daddy!" The younger woman frowned at him. "That's not very Christian of you. Besides, if Officer Buck or Officer Wanda knew Miss Jordan was the murderer, do you think she'd be standing here taking our breakfast order?"

I opened my mouth to speak when the man laughed. "I'm just ribbing her. No offense, Miss Jordan." He tapped his fork on the table. "But it needs solving."

I swallowed and started again. "It needs to be solved, all right. I'm sure the police will discover poor Stella's actual killer any hour now. And please call me Robbie. Now, what can I get you for breakfast?"

By the end of the hour, the first rush had ebbed and the air in the store was getting stale from all the frying, despite the exhaust fan going full-time. I swung open the front door until it was flat against the inside wall, pushed the screen open, and stood in the fall sunshine for a moment. The store was at the edge of town, and I was blessed with a slice of heaven for a view: red and yellow leaves decorating the woods across the street, and hills rising up in the distance. I closed my eyes, letting the light bathe my face in warm comfort, smelling wood smoke, dry leaves, and a hint of apple from the orchard down the road. The cyclic rhythm of their droning cider press suddenly was drowned out by the bells from the three churches on Main Street that competed in ringing their invitations to worship. Our Lady of Springs was nearest, followed by the popular Hope Springs Eternal Assembly of God, with Grace Zion a block farther down. A half-dozen other churches were scattered through the village. People in Indiana took religion seriously.

My bubble of respite popped when someone cleared his throat. My eyes flew open to see Buck in front of me. I groaned.

"That's not much of a good morning, then, is it?" he asked in his usual drawl.

"Sorry. I'd forgotten about Stella's death for a minute there."

"Wish I could forget. Yes, I sincerely wish I could."

"You're not here to arrest me, are you?" I smiled a little nervously.

"Not at this time, no." He cleared his throat again. "I wondered if I could get a bite of breakfast, though."

I laughed, my nervousness gone as fast as it'd come on. "That's what I'm here for." I gestured into the store. "After you, Officer." I let the screen bang behind me.

Buck ordered the Kitchen Sink omelet—peppers, sausage, cheese, salsa, the works—and biscuits, with a side stack of pancakes. I took it to Adele, whose hair was damp under her hat.

"Let me take over cooking again. You look beat. Go sit down, why don't you?" She was healthy and vibrant, but she was seventy, after all. My mom, sixteen years younger than Adele, had apparently been a late-in-life afterthought for their parents.

"It's a deal." She tossed her dirty apron in the makeshift hamper under the sink, poured herself a tall glass of orange juice, grabbed a biscuit, and took them to Buck's table.

Vera, meanwhile, slid a gigantic rimmed baking sheet full of brownie batter into the oven. Then she combined flour and butter in my industrial-sized food processor and mixed for half a minute. Adding a measure of ice water, she pulsed it for a few seconds. She turned to catch me watching her.

"Hey, it's the way Julia Child made pie crust in her later years. Worked for her, works for me." Despite looking the same age as Adele, Vera didn't appear quite as whupped.

"Not a problem for me, Vera. I'm just grateful you're here to help. Make sure you sit down soon, too, though, okay?"

"I will. Want to let this chill a bit before I start baking." She turned out the dough onto the pastry slab and deftly kneaded it for a short minute before making a disk, wrapping it in plastic wrap, and taking it to the cooler.

I whisked up Buck's breakfast in no time and brought it to his table. I accepted payment along with thanks and congratulations from the remaining group of customers, and cleared their table as the screen door *thwacked* shut after them. I was beat, too. I needed to cut out and bake the last pan of biscuits in case we were flooded with hungry after-church customers, but I thought I could sit for a couple few minutes, anyway.

"Join you?" I asked Buck, who waved without speaking at the empty chair across from him. Good thing he didn't try to talk with those cheeks bulging with omelet. "Any new developments in the case?"

"Listen to you," Adele said with a snort. "You sound like you're on one of those television cop shows."

"Well," I started to protest, "since I'm apparently a person of interest, as they say, I'm pretty interested in Buck and his colleagues finding who really did kill Stella."

Buck swallowed. "*Actually,*" he said, drawing out the word, "you're not a person of interest. That's a technical term."

"You asked where I was yesterday afternoon.

Sounded like you were interested." I watched him. "So Stella was shot from behind?"

He raised his eyebrows, then narrowed his eyes at Adele. "You tell her that?"

"Yeah," she said. "The news is all over town. Heard the weapon was a Bersa Thunder, although most people wouldn't know a Bersa from Adam's off ox."

"Like me," I said. "I've never even held a gun." I was amazed, but not really surprised Adele knew the make and model of the gun. She was one tough lady who'd lived by herself on a small farm for years. She'd had to shoot coyotes and foxes who preyed on her lambs. I only hoped whoever shot Stella didn't have anybody else in his very real sights. Or hers.

Buck groaned. "How in blazes that news got out, I'll never know."

I leaned forward. "So, Buck, your police department is pretty small, isn't it? You, Wanda, and the chief, and a couple others. I read that feature they did on you in the *South Lick Sentinel*. Are you equipped for a murder investigation?"

"Welp, that's kind of a sticky issue. We rightly called in the Brown County Homicide Unit. But they're not that big, either. And believe it or not, there was a murder way down in Becks Grove couple days ago and they're all-out busy with it."

"But you guys know what you're doing?" I pressed.

Vera carried a glass of water to the table and joined us.

Buck sat up a little straighter. "We were all trained in homicide investigation. You bet." He nodded as if that might convince him it was true.

"So, who are you looking at? Who would she have invited into her house?"

"Stella knew everyone in town, Robbie," Adele said. "She'd been the mayor's aide since before my two terms, and that was years ago, although she was pretty young then. Younger'n me, anywho."

"Rubbed a lot of them the wrong way, too." Buck sopped up whatever was left on his plate with his last biscuit and popped it into his mouth, washing it down with the rest of his coffee, then unfolded himself out of his chair. Laying a ten and a five on the table, he said, "Duty calls."

"That's too much money, Buck," I said. We weren't as inexpensive as some breakfast joints, but what he'd consumed sure didn't cost that much.

"Throw it in the tip jar, then." He ambled out.

"A tip jar," I said, staring after him. People left tips on their tables, but I could add a jar at the register. "Why didn't I think of that?"

Chapter 6

I didn't lock up and turn the sign on the door to CLOSED until after four. I'd planned to be open from eight to two on Sundays, but the lunch crowd never let up, and I realized lots of folks kept a later schedule than the early bird I was. Adele and Vera had graciously stuck it out, working their butts off, until I shooed them home at three-thirty. I'd cooked burgers and eggs at the same time, since I offered breakfast all day long. My helpers had served up the menu from pancakes to brownies, and Vera's apple pies had sold out, especially after she'd suggested serving pieces with a slice of Wisconsin sharp cheddar alongside. My fears of being shunned because of Stella's murder hadn't materialized.

But I needed to hire help and I hadn't received any responses from the craigslist ad I'd placed right after that girl quit. Who would want to work in an untested restaurant in a small rural town, anyway? I don't know what I'd been thinking, that I could both cook and wait tables. It exhausted even three of us. It was a good problem to have, I supposed, to be so busy, and the till was full of money. But I now saw I couldn't do it alone. Adele and Vera weren't young, and they had lives they wanted to live while they could. And Phil worked as the secretary in the IU music department. He'd said he didn't mind helping out now and then, and was willing to bake the desserts from home, but he couldn't work for me on any regular basis.

Speaking of the till, I emptied it except for Tuesday's starting change and secured it in the small safe back in my rooms. As a single-woman proprietor, I couldn't be too careful.

My stomach complained bitterly of neglect, so I loaded up a plate with an extra hamburger I'd cooked after miscounting and sank into a chair. I munched the burger, surveying the kitchen mess still to be cleaned. At least we'd be closed tomorrow, my compromise for staying open all weekend, and maybe I could get out for a long bike ride. After I swallowed the last bite, I laid my head on my arms. Cleanup could wait a little.

I must have dozed off, because I awoke with a start to a knocking noise. Sitting up, I wiped a drop of drool from the corner of my mouth and paid attention. The knocking started up again. Somebody was at the front door. A pang of fear shot through me. A murderer still walked free out there, as far as I knew. But would a murderer knock insistently at the front door? I laughed and tried to shake off the fear. Still, I made my way around the side walls of the store until I could see out the front window without being seen myself. It was a tall, slim young woman, with reddish gold dreadlocks pulled back in an unruly ponytail.

Fumbling for the lock, I finally opened the door to say, "I'm sorry, we're closed."

"I'm not here to eat. Are you Robbie?" she asked.

I nodded slowly. Adele had convinced me to add ROBBIE JORDAN, PROPRIETOR to the sign above the door.

"I'm Danna." She waited, head tilted to the side, one hand rubbing at the shoulder of the tie-dyed T-shirt she wore over long cargo shorts.

"Hi, Danna. Am I supposed to know you?"

She frowned, her light brows knitting above hazel eyes. "I want to work for you. I answered your ad, you know, on craigslist?"

Was I still sleeping? Or was she an angel arrived to answer my secular prayers? Then I realized what had happened.

"I haven't checked my e-mail in a couple days. We only opened yesterday, and—"

"I know. My mom was your first customer."

That explained her height. "You're Corrine's daughter? And you want to work for me?"

"Totally."

"Come on in, then. Let's talk."

After we sat, I said, "Do you have experience working in a restaurant?"

She started to roll her eyes, but she caught herself. "I attached my résumé to the e-mail."

"Which I haven't seen. Why don't you just tell me about yourself?" She looked to be less than ten years younger than me, but I suddenly felt like an adult. A tiny silver ring was laced through one of her eyebrows, and she wore an even tinier blue topaz stud in one nostril. At least it didn't sound like her tongue was pierced and no tattoos were in evidence. I'd never understood the piercing trend among people my age. And tattooing? Don't get me started.

"I've worked at Kowalski's Country Store restaurant

for three years. I'm nineteen, and my mom thinks I'm taking a 'gap year.'" She surrounded the last two words with air quotes. "But I'm just not sure I want to go to college."

"What does your dad say?"

"My dad? I don't have a dad." She folded her arms over her chest and looked over at the kitchen area.

Poor thing. She was trying to be nonchalant, but I thought I heard an undertone of hurt.

"Anyway," Danna went on, "when I saw your ad, I thought I could literally walk to work instead of driving into Nashville."

"What did you do at Kowalski's?"

"I bussed, then I waited tables. But what I really want to do is cook. They finally let me work on the line last year."

"So, why leave?" I set my forearms on the table and leaned on them.

She gazed at the same corner of the ceiling Buck was examining this morning, or was it last night? I was so tired I couldn't remember.

"Let's just say the environment there isn't so great." She tapped the table with her black-painted nails and didn't meet my eyes.

Something had clearly gone wrong at Ed's. "Will someone give you a recommendation?"

She looked at me again. "Yes. And my counselor at the high school will, too."

"Brown County High School?"

"I graduated in June. Robbie, I hope you'll give me a chance. I really want to work here."

I looked at her, wondering why she wanted to work for me so badly. She held my gaze, chin up. She demonstrated initiative. She wanted to cook.

She looked strong and healthy. "Let me check out your résumé and your references. I'm thinking this could be a good fit, but I'll need you to help with everything—clearing, waiting, cleanup, along with cooking. I'll do all of it, too," I added hastily as she started to look unhappy at what I'd said. "We can trade off. Sometimes I'll need to be out there with the customers and sometimes I'll need to be cooking. How does that sound?"

A slow smile spread across her face, the first sign of cheer I'd seen on this serious girl. "Good. It sounds good."

"I'll need you here on the dot of six-thirty every weekday except Monday, and on Saturday. Sunday's an hour later, and I'll pay time and a half. Okay?"

"No probs."

"We'll do a probationary period for a couple of weeks, though. Just to be sure we work well together."

"Whatever. Want me to start right now? Looks like a tornado hit in here." She surveyed tables littered with crumbs, an industrial sink full of dishes waiting to be rinsed, a grill needing scraping and oiling, a stack of baking sheets and pie pans awaiting a scrub. Not to mention the floor.

"You can't even imagine what a great offer that is." I proposed an hourly rate she seemed pleased with and showed her where I kept the aprons. Between us the place was spotless in an hour. She seemed able to work without incessant chat, but also was open to conversation.

Maybe I was going to pull this gig off, after all. If I wasn't associated with any more murders, that is.

* * *

After Danna left, promising to be here at six-thirty on Tuesday, I locked up again, then threw my apron in the hamper and carried the bin to the big washer and dryer I'd installed near the back door of my small apartment. I'd run out of money with all that needed to be done in the restaurant, so my personal space was pretty rudimentary: a linoleum-floored kitchen last remodeled in the 1950s, a small bedroom that fit my double bed and wooden dresser with little room to spare, a bathroom with a claw-foot tub and pedestal sink, and a little living room featuring big windows looking out on the old barn and the woods behind it. Still, I'd given it all a fresh coat of paint—a pale yellow for the kitchen, a light rose in my bedroom, and linen white for the rest. I loved light-colored walls to show off my few pieces of art, if I ever found time to hang them. I'd placed a house plant in every room, and my mom's sleek handmade tables and chairs filled the space with the beauty of fine wood. Despite chipped trim and cracked ceilings, the apartment was clean and mine, with about the best work commute in the world.

I started a load in the washer, then stood in the kitchen with aching feet, uncertain. I glanced at my vintage clock that read five-fifteen. What I really wanted was a glass of red wine and today's *New York Times* crossword puzzle. But I knew from long experience what I needed was a spin on my bike. Fresh air and exercise always cleared my brain and my energy pathways. I drank a glass of water and went to change into biking shorts and a long-sleeved biking shirt in neon yellow. Being on the western edge of the time zone in October meant it was still light until seven-thirty. The wine and puzzle would be here when I returned. I slipped the slim wallet I always carried and my cell phone into the pocket on the shirt's back, filled the water bottle that clicked into a holder on the frame, and slipped on the stiff cycling shoes that clicked into their own holders on the pedals. No good for walking any distance in, but the ride was a lot more efficient if you pulled the pedals up as well as pushed them down.

Lifting my lightweight Cannondale bike from where it hung on the wall in the back entryway—it was way too expensive to keep it in the barn and risk theft or weather damage—I wheeled it out the door, stopping to lock up after myself. I fastened on my helmet and was about to throw a leg over the cycle when I heard a plaintive sound from the antique lilac a long-dead shopkeeper must have planted a century earlier. I heard the sound again. It was coming from under the bush, whose leaves had turned a winey deep red. I leaned the bike against the wall and squatted to look.

A forlorn cat huddled there, its long-haired black coat lightened by a white face with one black eye patch. I'd never seen it before.

"Hey, kitty cat. Come here." I scratched the ground in front of me. "It's okay."

The cat made its way slowly toward me. But when I reached out to pet it, it retreated under the bush again, keeping its eyes on me with a hungry look. I stood, watching it.

"Whose kitty are you? And why are you afraid?" When I got no response, I unlocked the door and filled two small dishes, one with milk and one with water. I set them on the ground near the bush, made sure I locked up again, and set off down Main Street.

As I pedaled past Shamrock Hardware, I remembered what the proprietor had said—*What was his name? Denny? No, Don.* Don said he'd been friends with my mom. He implied it might have been a bit more than that. Maybe Adele knew the story. Mom had never mentioned him, but why should she? She'd left Indiana before I was born, after all. And who hasn't had a high-school fling? Don hadn't seemed any too happy with Corrine, that was for damn sure, or with Stella, either.

I thought I'd head out toward the village of Gnaw Bone, which would give me hill work. By the time I got back, I'd have done a strenuous twenty. I rode past the gazebo on my way out of town. What a treat it would be to head for a soak in a hot springs after this ride, after this weekend. Far as I knew, there weren't any still operating in town, though. As I cycled along the country lane, passing a sign for HAPPY COW DAIRY FARM, I felt my stress lowering even as my heart rate rose. The slanting light was particularly lovely on the leaves in shades of red and gold, and the cooling air smelled of cut grass and wood smoke, overlaid with a hint of manure. Maybe I'd even stop at the Gnaw Mart and indulge in a wet tenderloin. My stomach growled out loud at the prospect. The little store, the only one in town, mostly sold snacks and drinks, but their deli counter specialized in deep-fried breaded tenderloin dipped in gravy. Even though this ride wouldn't anywhere near burn up so many calories, it was okay once in a while.

But my plans took a big honking detour when a sleek black car sped past me on the two-lane road. "Hey, look out," I yelled as it veered way too close to my left side and forced me onto the gravel-strewn shoulder. My front wheel skidded. I struggled to control the bike, to stay upright. Instead, we both went down in a pile sideways. The brush growing just beyond the shoulder scratched my hands. My knee scraped on the gravel and then twisted, caught under the bike until my shoe released from the pedal.

I raised my head and caught a glimpse of the vehicle vanishing down the road, but I could only make out the last few letters of the vanity plate: *TOR.* After I extricated myself from the bike and stood, I assessed the damage. Thank goodness I'd worn long sleeves; scratches and scrapes seemed to be the extent of it. When I lifted my road cycle, it seemed intact, too, apart from its own scratches. I took a few steps, testing my knee, and was relieved when it wasn't damaged. *Damn that car.* It was almost like it sideswiped me on purpose.

I could no longer muster the energy for a vigorous ride. I'd create my own spa at home. I'd run a hot bath and take a long, hot soak in the tub with, yes, that glass of wine.

Chapter 7

Much refreshed by my bath, I sat at the kitchen table with a cheese omelet, a round-bowled glass of red wine, and the crossword. Mom had crafted the drop-leaf table out of a cherry that shone, with simple Shaker-style legs. I missed her when I sat there, but it was a perfect size for the small room, and I could expand it if I ever had more than one guest over. So far, I'd been too busy to invite anyone for a meal. I flashed on an image of Jim sitting across from me, candles glowing, a vase full of yellow alstroemeria behind them. That'd be nice. Maybe I'd see what he was doing for dinner tomorrow.

I was a bit out of sorts, though, because I couldn't find my puzzle pen. I always used the same pen when I did the crossword, the pen from Mom's shop. It was a gel pen I could get refills for, and the ink flowed out really nice. But the best part was the logo from her business, the one featuring the outline of a long table with JEANINE'S CABINETS written inside it. I'd looked everywhere. In the kitchen drawer, in my handbag, in the store. With the flurry of getting the store ready, I wasn't sure when I'd last had it, but I thought it was in the restaurant. I must have written down breakfast or lunch orders with it over the last two days. Oh well. I dug another pen out of my purse and set to work. It was tricky, being left-handed, not to smudge the letters, but I'd had plenty of practice.

I'd finished a quadrant on the crossword, filling in "strippers" for the clue *ECDYSIASTS,* when I heard a sound from outside. I cocked my head and listened, then realized it must be the kitty. The dishes I'd left had been empty when I returned, but the little creature had been nowhere in sight.

When I flipped on the porch light and looked out the door, there the cat was again, not quite cowering this time, but crouching in a wary stance. I grabbed the bowls and refilled one with water. I glanced at the clock. Eight o'clock was too late to go out and find dry cat food on a Sunday night, but I located a can of tuna in the cupboard and emptied that into the other bowl. When I set them outside the door, the cat came running up. It started scarfing down the tuna, which gave me the chance to see it was a *he*. He then proceeded to purr so loudly, he chirped as I petted his head.

"I guess you were just hungry, little guy. Where'd you come from, anyway?"

He didn't answer. When I switched off the porch light, I glimpsed a full moon rising above the trees and walked back out to get a better eyeful. I supposed it was the harvest moon, not that I was much up on farming lore. It was gorgeous, no matter what it was called. A wisp of cloud floated across the front of the golden orb and I half expected a witch on a broom to follow.

The kitty rubbed up against my leg. I reached down to pet him, which only produced more chirping.

"You sound like a bird, not a cat," I told him. Should I invite him in? I couldn't have him in the restaurant, for sure. Board of Health would shut me down in a New York minute. But I didn't see why he couldn't share my apartment with me. What if he already had a home, though? It wasn't cold out. I'd leave him alone for tonight and see if he was still around in the morning.

I locked the door behind me, smiling. I hadn't had a pet since I was sixteen and the old cat we'd had all my life died. Butch had been an affectionate curmudgeon, deciding on his own terms when he wanted to sit on your lap and letting you know quite vocally when he didn't. Now I heard another sound and cast my gaze around the apartment for the source. I dashed for the bedroom when I realized it was my cell phone, likely still in the pocket of the bike shirt. By the time I dug it out, the ringing had stopped, but I saw Jim's number on the display, which made me smile all over again.

I rang him back. "I was just thinking about you," I said after greeting him.

"Is that so?"

"Yup." I took the plunge. "How about coming over for dinner tomorrow?" When he didn't respond, I added, "If you want to." *Damn. Did I misinterpret his interest?* It seemed like a week ago, but I realized it was only last night he told me he only kidded people he liked. Maybe that meant people he liked as friends. *Why do I feel like I'm back in high school?*

"I want to. Thanks, Robbie."

Whew.

He cleared his throat. "I called to say hello, but I also wanted to share something I learned today."

"Oh?" I was only half listening, already planning what I wanted to cook for him.

"It might be connected to the murder."

I thudded off my romantic cloud and back to earth. "Oh." Now he had my complete attention.

"Well, I was in Nashville for a Rotary Club meeting this morning. Ed Kowalski was sitting across the room, and the woman sitting next to me mentioned he's been having trouble keeping employees."

"Huh. I hired Mayor Beedle's daughter this afternoon to help in the store."

"Danna?"

"The same. She's been working for Ed, and when I asked her why she left, she wouldn't really say. Only that the environment wasn't so great. Were you thinking Ed's employment problems mean his business is in bad shape, which would make mine seem like even more of a threat to him?"

"Exactly."

I shook my head. "I don't know. It's just such a stretch for Ed to kill Stella and then hope I'd be prosecuted for it. There'd never be evidence linking me to it, right?"

"Let's hope not. Wait, that sounded bad." He laughed. "What I meant was I hope the killer didn't plant something of yours at Stella's."

"But—" An image of my lost pen flashed across my brain. *No, I had to have just misplaced it.*

"Robbie, don't worry about it. You'll be fine."

"Whatever you say, Mr. Lawyer Man. I'll tell you, it's been the craziest weekend I've ever had." I yawned.

"Get yourself some rest, then. What time should I come tomorrow, and should I bring red wine or white?"

"Come at six. We are in the Midwest, after all. I'm not sure what I'm making yet. Red wine goes with anything, in my opinion. But then, nobody would ever call me a wine snob."

Jim laughed again.

"I should ask if you have any food allergies."

"Not a one."

"And even though you're a vegetarian, you eat seafood, right?"

"I do. Thanks for the invite, and sweet dreams, Ms. Jordan."

Sweet they would be. I was going to have my second date in a week. And for sure Buck and friends would nail the murderer soon.

With my digital tablet in hand, I checked the supplies in the walk-in in the morning, yawning out loud. I'd found an excellent restaurant inventory app linking me directly to my several purveyors. I clicked a couple of items that needed restocking and closed the door behind me.

I stood for a moment with my back to the door. Something felt out of place. I opened the cooler again. As the door clicked shut behind me, I surveyed the wire rack shelves. Dairy took up a big section in a restaurant like mine, with pound blocks of butter, several kinds of milk, bricks of cream cheese, and hefty chunks of cheese. I kept the meat in its own area, although I was still trying to figure out how much to use fresh and how much frozen. Bacon, ham, and sausages kept well, but I really needed to spend the afternoon making beef and turkey patties and freezing them. I'd created another section for fruit, and the last for vegetables, like green and red peppers, onions, and mushrooms for omelets, as well as lettuce and tomatoes for the burgers. The waxed boxes from the supplier lined up on the shelves like squat waiters ready to serve.

So, what was awry? I walked all the way in, checking every shelf, but I couldn't find anything. The dairy didn't seem quite as I'd left it, but then Adele and Vera had been helping all day yesterday. Either one could have rearranged things. A shudder ran through me and it wasn't from the cold air. As far as I knew, a killer still roamed free in town. And I was shut in alone in an extremely cold place. I shook my head. The big red emergency button perched on the wall next to the door, after all, and I held an Internet-connected tablet that got a signal even in this thick-walled room. I made my way out and pushed the heavy door shut, the thick latch clicking shut with a satisfying *clunk*.

I felt at loose ends. I'd planned Mondays as my day off, to relax, to catch up. Ever since I bought the store, I'd been pushing with all my energy toward opening day. But that day had now come and gone. I wandered back into my apartment, where the morning light streamed into the kitchen. I'd had coffee and munched an apple, but my stomach now called out for more.

As did kitty's, apparently. He mewed from outside,

so I opened the door. After I picked up his bowls, I propped open the screen.

"Hey, little guy. Come on in." I filled the bowls with milk and water and set them in the entryway.

He peered in, looked behind him, and moseyed in a few steps. Stopping, he gave a bite and a furious lick to his left shoulder, then licked his paw. With a little chirp, he continued in until he was lapping up the milk, purring like a tiny electric fan.

I watched him finish the milk and then give himself a bath all over. Finding a sack of dry cat food was apparently top on my list for my day off, and a few cans of wet food as well. Did I need to set up a litter box and all, too? As I turned toward where my purse hung from a hook, I jostled a chair, and kitty streaked out the still-open door. He could keep going to the bathroom wherever he'd been going up to now. At least until the ground froze.

I made and ate a piece of toast with peanut butter and honey, then grabbed my bag. I'd seen cat food in Shamrock Hardware. I could pick up a bag there, for starters. As I locked the door behind me, kitty sauntered up again, purring with his chirping noise.

"That's it," I told him. "Your name is Birdy."

He eyed me with an inscrutable gaze as he crouched, paws in front of him, looking for all the world like a tiny black-and-white Sphinx. A Sphinx named Birdy.

Chapter 8

"It needs fixed." The male voice one aisle over at Shamrock Hardware was insistent. "Don't got no insurance."

I cocked my head, but couldn't place the speaker.

"I'm not talking about this," he said. "I don't want all of South Lick to know my bidness."

I lowered my head again to stare at the array of cat treats. He was a local by the way he talked, but I hadn't heard another voice. I guessed it was a domestic spat being conducted over the phone.

Having no idea what kind of food my new buddy, Birdy, liked, and suspecting he wouldn't be picky, I threw a dozen little cans into the basket, then loaded up a sack of the most expensive dry food, the one saying it was made in the USA with organic ingredients. Only the best for my new family member. And from what I'd read about the dangers lurking in pet food made in China, the cost was worth it.

I wandered the narrow aisles, trying to think if I needed anything along the lines of actual hardware. It was an old-style store, with shelves to the ceiling, and a good deal of rather dusty inventory that could have been sitting there for a century: mousetraps, nasty chemical cleaners, cast-iron C-clamps. I added a few sponges and scrubbers to my cart, then searched out picture hangers. I hadn't gotten around to hanging any of my framed art and that could be another easy task for today.

After adding a couple of packets of hangers to my shopping cart, I passed a wide locked glass cabinet and stopped to examine it. It was full of guns. Small ones, big ones. I didn't know anything more about guns than the terms that were tossed around on the news and in books: rifle, shotgun, semiautomatic. Revolver, pistol, weapon. But it sure looked like they were all in there, and for sale, too, along with boxes of what looked like bullets. It gave me a chill to think the gun that killed Stella might have been bought here, and the ammo, too.

Heading over to Barb, the cashier, a trim older woman with perfect makeup and a short cap of salt-and-pepper hair, I spied the frowning proprietor emerging from a door labeled OFFICE: NO ADMITTANCE. I waved.

"'Morning, Don," I called.

When he saw me, he plastered a fake smile over his frown and walked toward me. "Robbie. How were your first couple days?"

"Very good, thanks. We had a great crowd both Saturday and Sunday."

"Heard about the biscuit." He leaned in and lowered his voice. "You know. In Stella's mouth. Bad news for you."

He had the nerve. I stood up as tall as I could. "Not at all. No one who ate in my store on Sunday seemed worried in the least that they'd die from one of my biscuits."

"I just thought . . ." His voice trailed off and his eyes got that worried look again.

"Do you have any idea who might have killed Stella?"

"Who, me? Not a clue." He cleared his throat and glanced into my cart. "So, did you find what you needed? Looks like you got you a cat."

"Just acquired one. Or he adopted me, I guess is more accurate."

A fond smile spread across Don's face and he finally stopped frowning. "I have three." He proceeded to tell me about each of his cats, their names, their habits. "Why, I gave your mom a little bitty kitten long, long ago. She took that guy on her drive cross-country when she moved out California way."

"Butch? You gave Mom our cat, Butch?" I was astonished.

"If that's what she went ahead and named him, why, then, yes, I did. So did you give this cat who adopted you a name yet?"

"I named him Birdy, because he almost chirps when he purrs."

"Well, he's yours now. You know what they say, once you name a stray, you ain't never going to get rid of him."

"So far, that's not a problem. He seems very swee—" I stopped speaking when Don turned his head sharply to the right.

"Roy," he said in a voice that would have put honey to shame. "Let me express my condolences on the death of your mother." Hand outstretched, Don approached a man a few years younger than me who looked like he didn't exercise much.

So this was Stella's son. Inconveniently named Roy Rogers. Well, maybe he was more typical of his generation than I was, and had no idea who the old TV singing cowboy was.

Roy shook Don's hand without really putting himself into it. "Thanks, Don."

Whoa. The guy I'd heard on the other side of the partition earlier. He looked over at me and squinted, running his left hand through hair so greasy it made him wipe his hand on his dark blue work pants.

"This the girl who robbed me of my store?" Roy asked Don.

Don held up both hands facing Roy. "Hold on a chicken-picking minute, Roy. She didn't rob nobody." He beckoned me over. "Kinda funny, that. Robbie here didn't rob nobody." He gave a grim little chuckle that neither Roy nor I joined him in. "Robbie Jordan, Roy Rogers. The late Stella's only son."

I took a deep breath. "Nice to meet you, Roy. And I'm so sorry about your mother's passing."

Roy snorted. "As if."

Don gave Roy a look. "Now, Roy, Robbie there lost her very own mother only last year. Haven't we talked about being nice?" He took Roy by the elbow and steered him away.

I watched them head toward Don's office. What was with the "haven't we talked about being nice?" Don's tone was that of an adult to a child. Curious. I approached the cash register and paid Barb for my purchases.

"How's the store going, now's you're open?" she asked with a big smile.

"Good, so far, thanks."

She leaned toward me. "Heared the sad news about Stella, may she rest in peace." She shook her head. "She was a tough customer, bless her heart. Hope they catch whoever did it, though. Don't much like a killer running around loose."

"I'm with you on that. Say, Barb, you don't know if anyone has reported a lost cat, do you?" I figured if anyone knew about Birdy, Barb would. She had a finger on everything that happened in town. "Little black-and-white guy?"

"Not as I've heared. Nobody's put up a poster here, anywho." She gestured with her head to the large community bulletin board near the door. "Let you know if I hear tell anything."

I approached Kowalski's Country Store on my bike an hour later. It was such a beautiful fall day, sunny and crisp, that I'd decided to ride to Nashville and take myself out to a second breakfast, one I didn't have to cook. Spying on the competition wasn't a bad idea, either. I'd looped up through Beanblossom on my way, and smiled as always when I passed the Mennonite church, which featured a prominent sign that read STRANGERS EXPECTED. I'd never gotten around to asking anyone what it really meant, but the words brought to mind science fiction or the magical realism I'd read in Gabriel García Márquez's works in college.

Stopping a couple doors down from Kowalski's, which sat just outside the artsy, touristy county seat, I put my foot on the ground and examined the storefront. It featured a porch overhang like mine, but so much kitsch clogged the porch there wasn't space for even one chair. I loved the refurbished rocking chairs in front of Pans 'N Pancakes, and folks had occupied them now and then over the weekend. Here an old wooden plow vied for space with an oak barrel short a few staves, a rusty hay rake, a low wrought-iron table that could use refinishing, or at least a paint job, and a boatload of other antiques, sort of. I squinted. There was actually a rocking chair amidst the junk, but no way to get close enough to sit in it. The paint peeled off the porch railing, and the middle of each stair tread swayed like the back of an old mare.

I rode the last few yards, locked my cycle in front of the store, and unclipped my helmet. A bell dinged as I pushed the door open. Not an actual bell on the door, though, but an automatic alert someone had entered or left. A long counter lined with round-seated diner stools faced the left wall, with the kitchen visible through a wide order window. Several dozen tired aluminum tables were arrayed in the middle of the space with chairs surrounding them; the restaurant could probably accommodate twice as many customers as mine. Most of the chairs were occupied by folks who looked like they often indulged in big starchy, greasy breakfasts. And since it was a Monday morning, they were either tourists, retirees, or both.

An older waitress dressed in black breezed by, saying, "Sit anywhere you want, dear."

First I scanned the room and located the restroom. I needed to wash up after my ride. A few minutes later I emerged with clean hands. I'd splashed water on my face, too. The restroom was dingy but clean. Whoever the decorator was, he or she must be long dead—the decor looked that exhausted. The walls of the hall where I stood were lined with framed pictures. I examined them, one by one, as I strolled by holding my helmet. They were mostly of Ed with various groups of townspeople: Ed with the current state representative; Ed receiving a Rotary Club award; Ed with four other men on the golf course; Ed with a cluster of Boy Scouts.

I stopped at one of them and peered more closely. It was of Ed in younger days, with his arm slung over Stella's shoulders. And Stella was actually smiling. I made my way to the counter and took a seat on one of the red vinyl stools.

The same waitress I'd seen earlier slapped a paper place mat doubling as a menu in front of me. "Coffee?"

"Please." I studied the menu.

She returned in a minute with a thick mug and a pot of coffee. "Was you wanting to order?"

"I'll take the blueberry pancakes with sausage, and a side of biscuits and gravy." If I was here to assess the competition, I might as well go whole hog. So far, my place was cleaner, brighter, and more interesting. But it was also in a much smaller town. Nashville brought tourists literally by the busload, especially at this time of year.

It didn't take more than a couple of minutes for a steaming platter of food to be set in front of me. I thanked the waitress and tucked into it. First I took a bite of pancake. It was of the white-flour variety that I didn't care for. These were particularly pasty and the blueberries tasted cooked, not fresh. When I threw berries into pancakes, I either used fresh or flash frozen, depending on the season.

My first bite of sausage was crispy on the outside and moist on the inside. Can't go wrong with links unless you let them dry out. I cut a biscuit in half and took a bite. Not bad. Warm and homemade, at least. No cheese in it, of course. That was my idea. Mom had baked cheesy biscuits since before I could remember, and I hadn't found any offered in other restaurants in the county. I poured the warm gravy over the other half biscuit, this time using my knife and fork to lift a bite, but the gravy was salty, lumpy, with little dots of pork, and it tasted like it came out of a can. A can some machine filled a long, long time ago.

I looked around at the other diners. Nobody seemed upset about their meals. People were sopping up egg yolks with white toast, demolishing stacks of pancakes, and crunching down pieces of bacon like there was no tomorrow. I glanced at the rest of the store as I ate the palatable parts of my breakfast.

Vintage shelves, like the ones in my store, lined one wall. I saw a collection of rusty tools and a section with what looked like antique dishes and pottery. But Ed also stocked new fishing supplies, snacks, and other supplies, and had a kind of beach corner set up, with flip-flops, sunscreen, hats, and beach towels. Somebody ought to tell him it was nearly mid-October.

Ed appeared out of nowhere at my elbow. "Taking a day off to slum with the competition?" His face was as ruddy as it'd looked on Saturday and his crooked-tooth smile bordered on a leer as he leaned in a bit too close. With a green tie knotted over a blue dress shirt, he sure as heck wasn't dressed for kitchen work.

"I decided to close on Mondays, since we're open all weekend." I moved as far away as I could from him without falling off my stool. "I was out for a ride and got hungry."

"How'd you like the breakfast?" He pointed at my

plate. "Looks like you weren't hungry. Everybody loves those blueberry pancakes."

I mustered a smile. "The sausages were so good I just filled up on them."

"I can give you the pancake recipe if you want." He pulled out a pen and held it above my menu with his left hand.

Another leftie. "No, thanks, I have my own recipe I like." I sipped my now-cold coffee. "Looks like you're doing a good business."

"The place is always crowded in the fall. Plenty of hungry tourists who also need to pick up batteries or a new lure."

"By the way, I hired one of your former employees yesterday. Danna Beedle. Said she wanted to be able to walk to work. Can you recommend her?"

He frowned and squinted so hard his small eyes almost disappeared. "We had a difference of opinion. She can be pretty standoffish." He relaxed his eyes. "But she's a good worker, that Danna, and was shaping up to know what she was doing in the kitchen."

"Great, thanks. Terrible news about Stella, isn't it? Looks like the two of you were friends." I watched him. He hadn't greeted Stella at my place Saturday. Not that I'd seen, anyway.

Ed's gaze darted about the room and back at a spot just beyond my right ear. "No. No, we weren't." He shook his head and cleared his throat.

"Isn't that a picture of you two in the hall by the restrooms?" I gestured with my fork. "You look pretty friendly, although it was a few years ago."

"Many years ago. Many, many years ago. We were . . . I was . . ." He swallowed and glanced at his big gold watch. "Would you look at the time? I'm late for a

Chamber meeting." He looked past me again. "Nice seeing you, Robbie. Don't worry about the bill. Your meal is on the house." He rushed off before I could even thank him, and muttered something to my waitress on his way to the door.

Somebody was nervous about Stella.

Chapter 9

Rolling slowly up Van Buren Street, I tried to avoid tourists wandering diagonally across the main drag without looking. Tourists had much to be distracted by: dozens of shops featuring quirky lawn ornaments out front, advertising fudge and salt water taffy, or offering hand crafts from purses to pillows to picnic baskets. I passed the Hobnob Corner Restaurant, which I knew served decent food all day long. The building had formerly housed a general store, and then a pharmacy. I glanced at the delightful Melchior Marionette Theatre, a brightly painted space open to the sidewalk. It advertised free popcorn and delightful entertainment. I'd wandered in one time and read a sign painted on an old board: AN ACT TO PREVENT CERTAIN IMMORAL PRACTICES. It referenced a law enacted by the second session of the state general assembly in 1817. Section 7 prohibited staging puppet shows for money, with every person so offending to be fined three dollars for each offense.

After I reached the Nashville Inn, I parked my bike and knocked on the service door around the back.

The big kitchen exhaust fan thrummed as loudly as usual, so I finally just pulled the screen door open and entered my former workplace. While I loved my new gig, I kind of missed the inn.

"Christina?" I called. I turned from the hall into the kitchen. "Anybody home?" Christina had been my assistant, and she snagged the job of chef when I left.

Nobody occupied the big industrial kitchen, but lunch prep was clearly under way. Stock simmered on the stove, and squash and carrots in the process of being chopped lay on the wide stainless-steel worktable.

Christina emerged from the front, a big smile erupting when she saw me. "Robert! You're back." She always played with my name.

"I was in town, thought I'd stop by." We exchanged a hug, and I watched as she washed her hands. "How's being head honcho treating you?"

She rolled her eyes and resumed chopping carrots. "You know. It's crazy. But I love it. How about you? You're both head honcho and owner now. Is it good? I hear you opened on the weekend." A straight blond ponytail hung down her back from a white baseball cap with the inn's logo on the front. Her slender hands were like machines with the knife, the carrots rapidly transformed into tiny cubes. "Sorry I couldn't make it over. Things were nuts here with the foliage fanatics."

"No worries. If you ever get a Monday off, come by and we can hang out." I plopped onto a metal stool.

"I'll do that."

"The opening weekend was pretty good. Nothing

burned up, and it was solid customers the whole time. Which reminds me . . . I have to get to the bank some-time today."

"Money to put in the bank's always a good thing. But what about this murder over in South Lick?"

I grimaced. "Stella Rogers. She came into my place for breakfast. The bad thing is, she was found with one of my special biscuits stuffed in her mouth. So the police think I might have done it."

"You kidding me? One of your signature cheesy bis-cuits?" She paused and looked up. "But you wouldn't hurt a soul."

"Of course not." I tapped my finger on the counter. "I have a question for you. Do you ever hear anything about Ed Kowalski's restaurant?"

"Other than that it's a plain-wrap, low-quality break-fast-and-lunch joint? Not really. Although people seem to love it. I'm only glad we don't do breakfast, other than the continental spread we put out for paying guests. Why do you ask?"

"I hired a local teenager yesterday to help out. She was working for Ed, but she didn't seem too happy about him. When I asked Ed how she was as a worker, he put on a big old frown and said she was stand-offish."

Christina laughed. "That lech? He'll feel up any-thing with boobs. It doesn't matter how old or how young. He has a hard time keeping female employees."

"That must be it. How disgusting. Danna isn't even twenty and he's gotta be fifty."

She rolled her eyes. "Way of the world, kiddo. Way of the world."

"Is he married?"

"Not sure. Betsy told me he grew up in South Lick, though."

"I saw a picture of him from a few years back with Stella, the woman who was killed," I said. "In the photo they were both smiling, but he claimed they weren't friends."

"He probably went to kindergarten with her or something."

"So maybe Ed grew up in South Lick. He came into the store Saturday with Don, the guy who owns the hardware store."

"Well, married or not, Ed's sure not my type."

I laughed. "Well, duh." I knew Christina's type was Betsy, a lean welder.

"Speaking of type, you found anybody your type lately?" She waggled her eyebrows. "It's time to get over Will, you know."

I nodded slowly. Even though I'd left Will behind in California, I'd poured out the whole story to Christina when we worked together. "Funny you should ask." I told her about my date with Jim. "I'm making him dinner tonight, actually."

"That's what I like to hear. Get out of here, now. I have work to do."

"Same here." We exchanged another hug and promised to see each other soon, somehow.

I checked the wall clock in my store and then my list. Three o'clock and many of my errands and chores were checked off. I was such a list person—if I forgot to add a task, but I'd already done it, I wrote it down simply to have the satisfaction of crossing it off.

I'd deposited the weekend's cash at the bank, picked up frozen shrimp at the market and local produce from the farm stand for dinner, bought a litter box and litter, and cleaned the kitchen and living room. Working in the restaurant, I'd made tomorrow's miso gravy, prepped the biscuit dough, and cut up pineapple, melon, and grapes for a fruit salad I'd add to the Specials menu on the chalkboard. I was pretty sure business on weekdays would be slower, but I still wanted to be ready. As I was washing up, someone knocked on the store's front door. Walking over as I dried my hands on a towel, I spied Phil.

"Hey, feeling better?" I opened the door and stood back. He wore an old red IU sweatshirt with ratty jeans, and he held two wide trays stacked on top of each other.

"I am, thank the blessed Lord." He handed me the trays, which were sealed with plastic wrap. "Take these. Be right back." He turned, leaned into the back of his old Volvo station wagon, and drew out two more, then followed me into the store, setting them on the counter next to where I'd put the first two.

"Sit down for a minute?" I asked. "You must have taken a sick day."

"I did. Whew," he said, shaking his head as he sat. "I don't recommend the twenty-four-hour stomach bug to anyone." Somehow his dark skin looked pale and his eyes watered.

"Thanks for baking. Are you sure—"

"That I didn't infect the brownies?" At least his wicked grin was his usual. "Yes, ma'am. I was over it by this morning. I wiped down my kitchen with disinfectant just in case, and I washed my hands about every two minutes as I was cooking."

"Well, I appreciate it. We missed you Sunday, but by some miracle a competent young woman answered my ad and I hired her on the spot. Madam Mayor's teenaged daughter, Danna."

Phil laughed. "I used to babysit her, even though I'm only a few years older. She was a handful. Smart, but a bit too adventurous sometimes."

"That's funny." Then reality dawned and I felt the smile drain off my face. "You heard about the murder, I assume. Hard to believe."

"Stella. She never seemed happy, anytime I saw her."

"You seem about the same age as her son, Roy. Did you go to school with him?"

He nodded. "That one donated his brain to science before he was done with it. He'd lose a debate with a doorknob."

"That's not very nice, Phil. But Roy's odd, for sure. I ran into him in the hardware store this morning. What was it Don said to him? Something about being nice, like Don had tried to help him before."

"Don coached his Little League team and he's kind of looked after Roy ever since."

"Roy didn't seem too broken up about his mother being killed."

"I don't know if he's got Asperger's or if he simply has different reactions than most people." Phil shook his head. "His dad died when he was a kid, and that was tough on him."

I wrinkled my nose. "I never even thought about Stella having a husband. What did he die of?"

"I don't remember. I was a kid, too." He raised his eyebrows and stood. "I'm off. Rehearsal tonight."

I stood as well. "What's the show this time?"

"It's Copeland's *The Tender Land*. Absolutely gorgeous. And I have the male lead." He grinned.

"Get out. Really? That's awesome." I knew he aspired to a career in opera. "Thanks again for the desserts, Phil. You'll do more on Thursday for the weekend?"

"You bet." He left, humming as he went.

Chapter 10

Yikes. It was five-thirty already and I still hadn't changed for dinner. I finished whisking the rosemary vinaigrette together, fussed once more with the silverware and cloth napkins I'd laid on a vintage floral tablecloth, and turned the shrimp kabobs in their marinade one last time. I rummaged in a drawer, coming up with two red candles left over from Christmas. I stuck them in glass candleholders and decided they'd do just fine.

I ripped off my jeans and T-shirt and raced through a super-high-speed shower without washing my hair, to rinse off the sweat of biking, cleaning, and cooking. But now what to wear? I slipped on a pair of black leggings and searched my crowded bedroom closet, finally grabbing a long silk shirt in fuchsia from a hanger, since bright colors lit up my Mediterranean skin. I brushed my hair out loose on my shoulders and added silver earrings, a chunky silver necklace, and a touch of lip gloss. Satisfied, I left it at that.

Back in my apartment kitchen, I ruined the look by adding an apron over the silk top. Better that than stains. I poured a half glass of wine from the open bottle on the counter, sipping it as I thought of what was left to prepare. I sliced a couple of the last heirloom tomatoes of the season onto the salad and had just put pasta water on to boil when I heard a knock at the back door, the only door to the apartment besides the one leading into the store.

When I pulled the door open, Birdy streaked in ahead of Jim, who carried a bottle of wine in one hand and a fat paper-wrapped bunch of flowers in the other. He was wearing a pressed pink button-down shirt untucked over jeans and once again looked good enough to devour.

"Whoa, what was that?" he asked.

"I just adopted a cat. Actually, he just adopted me. His name's Birdy." I smiled back, trying to keep my nervousness from showing. Or maybe it was my lust I was trying to hide. "Come on in."

"First this." He leaned in and kissed my cheek. "Thanks for inviting me over." He smelled like fresh air and rainwater, with undertones of healthy male.

Flustered, I said, "You're welcome." I stood there for a second, looking at him.

"Are we having a standing meal?" he asked with a laugh.

I whacked my forehead and turned, leading him into the kitchen, where Birdy posed at one of his bowls and gave me a quizzical look. I tore open the cat food sack and scooped a cupful of dry kibble into his bowl. He fell to crunching.

"Looks like he was hungry," Jim said as he extended his offerings. "Flowers for the lady, and red wine, as per your expert recommendation. It's a very fine Cabernet, if I may say so."

I thanked him and set the wine on the table. When I unwrapped the flowers, I looked up in astonishment.

"How did you know I love yellow alstroemeria?"

"Just a hunch." Jim stuck his hands in his pockets, his eyes taking me in like a couple of thirsty emeralds. "You look really nice, Robbie. That color is stunning on you."

Now I was blushing. "Thanks." I cleared my throat. "How about if I open the wine?"

"Looks like you got a head start." He tilted his head at my half-full glass. "Just pour me a glass of whatever that is and hand me the opener. This one can breathe until we're ready for it."

I filled a glass and handed it to him, along with the folding corkscrew, then dug out my best vase, a trumpet-shaped heavy crystal that had been my grandmother's. Clipping off the bottoms of the stems, I said, "How was your Monday?"

"Unh." The cork popped out. "It was a Monday. Had a closing. Wrote a will. Ate lunch with Buck."

I'd been half listening as I clipped. "That's nice. . . . Wait, what? You had lunch with Buck?"

"Yup." He poured wine into his glass and topped mine up, too. "I ran into him at the courthouse in Nashville and we grabbed lunch at the Chili Shack."

I finished arranging the flowers before I spoke. I was dying to know what they'd talked about, but did I want this date to turn into a discussion of murder?

"How was the chili?"

"Great. Triple alarm." He fanned his open mouth, then took off his glasses and polished them on a corner of his shirt. "Poor old Buck can't eat spicy chili unless he gets heartburn."

I took a sip of my wine. "You mean he can't eat chili

because it gives him heartburn, right? You're talking like a Hoosier." I laughed.

"Hey, I am a Hoosier. I grew up here. You'll pick it up, you just watch."

"You don't usually talk that much like a local."

"It's because I'm a lawyer. Plus my folks are from Chicago and I was back East for law school. I kind of trained it out of me."

I glanced at the clock. "Time to start the coals." I grabbed my wine and a box of matches and headed out the door. I stuffed newspaper in the bottom of the cylindrical chimney and poured coals in the top. As I lit the papers, Jim strolled out, glass in hand, and leaned against the wall.

"You know what you're doing."

"Yeah. I like grilling." I dusted my hands of charcoal dust before I sat on the bench, patting the seat next to me. The low sunlight slanted through the half-clad swamp maple. The air brushed softly on my arms, but I knew the temperature would drop as soon as the sun did.

Jim joined me. "What were you up to today?"

I told him about my encounters of the morning: Don and Roy at Shamrock Hardware. Ed, his picture with Stella, his reaction to my asking, and what Christina said about Ed's habits. Phil's assessment of Roy.

"I've heard similar things about Ed. So far, nobody's brought charges."

I cocked my head and listened. "Water's boiling. Be right back." I hurried inside, poured a box of orzo into the steaming pot, stirred it, and turned down the heat. The coals would be ready soon, so I brought the long, narrow dish of marinating kebabs outside and set them on a little table I kept next to the kettle grill.

Unable to resist, I said, "Want to tell me about lunch with Buck? Has he locked up Stella's killer yet?"

Jim looked at the old barn behind the store, which I used for storage, then at me. "He asked me not to talk about it."

"But I'm your client. Or . . . maybe I'm not? I guess we haven't talked about what happens if they actually arrest me."

"If you're arrested, which you shouldn't be, you need a criminal lawyer, not a real estate and probate lawyer. And I'd recommend someone I know." He stared at the barn again.

Frustrated, I stood and dumped the hot coals onto the bottom rack of the grill with a bit more vigor than they needed, jumping back to avoid a spark landing on my shirt. I set the top grill rack on to heat and headed for the kitchen.

An hour later our plates were empty and the candles on the kitchen table were half the size from when I'd lit them. A half-dozen empty skewers attested to some pretty tasty grilled shrimp with crimini mushrooms, Vidalia onions, and sweet yellow peppers. A limp lettuce leaf hung off the edge of Jim's plate. On mine a few green-specked torpedoes of orzo vied with an errant translucent pink shell I missed when I prepped the seafood.

I'd managed to get a handle on my mood as I threw together the orzo and my special basil pesto. If

Buck asked Jim not to share a secret, then I should be admiring his integrity. I'd closed my eyes and taken three slow breaths in and three slow breaths out. Calmer, I'd gone back out to grill the kebabs, and we'd been chatting about everything except murder since then.

Now I said, "How can you call yourself a vegetarian if you eat seafood?" I set my chin on my hand. The room had darkened as we ate, and we sat in a circle of candlelight, the rest of the world lost to the night. Jim's skin glowed and the light flickered in the wineglasses.

He leaned back in his chair. "I've been a vegetarian since college. But a few years ago I was feeling kind of *meh.* I consulted a nutritionist, who told me I needed more high-quality protein. So I eat fish and other seafood on occasion. I prefer wild rather than farm raised, but when I'm out"—he gestured at the table— "I get off my high horse and eat what I'm served. Which was delicious."

"Thanks. I thought it was pretty good, too. It's a marinade I developed when I was cooking at the inn." I felt Birdy rubbing my ankles. I reached down to stroke him, which produced his chirping purr again.

"Lime, soy, maybe wine?" Jim raised his eyebrows.

"Good detective work. Plus ginger and sesame oil. But I can't figure out why eating fish doesn't disqualify you from being a vegetarian."

"You're right—it should. Somehow the fact that fish are wild and don't have legs seems an important distinction." He gazed at me. "You're kind of wonderful, you know that?" He leaned forward now, folding his arms on the table, gazing at me. "You can cook. You can build things. You can dance and solve puzzles. You bike all over the place. What can't you do?"

"Don't ask." I laughed to soften my answer. I couldn't hold on to a first husband, for one. "I'm miserable at foreign languages. I didn't even catch on to Spanish. In California." I shook my head. "My eyes glaze over at talk of the stock market, and I hate writing. I can't type for beans and I don't even like writing thank-you notes or birthday cards. There's more, but I don't want to spoil my reputation."

Jim topped up my wineglass. After holding the bottle up to the light, he drained the rest into his glass. He took a sip, then set his glass down.

"You're a successful lawyer," I said. "You can dance. I'm sure there's lots more you're good at. So what are your failings?"

He laughed. "I hate reading fiction. My brain just can't suspend disbelief and stop analyzing why the people in a story would never, ever do something like that. And I bit my nails until a year ago."

I glanced at his hands. Sure enough. His nails were short, but they were trimmed rather than ragged. "That's not so bad. Nothing else?"

A cloud scudded over his eyes. "You don't want to hear the rest." He cleared his throat and mustered a smile.

"Gotcha." I stood and collected our plates. "Apple crisp?"

"Absolutely." While I cleared the rest of the dinner things, Jim wandered into the living room. "Okay if I put on music?" he called in. Soft light shone in from the doorway.

"Sure. Help yourself." I cut two pieces of crisp, adding a scoop of vanilla bean ice cream to each before I set them on the table.

The tune of "Ya Gotta Dance" filled the room. Jim appeared next to me and pulled me into a close dance position. "Shall we?"

"The ice cream is going to melt," I murmured into his shoulder.

"Let it."

Chapter 11

Sure enough, Tuesday morning wasn't quite as busy as the weekend. But Danna showed up on time and ready to work, her dreads neatly tied back with a turquoise scarf, and a steady stream of customers came through, despite the rain that began to fall right when we opened. The two of us were shaping up to be a good team. Locals who came in seemed pleased to see Danna, and she knew every one of them, of course. She even pulled an empty half-gallon Mason jar out and hand lettered a TIPS sign she taped onto it, setting it next to the cash register. I'd had a few requests for take-out orders, so the jar could come in handy.

Cooking and greeting kept me too occupied to dwell on last evening's delicious end, but a rosy feeling still held me. Jim and I had danced and, well, just plain made out. We never did get to our dessert. And then I'd reluctantly sent him along home. I knew I had to get up early. But Jim said he'd see me this week and I believed him.

Corrine Beedle sailed through the door during the

nine o'clock lull. Stella's death hit me again. Last time the mayor was here, Stella walked in right behind her. I waved from the sink and called out a greeting.

"You got somewhere I can put my umbrella?" She stressed the first syllable like it was a dignitary.

I pointed at the umbrella stand right next to her.

Corrine deposited the flaming red but soaking wet umbrella, hung her raincoat on the wrought-iron coat tree near the door, and sauntered to a table, this time clicking on blue heels matching her suit. Danna was at the grill, so I pulled an order pad out of my apron pocket.

"Thanks for coming back," I said. "What can we get you today?"

"I'm just spying on my baby there. Hey, baby," she called to Danna.

A couple of customers who were tucked into their omelets looked up and smiled. Danna didn't turn from the grill, but she lifted a spatula and waved with it. I expected she was used to being embarrassed in public by her bigger-than-life mom.

"But I am just a touch hungry," Corrine said. "Why don't you give me two eggs over easy with bacon and hash browns. You got any fried biscuits with apple butter?"

"'Fraid not. You're not the first person who's asked, though." Deep-fried biscuits might be a local delicacy, but my hands were full enough keeping up with the regular old nonfried version. I took the order over to Danna and carried the coffeepot back to Corrine.

After I poured, she gestured at the chair across from her. "Take a load off, honey."

"Just for a minute, but thanks." After I eased into the chair, my feet expressed their extreme gratitude.

I was going to have to build in break time. "Danna's been a godsend. She works hard, knows how to cook, and is easy to be around."

Corrine smiled like she knew what I was talking about. "Always been her own person, that girl."

"I should offer my condolences on the death of your assistant. Her shoes will be hard to fill." I wasn't sure about that, but I thought it sounded like the right thing to say.

Apparently, it wasn't, because Corrine snorted. "Stella? I'm sorry she's dead, but she was a real bitch."

I must have looked surprised, because she went on. "Well, she was. And somehow she'd gotten her job written into the town bylaws so she'd have it in perpetuity." She shook her head. "Doncha think a new mayor might ought to be able to bring along her own admin? Couldn't believe it when Stella told me I couldn't. I'm glad to be rid of her, frankly." She drummed long blue fingernails on the table, over and over.

"She was a little difficult to deal with," I said.

"'Difficult' is kind of an understatement. I heard tell she was blackmailing half the men in town."

My eyes flew wide open like little strings pulled them up. "Really? For what?"

"Oh, this and that." She patted her hair, today done up in a kind of twist, the front swooping low across her forehead. "Is there a man alive who don't have something nasty in his past? Stella knew everybody's secrets."

I hummed to myself as I did final cleanup. I'd sent Danna home a little while ago after a good day of working together, and had flipped the sign on the door to CLOSED, since it was after two-thirty. I emptied the compost bucket in the bin outside the service door on the left side of the store beyond the kitchen area. I made sure the door was locked when I went back in.

Corrine's gossip about Stella blackmailing town residents didn't sit well, but I'd been too busy to dwell on it. And it wasn't my business, anyway. Let Buck and his cohort weasel out which among her victims might have been the one to turn the tables on Stella.

I whirled when I heard the door bell jangle, and then lit up inside as I saw my visitor was Jim, even though I was tired and a day's worth of cooking odors clogged my pores. I wiped my hands on a towel as I strolled toward him.

I smiled. "Nice to see you."

He sank into a chair and didn't speak. He didn't smile back, either.

Uh-oh. I sat, too, and waited.

He brushed raindrops up off his forehead and into his hair. "I have some bad news. Did you happen to lose a pen recently?" He gazed over at the shelves of cookware.

I nodded, as slow as a bobblehead in a slo-mo video.

"A pen with 'Jeanine's Cabinets' printed on it? Your mother's shop logo?"

"Yes. Did you find it?" I did not have a good feeling about this.

"Buck did. In Stella's apartment. They're testing it for DNA and prints now." He finally looked at me.

Astonished, I sat back and let his news sink in. I shook my head, hard. "But it's my pen. Of course it'll have my identity all over it. Plus I taped a red plastic flower to the end so nobody would walk off with it. What Buck should be doing is figuring out who stole it and left it there." I stood and paced to the cookware area and back. "Somebody really is trying to make it look like I killed Stella."

"Appears that way. When's the last time you used the pen? Or noticed it was missing?"

I thought for a minute. "I remember missing it when I wanted it for my crossword."

"You do crosswords in pen?" Jim's voice lost its edge and he smiled a little.

"Of course. Even though I'm a leftie. But I'm careful. Anyway, that was Sunday night. I must have been using the pen to take orders Saturday morning. Mom would have loved this place, and I remember putting the pen in my apron before we opened, so she'd be part of it. Anyone could have taken it on Saturday . . . and then planted it in Stella's house." I gripped the back of the chair I'd been sitting in. I was steaming at the thought of Mom's pen being defiled. First stolen, then used to deflect guilt for a horrible crime.

"Pretty much the whole town came through here the first day," Jim said with a grimace.

I sat again and fixed my gaze on an antique meat grinder on a shelf across the room, next to its little box holding disks with various-sized holes. The cast-iron device, with a conical hopper, a long grinding handle, and a vise at the bottom to attach it to a table, was a silvery color and looked comfortingly substantial. Way more substantial than my life felt at the moment.

"Would anyone else have one of those pens?" Jim folded his arms. "Adele maybe?"

"She might. Mom might have sent her one and the killer could have stolen it. I can ask her." I scrabbled in the apron for my cell phone.

Jim held up his hand. "Later. No one else?"

"Hmm. Don at the hardware store said he was friends with Mom long ago, but he made it sound like it was more than just friends. He gave her our cat, Butch, too. I never knew that. I don't think they'd been in touch, but maybe they were. Maybe she sent him a pen. For all I know, he'd been out to visit her in the years since I left home."

We sat in our bubbles of thought for a few moments. Mine was filled with both angst and ire. My happy new life as restaurateur and proprietor was exploding in my face. My exciting new romantic life seemed to have gone up in a puff of smoke, too.

I looked up and swallowed. "So now what? Am I going to be arrested?"

"No, but Buck wants to talk with you." He cleared his throat. "I told him I'd bring you down. And I'll stay there until we learn if you need a criminal lawyer or not."

"Buck wants to talk with me now?" My voice angled up.

"This afternoon."

"I need to clean up." I glanced at the wall clock. "I'll be ready in an hour."

"Okay. I'll be back at four."

I untied my apron and started toward my apartment. Then I stopped. "Wait a minute." I turned back.

Jim rested a hand on the door. He looked at me.

"You knew about this last night. That was what Buck told you yesterday, about my pen." I couldn't believe it. "And you wouldn't tell me."

"I'm sorry." He blew air out through his lips. "I didn't want to spoil our dinner."

"Well, you've spoiled it now."

Chapter 12

I tapped my fingers on the metal table in the police station interview room. Jim sat catty-corner from me doing something with his phone. I didn't want to be here, and I sure didn't want to be here with him. Knowing he was aware last night of me being under suspicion and not telling me left the taste of spoiled lemonade in my mouth. You want it to be sweet, but instead it's acrid and half fermented.

All the time while I'd showered and dressed, my mind was a boiling pot of thoughts. I searched the little I knew about Saturday's customers for who'd had the chance to steal my pen, and then who had reason to leave it at Stella's house before killing her, but I came up with almost nothing. Possible suspects included Corrine, because Stella was a bitch. Don, because he hated Stella for blocking his election. Ed, because I was his competition. But then why kill Stella? Why not murder *me*? For all I knew, Stella herself took the pen out of spite.

After stewing about what to wear to a police interview, I'd pulled my hair back in a severe knot and dressed in a dark sweater, skirt, and boots. A kindly female professor had told me once, when I was worried about presenting a paper, it was always better to be overdressed when you were nervous. This pretty much fit the bill.

Now, though, I was even more nervous, because we'd been sitting here for half an hour. My stomach was a winter nesting ground for butterflies. Out of the corner of my eye, I saw Jim look up at me, but I didn't look back.

"Robbie, I know you're upset with me," he said. "But when Buck comes in, try to stay calm. Answer questions as simply as you can. A 'yes' or a 'no' will suffice, and don't elaborate if you don't have to. Okay?"

"Yes." I clasped my hands on the table and willed them not to fidget.

Finally the door pushed open. Buck sauntered in, followed by a female police officer.

"Robbie, Jim. You know Wanda, right? I mean, Officer Wanda." He gestured at her.

He spoke so slow I thought maybe he was about to nod off midsentence. Wanda stood in front of the door without looking at us, her hands behind her back and her feet apart. Her distinctly female body was stuffed into the male-cut uniform like a sausage, and her hairdo matched mine, except hers was gelled into submission.

Buck sat across from me, stretching his legs out, as always, and laid his tablet on the table. Scratching the back of his neck, he checked the corners of the ceiling.

"All righty, then." He pressed something on the

tablet, spoke his name and rank, and stated the date. "Roberta Jordan, do I have your permission to record this interview?"

I glanced at Jim. I hated to admit it, but I needed his help now. When he nodded, I said, "Yes."

Buck asked me to state my name and address.

"Roberta Jordan, 19 Main Street, South Lick, Indiana."

He went through the same questions as Saturday night: Where had you been? Did you kill Stella? I answered him the exact same way.

"Do you own a pin with a picture of a table and the words 'Jeanine's Cabinets' on it?" He looked me in the eyes.

I sat up straight. "I own a *pen* like that. Not a *pin*." That was how he'd said it, even though it was rude of me to point it out.

He gave an exasperated sound. "Don't get fresh with me, now. Do you currently know where your *pen* is at?" He stressed the word, but it still sounded like "pin" to my ears.

"No. I—" I cut myself off. Jim had said not to elaborate.

"When was the last time you're aware you were in possession of the pen?"

"I put it in my apron pocket before the store opened Saturday morning."

"Did you have it Saturday night?"

"I don't know."

"When did you realize it was missing?"

"Sunday night."

"Do you agree to let us test your DNA?"

"Of course." I opened my palms and leaned forward. "But listen, Buck. If it is my pen, my DNA will be all over it. Fingerprints, too. Which doesn't prove . . . anything." I thought it would be prudent not to let loose with a string of obscenities, but my anger had taken over for my nerves. "You need to find the DNA of the idiot who thought they could frame me for a crime I didn't commit."

Buck sighed with a deep, mournful sound. "Do you know of anyone else who owns such a pen?"

"No." I glanced at Jim. *The heck with his instructions.* "You should ask Don O'Neill if he has one. He used to be friendly with my mother." I wasn't going to suggest Adele might have one, though. Let them figure that out. The murderer could be trying to frame her instead of me, and she'd been baking biscuits all morning Saturday.

Buck raised his eyebrows all the way up to Canada. "I'll ask you not to talk to anyone about this pen business," he said. "Do I have your word?"

"Of course, whatever. But there's another thing." Now I was on a roll. "Yesterday Corrine Beedle told me she heard Stella was 'blackmailing half the men in town.' Her words. There's gotta be people around here with an actual reason to kill Stella. I sure didn't have one."

Buck cleared his throat. "You might not know this, Robbie, since you're still a newcomer to the state and all like that."

"I've lived here for three years."

Buck ignored me and went on. "We have a law against spiteful gossip."

Jim stared at him, swallowing as if he was trying not to laugh. He looked at me. "It's true."

"You'd better tell Madam Mayor, then." My breath was coming fast and furious now, with "furious" being the key word. "I'm just passing on what she said. She's the gossiper, not me."

Chapter 13

By the time Jim dropped me at home, the earlier gentle rain had turned into a real storm. I longed to head out on my bike, and let some sweat and some hills make me forget about the mess my life had become. But no way I was riding in this wind and rain, plus it was getting dark. I sat at the laptop in my apartment and prowled the Internet until I found a bike trainer that transformed a road bike into a stationary model. I'd seen the simple stands that the back wheel clicked into, with selectable resistance levels, and I ordered one on the spot. It'd be useful all winter, and was way cheaper than a gym membership. Nashville had a YMCA, but I preferred exercising alone.

I heard a scratching at the back door and froze. *Someone trying to get in? Or maybe a branch in the wind?* I was sure I'd locked it, but it only had a simple lock in the doorknob. If somebody really wanted to get in, I had no doubt they could. I reached out and switched off the lamp on the desk so I couldn't be seen. The motion-activated light outside was lit up, although that could be from the branches waving in the wind.

Or maybe from a murderer skulking around my windows. I shivered and grabbed for my bag, scrabbling in its depths for my phone.

I heard the sound again. The loud *meow* that followed made me laugh at myself. I turned the light back on before I got up and let Birdy in, who gave the expression "as wet as a drowned rat" new meaning. His fluffy black fur was soaked and made him look about half the size he usually did. I found an old towel and rubbed him as dry as I could get him. I made sure I locked the door again, just in case the next sound wasn't so innocent. Maybe my next purchase should be a dead bolt. And a cat door.

I was still restless. I hated having to go to the police station. I couldn't stand that I was living under even a hint of suspicion. Buck hadn't given my ideas much credence, either. I was still upset with Jim at having withheld his knowledge of my pen's discovery. And a killer was out there somewhere, a person who'd found it within himself or herself to take another person's life.

I paced my apartment, then went into the store. Wielding a feather duster, I wandered among the shelves of cookware. While everything was vintage, that didn't mean it should be covered with dust. Reaching up, I dusted the top shelf, where I'd arrayed colorful cookie tins and trays. I straightened a collection of pastry cutters and another of choppers. I moved a couple of tart pans from the measuring-spoon section back to the shelves of baking pans. When I came to the meat grinder, I paused. I wanted to insert the *Find the Murderer* disk, pour all the information I'd learned into the hopper, and grind out the answer. Too bad life didn't work that way. And so far, my puzzle master hat wasn't really working, either.

When my stomach notified me in no uncertain terms it was time for dinner, I put away the duster and returned to my personal kitchen. Birdy ran to his food bowl and gazed up at me with hopeful eyes. Looked like it was his dinnertime, too. I scooped out a cupful of dry food, but he bumped my hand as I poured it into the dish and half of it scattered on the floor.

"Silly cat," I said, kneeling to gather up the food and get it back into the bowl, where it belonged. I heated up the rest of the orzo for my own supper, then I grabbed the grater and added Parmesan on top. That and a glass of red was plenty. I brought the crossword I was working on to the table, but it didn't feel right to do it without Mom's pen. I should have asked Buck if I'd ever get the pen back.

I took a bite of the orzo. Even though the basil in the pesto was still fragrant and the mouthfeel of the slippery little pasta shapes was usually something I loved, I barely tasted it. Despite the delicious ending to last night's dinner with Jim, the about-to-sprout romance looked like it'd dried up and withered away. I shook my head. I'd lived without love in my life for more than three years. I knew how, whether I liked it or not.

As I ate, I stared at the grid of squares on my clipboard. Some empty, some black, some I'd filled in. I looked at the clues, 110 of them in the *Across* list, and 114 in the *Down*.

Clues. What about the Stella Murder *puzzle? What would that one look like?* I snapped my fingers and rose to dig a pad of graph paper out of my desk drawer. I'd bought it when I was designing the layout for the restaurant and store. I brought the paper back to the table, along with a sharp number two pencil and a clear blue ruler. I supposed there was an interactive puzzle design website out there somewhere. Wasn't there an app for everything? But for me, using my hands with something more tactile than a keyboard engaged my brain in a different way than using my eyes on a screen.

I drew a grid. I started jotting down what I knew under the clues section. Corrine disliked Stella intensely. Don hated Corrine for beating him in the mayoral race and, by extension, hated Stella. Ed's restaurant now faced competition from mine. Someone either had access to Stella's house, or was a local she knew well enough to let in. Roy Rogers was an odd bird.

Then I added what I didn't know: *Who did Stella blackmail? Was Ed sexually harassing his female employees? Who stole my pen? Who killed Stella?*

By the time I ran out of facts and questions, my plate was empty and my glass was, too. No answers were apparent, but my mind was more at ease for laying it out in a format that was as familiar to me as my own name. I stood and headed back into the store to do prep for tomorrow. I had tables to set, biscuit dough to prep, gravy to make, and my alarm was going to ring loud and early. At least now I thought I'd be able to sleep.

I unlocked the front door of the store at a few minutes before seven, turning the CLOSED sign to OPEN. Danna had arrived promptly again, and we'd been working together for half an hour. I pushed the door open wide and took a deep breath of the fresh morning air. The storm had blown through, leaving a chilly but sparkling clean fall morning. The trees looked cleaner, too, since last night's wind had blown off half their leaves. We might have just slid past peak leaf-peeking. Adele's old Ford Explorer rattled up, the sides streaked with mud. She climbed out of one side, while Vera emerged from the other.

Adele and I exchanged a hug. "Couldn't stay away?" I smiled at her and greeted Vera.

"We're hungry," Adele said. "We've been out birding already. Thought we'd better fill up the tanks before we head back out."

They both wore sturdy outdoor boots and warm coats. Vera's neck was wrapped in a brilliant purple scarf and I spied a field guide stuffed in her coat pocket.

"See anything good?" I asked.

"We got the Wilson's warbler, and a Savannah sparrow." Vera patted her pocket. "That one's a life bird for me."

"I'm happy for you. No idea what either of those birds is, but come on in." I gestured them in ahead of me. "You're the first customers of the day."

Vera headed for the restroom as Adele strolled to the grill. "'Morning, Danna." She smiled at the young woman busy turning sausages. "You the new kitchen help?"

"Hey, Ms. Jordan." Danna gave her a big smile. "Robbie's trying me out."

"Of course you know each other." I shook my head. "Does anybody in this town not know everyone else?"

"Nope. Danna's school used to bring the kids out to see my lambs every spring." Adele snitched a hot sausage and tossed it back and forth between her hands before biting off half of it.

"Hey, sit down and order, lady." I shooed her over to a table, then brought the freshly brewed coffee and poured. "Vera too?"

Adele pointed to Vera's cup as she chewed the sausage. I looked over. Vera still hadn't emerged, so I leaned closer to the table.

"Did my mom ever send you one of her pens? You know, from the shop?"

She cocked her head. "That's a funny question. But yes, she did."

I must have looked interested, because she went on. "Don't get your hopes up. It got run over once and I threw it away. Why do you ask?"

I gazed at her for a minute. "My 'Jeanine's Cabinets' pen was found in Stella's house. Somebody stole it and planted it there."

The door pushed open with a jangle and three workmen clomped in. Bacon sizzled on the grill, and the timer dinged, telling me the biscuits were done.

Adele shook her head, looking as somber as a funeral director. "That's bad news, honey."

"Don't I know it." I headed over to the new customers. I called over my shoulder to Adele, "Come back during the morning lull if you can? I need to talk to you, but I can't now."

"Will do."

"'Morning, gentlemen." I mustered my inner cheery proprietor and came up with a smile for the workmen, who wore the green-and-white REA logo on their shirts. I'd had great service from the Brown County Rural Electrical Association. "I'm glad you've stopped in for breakfast. Can I start you off with coffee?" After they nodded, I poured from the pot I still held in my hand, emptying it. I took their orders and headed back to the grill area.

So the only pen in town was mine. Damn. Unless Don owned one, of course. But how could I find out?

Danna took the biscuits out and slid them into the shallow warming oven. I clipped the new orders to the wheel, started a fresh pot of coffee, threw a waiting pan of biscuits into the oven, and finished slicing the mushrooms I'd been working on when seven o'clock had rolled around. My brain was as busy as my hands, though, and it wasn't thinking about breakfast.

In a couple of minutes, the three orders were done and I carried two platters to the table. "Pancakes and sausage," I said, setting it in front of one man. "And the Kitchen Sink omelet with biscuits, gravy, and bacon?"

"Mine," said the heftiest one of the three.

I left his order and brought over the final breakfast, two scrambled eggs, with home fries and fruit salad.

"Looks super, miss," said the recipient. "This is George, and Ray, and I'm Abe. Abe O'Neill." He smiled with big brown eyes, a dimple creasing his right cheek. Looking to be in his thirties, he was lean and tan with wavy hair the color of walnuts, and his left hand was bare of gold. A little flutter of attraction in my midsection shouldn't have been as much of a surprise as it was.

"Nice to meet you all. I'm Robbie Jordan. And I love REA. You all were really helpful when I was setting up here over the last few months."

"We're a cooperative. Being helpful is part of our mission," Abe said. When George rolled his eyes, Abe said, "It is, truly."

I took a closer look at him. He looked familiar on top of the cuteness. "Are you related to Don?"

"One and the same. I'm his little brother."

"You two have the same eyes."

"And you're Jeanine's daughter, right? She used to babysit me back in the day, long time ago when she was dating Donnie." He laughed—a delightful, low, rolling sound. "Boy, did I give her hell."

When Mom was dating Don. So I was right about that. Maybe Don did have one of Mom's pens.

Abe's expression turned serious. "Sorry to hear about Jeanine's passing. That must have been tough for you." He watched me with the kindest gaze I'd gotten from a man in a long time. Maybe ever.

My throat thickened. I managed to swallow and say, "Thanks. I miss her. Boatloads." I mustered a smile. "And thanks to you all for coming in. I hope you'll be back."

"We will," Abe said. "I will, anyway." He kept those big browns on me until I turned away.

Chapter 14

I slid tea bags into three mugs as the clock chimed ten, filled them with hot water, and carried them to the table where Adele sat. She and Vera returned, as promised. Vera wandered the cookware shelves, picking up items and exclaiming. The restaurant was empty except for us and Danna, who hummed to whatever was in her earbud as she scrubbed the morning's pots and pans. The air was warm and still held aromas of spicy sausage, sweet syrup, and old wood.

"How was the birding?" I asked as I sank into a chair. It'd been a busy morning, thank goodness, but my feet ached. I'd been so occupied I hadn't had much time to worry about murder, but now it all flooded back into my brain.

"Decent. We never got the Carolina, although we heard him. So, what's up? Has something to do with your mom's pen, I guess."

"Buck questioned me about it yesterday. Do you

remember seeing me take orders with it Saturday morning?"

Adele shook her head. "I was pretty busy on the grill. Can't say I do or don't remember."

"Someone who was in that morning must have stolen it and left it in Stella's house. Either accidentally or to make it look like I was there. I didn't even know where Stella lived until Buck told me on the night she was killed."

"Hmm." Adele fished the tea bag out of her mug and laid it on a napkin, then measured four heaping spoonfuls of sugar into the mug.

A giggle burbled up out of me. "My teeth hurt just watching you sweeten that thing up."

She stirred, took a sip, and smiled. "I've always had a thing for sweet tea. But back to business," which she pronounced as "bidniss." "What we have to figure out is who wanted Stella dead."

"That's for sure. Believe me, my brain's been heating up trying to sort that out. Corrine was in here yesterday, said Stella was blackmailing half the men in town. Think it's true?"

"Could be. Wouldn't surprise me one iota." She tapped the side of the mug with her spoon. "She was a snoopy bi . . . broad."

I laughed. "Go ahead. Corrine called her a 'bitch.' You might as well, too."

"I'd always catch her listening at the door during the time when I was Madam Mayor. And it all got stored in her brain. Steel-trap memory, that one." Adele glanced at Danna as she worked. She lowered her voice and went on. "'Course Corrine herself doesn't exactly get along with everybody."

"Do you think Stella was blackmailing Corrine?"

"Possible." Adele nodded. "Coulda happened."

"What would there be to blackmail her about?"

Before Adele could answer, Vera walked up, holding a cast-iron muffin pan, with a delighted expression on her face. "I've been wanting one of these for years. Who doesn't love a corn-shaped corn muffin?" The heavy black rectangle featured indentations that looked like ears of corn.

"The muffins come out with nice crisp crust on them," I said. "Oil the pan and heat it up as you preheat the oven. Oh, and here's tea for you."

"Sold." Vera set the pan on the table and sat. "Hot tea's perfect, thanks. A bit chilly out there." She rubbed her hands together.

"Winter's on its way." I gazed out the front window as a gust of wind blew a collection of leaves sideways down the street.

Despite having a lineup of patties ready to cook and a red-skinned potato salad using local spuds on the Specials menu, lunch was slow. I finally sent Danna home at one o'clock. I could handle two customers here, one there, which was all we'd had since eleven-thirty. I hoped this was only a small Wednesday bump in the road and not a pattern.

The last customer to come in, a blond woman on the far side of forty, sat alone with a book, reading as she ate. I moseyed over, pot of coffee in hand, to see if she needed anything. She glanced up.

"The potato salad is right delicious. What're these small little goobers?" She used her fork to prod a caper. "They taste kind of like pickles."

"Capers. You're right, they're pickled. I like the flavor," I said. "And I'm pleased you're enjoying the salad. Can I get you anything else?"

"You might could top up my coffee, if you don't mind." She wore dark pants and a tailored green jacket on her well-padded figure. Her hair color, however, came out of a bottle, and it looked like she did it at home.

As I poured, I said, "I feel like I've seen you around town, but can't quite place you."

"I'm Georgia." She laughed. "I work at the library."

"That's it. It's nice to meet you, Georgia. I'm Robbie Jordan, and I'm sorry for not remembering where I'd seen you."

"Not a problem, hon. I'm no librarian, only an aide. But I love working there. I'm a reading addict." She winked.

I didn't think anybody younger than grandparents winked at people, but maybe I was thinking of California. I definitely wasn't in California anymore.

"Say, heard you're in a spot of trouble with this murder thing." Georgia raised her thinly plucked eyebrows.

"I'm not in trouble, exactly. But it seems like someone's out to make it look like I killed Stella."

"The biscuit. And now your pin."

By now I knew she meant "pen," but I was a little bit astonished she knew those details. Not really, though. Everybody in South Lick knowing everything no longer surprised me.

"Too bad all this came up right about when you opened over here." She shook her head. "I usually eat lunch with my girlfriends on Wednesdays. But they wouldn't join me today when I said I wanted to try your place out. Said you might poison them."

"Are you kidding me?" I stared at her. *I guess I am in trouble. Deep doo-doo trouble, if potential customers are boycotting me.*

"I told them they were being ridiculous." She waved her fork in the air. "And they are. This lunch was the best I've ever eaten in town. I'm going to tell everybody to get their suspicious butts over here and make sure you stay in business." Only a scrap of sesame bun remained from her cheeseburger and she'd done a good job demolishing the potato salad, too.

"I really appreciate that."

"And it doesn't even compare to what Eddie makes over in Nashville." She wrinkled her nose. "I won't eat at his so-called country store anymore, and it's not only the lousy food. That man's got problems."

"Oh?"

"Yes, ma'am. It's not Christian to speak ill of others." She patted her hair. "But he should be arrested for sexual harassment." She wiped the corners of her mouth with a dainty move of her napkin and stood. "What do I owe you, dear? I need to be getting back to work." She stuck her book into an enormous yellow faux-leather handbag and pulled out a wallet.

I handed her the ticket. When she handed me a twenty, I fished in my apron pocket for change until she held up her hand.

"You go on and keep the rest. I feel bad for you, losing business for nothing. I'm going to tell everyone I run into they should come eat here."

"Thank you, Georgia. I appreciate that." As she walked toward the door, I stacked up the dishes and silverware from her table. The bell jangled as I set them in the sink and turned on the water to rinse them. Man, if I was losing business over being questioned by the police, it could be bad. I whistled out loud, wet a cloth, and turned back to wipe Georgia's table.

And then jumped about a foot off the ground at the sight of Jim standing directly in front of me.

"Eep! Don't you know how to announce yourself?" I let out a breath and leaned against the counter behind me. He must have come in the door at the same time Georgia went out, or I would have heard the bell again.

He stuck one hand in the pants pocket of a well-tailored gray suit. He lowered his chin and gave me an abashed look over the top of his glasses. He wore a blue silk tie the color of cornflowers knotted over a black shirt, and kept his other hand behind him.

Recovering, I cocked my head. "You sure look like a lawyer today."

"Been in court all morning. But I wanted to apologize to you. And I'm also starving. Any chance of lunch with a side of forgiveness?" He brought a compact white box the size of a brick out from behind his back and extended it to me.

"What's this?" I accepted the box, holding it in both hands.

"I took a wild guess and got you dark chocolate fudge from the Nashville Fudge Kitchen."

"Jim. You didn't have to do that." Now I was the sheepish one.

"No, you were right. I should have told you Monday night. I don't think anything could have spoiled that evening."

I cocked my head, regarding him, set the box down,

and extended both arms toward his shoulders. "Hug and make up?"

He wrapped me up tight as I leaned into the smooth cloth of his suit jacket. I inhaled him as his heart beat beneath my ear. He stroked my hair with one hand, a touch that felt as intimate as if we were naked. I didn't want to surface, ever, but I had to. Customers could come in at any moment.

I pushed away, smiling up at him. "What was that about lunch?"

He sank into the nearest chair and set his chin in his hand, elbow on the table. "You're a lot easier on the eyes than Judge Zimmer." Using his other hand, he rubbed the tips of his fingernails with his thumb.

I laughed, but I was glad I'd worn my favorite skinny jeans with a deep peach-colored shirt that set off my skin. "Poor judge. Now tell me what you want." I pointed to the blackboard and told him about the potato salad.

"That and a mushroom veggie burger. And a glass of lemonade."

"Coming right up."

As I worked, he sauntered over and leaned against the sink. "Quiet in here today."

I pursed my lips. "Yeah. Not any lunch rush to speak of. A woman named Georgia came in, said her friends stayed away because they thought I might poison them."

The smile slid off Jim's face. "That's outrageous. I suppose they heard about Buck's questioning you."

"Who hasn't? Maybe I should have bought a store in Nashville, or even in Bloomington. A town this small—well, it's good and it's bad."

"You got that right."

"I feel like I should post a big sign in the window saying, 'The Cook Is Not a Murderer.'" I shook my head. "Anyway, a guy came in this morning. Don O'Neill's brother." I ignored the teeny-tiny pang of guilt stabbing me for having thought Abe more attractive than the common bear. Or the common Hoosier, at least.

"Abe?"

"Right. He said Don used to date my mom. So Don might have one of her pens. And, apparently, everybody knows Corrine and Stella didn't get along."

Jim picked up a spoon and tapped the sink.

"Do you know what kind of dirt Stella might have held on any of these people?" I asked. "Corrine? Don? Ed? Or anybody in town, for that matter."

"I was away at school for quite a while, what with undergrad at IU and law school in Massachusetts. I've only been back for about five years, so I'm sure I missed lots of news. Or secrets, as it were."

I flipped his burger and stirred the sautéing mushrooms around on the grill. I reached for a clean plate, laying a pickle and a big scoop of potato salad on the blue-and-white concentric stripes. I opened a bun onto the grill as I thought.

"I wish I knew what happened between Don and Mom. I don't think he'd tell me even if I asked." I assembled the burger and laid it on the plate. "Come on, eat your lunch. I'll get the lemonade."

He took the plate and sat. He managed to squeak out a "thanks" before chowing into his burger like he hadn't eaten in a week. After I brought his lemonade,

I realized I hadn't eaten in a long time, either. I dished up a scoop of potato salad for myself, grabbed a couple of leftover sausages, and took the seat next to him.

"News and secrets," I murmured as I chewed, not seeing my plate, not tasting my food. "Secrets and news."

"What?"

I glanced at Jim, who looked like he was waiting for an explanation. "Oh, I was just thinking about this puzzle." I fell silent for a moment. When my puzzle brain is engaged, I can barely carry out normal interaction. I forced myself to focus on his face and went on. "You mentioned missing news while you were away. I think I might hit up the library, see if I can find newspapers for the time right before Mom moved out West."

"Good idea. I'm not sure the South Lick Public Library has much of an archive. But Nashville will if they don't."

I scrolled through the archives of the *South Lick Sentinel* after Georgia happily set me up with the microfilm from a couple of decades earlier. I sat ensconced at a desk in a carrel on the second floor of the small but decent library, which was housed in a renovated boardinghouse built in the late 1800s.

Georgia watched me work for a minute. "We also have Nashville's paper, the *Brown County Democrat*, online." She showed me how to access it.

I thanked her, but I kept my gaze on the screen. My

puzzle brain had taken over again and I didn't want to engage in small talk. I was glad Jim had been wrong about the South Lick library archive, though. They seemed to have everything I needed, and I'd been able to walk the three blocks here.

Mom had moved to the Santa Barbara area before I was born, but I wasn't exactly sure how long before. Was she pregnant when she left her hometown? Had she met my birth father in California? I couldn't believe she'd never told me, although we hadn't really talked about my father. I'd had a brief flurry of curiosity after I started elementary school and realized other kids had dads at home and I didn't. She'd told me the man responsible for my hair and coloring was a decent man, but he wasn't able to be in our lives. After that, I was so happy with only the two of us I didn't really care. But living in South Lick, seeing Don's reaction to realizing I was Jeanine's daughter, and now the business with the pen had my interest in the past rekindled, and that fire wasn't getting doused by anything but the truth. I could have asked Adele, but I didn't want to interrupt my train of thoughts to step out and try to call her now.

I brought up issues of the paper from twenty-eight years ago. I was twenty-seven, so I'd start there and go backward in time. I scrolled through page after page, but had no idea what I was looking for. No, I knew what I wanted to find—any tidbit involving Don and my mom, or even her and a dark, curly-haired mystery man. A picture, maybe, or something newsworthy. But that was too nebulous, and the software didn't let me enter a search term. Heck, if I had a search term, I could have just used the Internet.

The *Sentinel* was a weekly paper. After an hour I'd browsed about three years of papers with no results. I stood and stretched, trying to unglaze my eyes. I strolled over to one of the many tall, graceful windows, and passed a wall clock with the hour hand just reaching four. I needed to prep for tomorrow, but I thought I'd give the search one more hour. As I looked at the street below, an unmistakable Corrine Beedle strode along the sidewalk, with an equally unmistakable Roy Rogers at her side. He seemed to be haranguing her, throwing his hand in the air and facing her as he walked. He tailed her when she marched up the steps to the front doors of Town Hall, but he remained outside after she pulled the door open and disappeared through it. He stood there for a moment. Then he rubbed his face with one hand and stomped down the stairs.

I didn't know what that was about, but my priority was right here. I returned to the carrel. This time I brought up the *Brown County Democrat*, the local daily paper for a century. I supposed local Republicans might not like the name much—and they were a major force in this part of the country—but the *Democrat* it remained. Once again I started with an issue from twenty-eight years ago, although the going was a lot slower, both with it being a daily paper and one serving the entire county.

I was up to March 10 when I caught my breath and stopped scrolling. On the screen in front of me was a grainy photograph of Don O'Neill, my mom, and another man. The arms of the three were draped on each other's shoulders as they grinned into the camera, with Mom in the middle. The caption read: *Locals welcome Rotary scholar from Italy, Roberto Fracasso.* I squinted and leaned in to examine it. Roberto's dark hair curled over his collar. He was Mediterranean. I'd never seen him before, but his smile looked familiar, like I'd seen it in the mirror.

Chapter 15

I sat at my kitchen table and stared at the printout: *Locals welcome Rotary scholar from Italy, Roberto Fracasso.* I'd been so stunned at the library, gazing at a picture of a man who looked just like me, all I managed to do was send that page to print and walk home with it. I'd forced myself to work in the restaurant prepping for tomorrow until I was done, but my mind was racing the whole time.

I sipped from a Cutters beer and read the article for the umpteenth time. It said Roberto, twenty-four, was a graduate student sponsored by the Rotary Club of Brown County, and the O'Neill family in South Lick were making room for him in their home while he studied the geology of the area. And then the story frustratingly veered off into what sounded like an advertisement for the Rotary and their international scholarship program, a story probably taken from a press release they'd sent out. Birdy munched a bite of food, jumped up onto the chair next to mine, and proceeded to wash.

Running my finger over first Mom's light wind-blown hair and then Roberto's dark curls, I tried to imagine that time. Mom must have been a couple of years younger than I was now, the same age as handsome Roberto. Who wouldn't fall for an attractive visiting Italian? But so many questions remained. Did she even tell him she was pregnant? If so, why didn't he want to be part of our lives? If she didn't tell him, why not? Maybe she moved to California and then discovered she was carrying a child. But wouldn't she contact him? It was the early days of the Internet when most people didn't use e-mail, but she could have written him a letter. Or phoned. And Don? He looked awfully friendly with Mom, too. Did she dump him for Roberto? Or maybe I was all wrong about Roberto being my father. She could have met someone in California who reminded her of Roberto and conceived me with him.

I sliced sharp cheddar and a ripe tomato and threw together a sandwich on thick slices of sourdough for my dinner, bringing it to the table so I could obsess over the picture some more. But I put the sandwich down after two bites. Where was my brain? Adele should know the answers to all these questions. I found my phone and pressed her speed dial number. When she didn't pick up, I left a message asking her to call. I didn't specify why. This was way too complicated to talk about in voice mail.

As I finished my dinner, washing down the last bite with a swallow of beer, I realized the Internet might have answers for me, now that I knew what I believed was my father's name. I headed to the desk in a corner of the living room and typed his name into the search bar on my laptop. I then groaned when a halfdozen links popped up, all in Italian. I tried looking for images of that name, but if he was still alive, he'd look different than he did almost three decades ago. I saw one picture I thought might be him, a distinguished-looking man with wavy silver hair, but I couldn't tell for sure.

And what I really wanted to know was what happened back then. I added *South Lick Indiana* to his name in the search bar. Now we were getting somewhere. The three top links were to news articles from June of that year, with an article from the *Bloomington Herald-Telephone* of June 15 as the top link. I clicked it.

The headline read QUARRY ACCIDENT INJURES ROTARY SCHOLAR, AREA MAN. A picture showed the well-known Empire Quarry, southwest of here, near the town of Bedford, and the story described how Don had driven Roberto there to show him where the limestone for the Empire State Building was mined.

Don was quoted: *"He'd heard about swimming in the quarries and wanted to give it a try. I told him he shouldn't, but he jumped in, anyway. When he came to the surface and cried out, I dove in after him."* The story went on to describe the rescue effort, that a woman called for an ambulance, and that the Italian was hospitalized in Bloomington for multiple injuries, including possible damage to his spinal cord.

At that, my hand flew to my mouth. Had he been paralyzed? Or sustained damage to his brain? The woman who called it in must have been Mom. The article made it sound like Don came out the hero. He was noted as having injured his arm, but not seriously. I read the rest of the report, but didn't really learn anything more except that Roberto was taken to the hospital in Bloomington. The other links were simple rehashes of the story in smaller papers, including the *Brown County Democrat*.

I refreshed the search, adding "accident" and "Empire" and removing South Lick. But no subsequent stories appeared, only the original three links. Odd. Maybe a quarry accident with a visiting Italian wasn't really newsworthy in a month of local weddings and graduations. People without enough sense to read the posted warning signs were injured or killed in illicit quarry swimming all the time. Maybe those signs hadn't been posted back then. Or maybe Roberto hadn't understood the English. If so, Don should have done more to keep him from jumping or diving or whatever he did.

Clicking back to the images for Roberto Fracasso, I studied the older gentleman again and tried to make sense of the words in Italian. I thought you were supposed to be able to translate anything instantly, but I couldn't find the button. And since I was a fail at foreign languages, I wasn't going to be able to understand the text when my last language class had been second-year high-school Spanish. If he was my father, at least he was alive. And good-looking, too. *Damn.* Here I'd been trying to ferret out information about Don and if he was involved in Stella's murder. Instead, it looked like I'd found my long-lost father, the one I didn't even know I'd missed. I tried to search for an e-mail address or phone number for him, but I came up empty.

My cell rang from the kitchen, where I'd left it. I

strode in and checked. *Adele.* I connected and skipped the niceties.

"Adele, was my father an Italian named Roberto Fracasso?"

"Good evening to you, too, Robbie." She exhaled. "Yes, he was."

"Why didn't you ever tell me?" I heard my voice crack.

"You never asked. And Jeanine didn't want me telling you if you didn't want to know. She did name you after him, after all."

That stopped me. Of course she did. "You must have met him when he was here. I have so many questions about what happened—" I paced to the door and back, stopping to scratch Birdy's head when he looked up at me like he could use a dose of affection.

"Honey, I was gone that year. I did a stint volunteering with Heifer Project International in Arkansas, when I wanted to learn about raising up animals. That was before I got my sheep. I never did meet Roberto." She cleared her throat. "We should talk in person about this, but Vera and I are heading out to catch a show in Bloomington."

"Okay," I said around a lump in my throat that had sprung up from nowhere.

"You going to Stella's funeral tomorrow?" Adele asked.

"Tomorrow? I haven't heard anything about it." *How come I didn't know about this?* I gulped down a swig of beer and sat.

"Visiting hours are tonight. Funeral mass tomorrow at Our Lady of Springs. Eleven o'clock, with a reception following."

"How can I go? That'll be during the lunch hours."

"See if Phil can help out. He wouldn't be going. And Danna's all broken in, right?"

I supposed she was, even though it'd only been two days. I blew air out. "Phil probably has to work, but I'll ask him. It'd be too much to ask Danna to do it all. Or would Vera be willing to work again?"

"I'm sure she would, but she's leaving in the morning. Has to get home to Frankfort, up north of Indy. She's got little grandkids coming to visit."

"I'll give Phil a call. You'll be at the service, I assume?"

After she said she would, we said our good-byes. After I disconnected, I laid my head on the table. My world was exploding around me and I wasn't sure I was capable of gathering up the pieces and gluing it back together.

Chapter 16

Mixing up pancake batter early the next morning, I was glad I'd made it dozens of times before, because my mind was not on the task at hand. I'd slept as restlessly as a hummingbird, my thoughts racing from murder to worries about the store to the discovery of a newfound father. Unlike when the tiny birds sucked sustenance from every flower they flitted to, I wasn't getting nourishment from any of my thoughts. At least Phil had agreed to cover the lunch crowd, saying he could take a personal day. He was bringing in desserts, too.

I sliced bananas and gently folded them into the big bowl of whole wheat batter, covered it, and set it aside. Good. That was done. I put caf and decaf on to brew, and set to cubing potatoes for home fries. I'd done the peppers, onions, and mushrooms yesterday. I already bought grated cheese. Maybe I should look into buying prechopped vegetables. Too bad one couldn't also order up solutions to murder.

After Buck questioned me at the station on Tuesday, I'd consented to a swab of my gums. Apparently, saliva was a good place to find DNA. But I hadn't heard back on the results, and it was making me nervous. As I mixed up the miso gravy, I thought of vegetarian Jim. We hadn't really talked about my involvement in that aspect of the case when he'd stopped in yesterday.

When Danna ambled through the door at six-thirty, yawn in progress, I was in the middle of cracking a couple dozen eggs into the omelet bowl. I greeted her. She mumbled something back, donned an apron, and washed her hands.

"You can set the tables, okay?" I said.

She moved like a zombie to the shelves where we stacked the dishes.

"Tough night?"

She rolled her eyes. I hoped she'd wake up once customers arrived.

"Listen, I need to go to Stella Rogers's funeral later this morning."

At that, her eyes finally popped all the way open. "My mom told me I should go, too. I was like, *seriously?* I didn't even know the lady. I mean, I know she was Mom's assistant, but Mom couldn't stand her. I'm surprised she didn't shoot her herself."

Clearly, Corrine hadn't hidden her feeling about Stella from her daughter. "Does your mom own a gun?"

"Oh, yeah, a couple of them. She's literally always down at the Beanblossom Firing Range practicing, too. She goes with Ed sometimes. I don't know how she can stand his company. But don't worry, she keeps the guns and ammo all locked up at home."

It was bad news for me if Danna planned to be at the funeral, however. "Are you going to go to the service? I got my friend Phil MacDonald to agree to come in to replace me. But if you're not here, either, it'll be too much work for him."

"No way I'm showing up at some depressing church ritual," Danna scoffed, giving her head a quick shake in a young person's dismissive gesture. "I'll be right here. And I know Phil. I'm kind of embarrassed he used to babysit me. He's awesome cute."

"That's him. It's a big relief to me you'll be around. Thanks." I paused in my egg cracking. I'd never gotten around to checking out Danna's references beyond talking to Ed, but I didn't care. "I know it's only been a couple of days, Danna, but I'd like to offer you this job as a regular thing. You're doing great and you're a huge help to me. As far as I'm concerned, you're no longer here on a trial basis. That work for you?"

Danna smiled at the fork she was carefully placing on a blue napkin. "For sure." She glanced up. "Thanks for giving me a chance, Robbie."

We returned to our respective jobs. At least one thing was going right.

An hour later I had delivered a plate of pancakes and bacon to a customer when my cell phone rang in my apron pocket. I turned away and connected, walking to the front window.

Jim greeted me and asked how I was.

"I've been better. I learned something pretty interesting yesterday, but I can't talk about it now. This place is bustling."

"So you're not going to Stella's funeral?" His voice trailed downward and sounded disappointed.

"No, I am. Phil's going to come in and relieve me. I'll see you there?"

"You bet. Want me to pick you up?"

I laughed. "Jim, it's four blocks away." I glanced out the window at another sunny, breezy day. "I'll walk over. I can use the fresh air."

"I'll save you a seat, then."

I emerged from my apartment into the store at ten-thirty. It was empty except for Danna and me until Phil waltzed in through the door a minute later, carrying his dessert trays and singing at the top of his lungs.

"'I believe,'" he belted, "'that the Garden of Eden—'"

"Yo, pipe down," Danna called from the stove. "You'll scare away the customers." She looked at Phil and laughed.

"No way. *Book of Mormon?* People around here love it," Phil answered. He set the trays on the counter. "Hey, Robbie, you look nice."

I glanced down at my black skirt, which I'd paired with a soft purple top and a short black jacket. My hair hung loose on my shoulders, and I wore low black boots with tights.

"Thanks. And major thanks for bailing me out like this. I owe you."

He batted his hand down. "I'll catch you up on that one of these days. Now get out. Danna and I have some catching up of our own to do." He slid an apron off the shelf and popped it over his head.

"The hamburger patties are all prepped, and—"

"Go, Robbie. We got it covered," Danna said. "We'll be here when you get back."

Thank goodness for competent helpers, I thought as I walked down the street. And now I had a minute to myself, it hit me like a jackhammer that Don would certainly be at the funeral. I could ask him about Roberto, but did I want to? He hadn't told me about the visiting Italian and the accident. Even if my mom hadn't ever informed him who my father was, he had to know by looking at me and putting the dates together. I thought back to when I met him on Saturday. He'd looked at me a little strangely and commented I didn't resemble Mom. I'd been used to that back home, but there nobody knew my father. Then again, it was a long time ago. Maybe he thought Mom met somebody in California who looked like Roberto.

The wind gusted my hair into my eyes and I raised my hand to push it back. As I did, a black car raced way too fast down the street in the same direction I was headed. This was Main Street in a small town, with all kinds of people going in and out of businesses and crossing the streets, with school children, too, in the afternoons. It was no place for speeding. More importantly, though, the car resembled the one that nearly ran me off the road as I was riding the other day. Once again I tried to see the plate, but my hair was still in my eyes and I missed it.

I stood in the back of the ornate church, scanning for Jim, five minutes later. An organ droned church music and people rustled their programs and spoke in hushed tones. A uniformed Officer Wanda stood in position in the back left corner, hands behind her back, also scanning the pews. I gave her a nod, which she barely deigned to return. Don was up near the front on the right, sitting next to Ed Kowalski. Roy sat with bent head, alone, in the first row not far from the casket, which was draped in a white cloth with a gold cross on it. I didn't see Adele anywhere, but when I spied Jim, I made my way up the side aisle to where he sat on the left and slid in next to him. He wore a dark blue suit today, with a green tie the color of his eyes.

He laid his hand atop mine on the seat and gazed at me. "You look lovely," he whispered.

"Shh," I answered, smiling. Someone tapped my shoulder and I twisted around to see who it was.

Abe O'Neill was leaning forward from the pew behind me. "Hi," he said in a soft voice. Mr. Lean and Tan was now in a blazer, slacks, and a purple tie, which matched my top.

I returned his greeting and faced front again as the music changed and a priest walked up to the podium, or whatever it was called in a church. I didn't frequent one, myself, and never had. Mom and I used to take breakfast to the beach on Sunday mornings: fresh strawberries, cheesy biscuits, creamy yogurt, plus cappuccino for her and hot chocolate for me. A big sky, warm sand, and the Pacific Ocean were all the religion I needed. I missed her again like a punch in the gut, with the fierce pain that sometimes grew fainter and then popped up again at unpredictable moments like this one.

Chapter 17

I stood with Jim on the steps of the church. We'd moved to the side to be out of the way as mourners and curiosity seekers alike emerged through the wide doorway bringing a hint of incense with them. Roy fidgeted next to the priest, shaking hands and speaking with townspeople, but he wasn't making much eye contact and his left hand worried a little pleat of cloth at the side of his pants leg.

Leaning toward Jim, I said in a low voice, "Stella didn't seem to have anyone who loved her besides Roy." I'd been shocked no one rose to offer fond memories of Stella during the allotted period. "No girlfriend, no cousin, no childhood buddy, no college pal."

"That's right. There's usually someone, at least."

"People must have been following the rule 'If you can't say something nice, don't say anything at all.'" I shook my head. "At my mom's memorial service, a few dozen insisted on speaking about her." An image of her service, so different from this one, flooded over me. We'd held it in a modern Unitarian Universalist church built on a bluff above her beloved Pacific, a church where the minister was Mom's best friend, Ann. Half the walls were of glass looking out at the ocean, and the wood inside was a light ash with simple curving lines. Bunches of coastal wildflowers had filled small vases throughout the space. An ocean breeze had spread the fragrance of the gardenias tucked into them, blooms I'd gathered from the five-foot-high gardenia bush outside my childhood bedroom window. The memories made me miss my home state as much as my mom. I liked southern Indiana a lot, but it wasn't California.

Jim interrupted my reverie by saying, "I wish I'd known her." He smiled at me.

"You would have been a little kid when she left." I was pretty sure Jim was only a few years older than me. "Uh-oh," I whispered as Buck ambled toward us, the wind making his hair point skyward.

He greeted both of us. The tall officer wore funeral gray today instead of uniform blue, his suit jacket neatly buttoned.

"What's happening, Buck?" Jim asked before I could speak.

"Nothing I can talk about." He took up position next to Jim, sliding his hands into his pants pockets.

I watched him check out the crowd, his gaze lingering on first this person, then that. For all Buck's slow country bumpkin manner, I didn't think much slipped past him. His eyes finally landed on me.

"Been staying out of trouble anymore, Robbie?" he asked.

"What's that supposed to mean?" I looked up, way

up, at him. "I run a business. Too busy to get into trouble."

"Heard you were digging in the library archives yesterday."

"So? It's a public library." I smiled to try to soften my remark. No point in getting heated up about a police officer asking me questions. "A very nice public library, too."

"Yup."

"Have you made any progress in finding Stella's murderer?" I asked.

"We're working on it."

"Is there something specific you wanted to ask Robbie?" Jim asked with a frown.

"You don't need to go all lawyer on me now, Shermer. I was only making polite conversation."

Right. I gave a little laugh, then spied Don walking toward us. *Uh-oh, again.* I was not going to ask him about my father . . . or about the quarry incident. I was not. Not here, not now.

"What a beautiful service it was," Don said with a mournful air after he'd said hello. "Just beautiful." He wore a dark suit with a tie featuring little pictures of his hardware store on it, and the wind wasn't being nice to his comb-over.

I looked at him. I wanted to say, *"Seriously?"* But I kept my mouth shut. The service struck me as impersonal, full of institutionalized ritual meaningless to me, and the church had smelled of funeral flowers. Well, who knew? Maybe Don really had found it beautiful. And I supposed the faithful of the church found comfort in the ritual.

"How are you, Don?" Buck asked.

"Just feeling sad about poor Stella, bless her soul."

He shook his head. "And poor Roy, there." He pointed with his chin.

I glanced at Roy and a bad thought popped into my head. "Does he inherit Stella's house?" I asked, looking at the three men one by one. Roy wouldn't have killed his own mother to get her house. Would he? He was the one who found the body, after all.

"I would assume so," Jim said. He narrowed his eyes and studied my face like his brain just lit on the same idea as mine. "Depends on if she left a valid will. If not, he's next of kin. Buck, you know anything about a will?"

Buck hesitated for a tiny, little minute. "Not at liberty to say at this time."

I'd bet a gold-plated sand dollar his hesitation meant he didn't know bug-all about the will.

My stomach let me know in no uncertain terms it was lunchtime as I surveyed the funeral reception spread laid out in the American Legion hall. I didn't see a sign indicating who the caterer was. Somebody must have paid a nice chunk of change for all this food, though. I slid into line behind Corrine Beedle, who was too busy chatting up the man in front of her to notice, and grabbed a plate. A couple of minutes later my plate was heaped with crispy fried catfish from a chock-full warming pan, a pile of coleslaw glistening with mayo, and a nice mound of potato salad. Holding a plate with the same offerings, as well as a couple of rolls and a hunk of the squash casserole I'd taken a pass on, Corrine glanced to her left and noticed me at last.

"Robbie, good to see you." She held up her plate.

"Food looks good, doesn't it? Come on, let's sit down together."

I said hello, while at the same time noticing Jim waving from a table across the room. "Join Jim and me, then." I led the way, with Corrine's heels clicking on the linoleum behind me. Two men approached the table before we got there. Don, holding a bottle of beer, sat and began talking to Jim. The other stood with his back to me. When we drew closer, I saw it was Ed Kowalski.

"Ah, Robbie, Corrine." Ed, also gripping a beer bottle, raised his Stroh's in salute. He wore a pin on his lapel that looked like a cat's pawprint and had BCAS written across it.

"Ed, Don, lovely to see you both," Corrine said. "Sit on down, Ed."

Ed turned a chair around and straddled it.

Don smiled at me, but he didn't include Corrine in the afterglow. "Madam Mayor," he said curtly.

"Well, I'll be a corncob's cousin. So you're finally talking to me again, Don?" Corrine set her plate on the table and extended her hand. "What's past is past, right?"

Don shook her hand, but it looked like it was the most reluctant move he'd made in a long, long time.

"No hard feelings?" Corrine kept hold of his hand for way longer than necessary.

"No hard feelings," Don said, grimacing. After Corrine relinquished it, he wiped his hand on his pants leg and loosened his tie.

"What's the pin for, Ed?" I asked.

His face softened as he patted the pawprint pin. "Brown County Animal Shelter. I volunteer with the cats and dogs nobody wants. I feed the strays and pet them. Take them to get their shots. Animals are so much easier to deal with than humans, don't you think?"

"I just took in a stray this week," I said. "You remind me that I should get him to the vet to make sure he gets whatever shots he needs." I sat and took a bite of the catfish. The coating was crisp and the flesh firm and succulent. I tasted a hint of dill and maybe a dash of hot pepper.

Ed cleared his throat. "How are you all liking the catfish?" His face looked redder than usual. Maybe that wasn't his first beer of the day.

I swallowed the bite in my mouth. "It's delicious."

"Great catfish," Jim mumbled through a mouthful.

"Do you know who catered?" I asked.

"Why, we did. Kowalski's Country Store." He beamed. "Usually, the ministry buys and cooks the meat, and supplies bread and drinks. Other church members are called to provide side dishes and desserts. To the family of the deceased, this is a great blessing in their time of sorrow." He appropriately lost the smile. "But as a prominent business owner and permanent deacon of Our Lady, I was asked to take over the ministry's role. I told them I might as well provide the sides and desserts, too. It was the least I could do." He folded his hands around his beer bottle as if it were a holy icon.

"That was very generous of you, Ed," Jim said with a wry smile.

A full-figured young woman in a black skirt and white blouse straining at the buttons circulated with a tray of full plastic glasses. "Wine or cider?"

I took a cup of red wine, as did Jim, while Corrine helped herself to cider.

"I'm on the job, you know," she said. "The mayor is always working."

Don grimaced and looked away, taking a swig of his beer. Then he looked back at Corrine. "I'm surprised you didn't offer remarks during the service. About your valuable assistant and how much you'll miss her."

Jim and I exchanged a quick glance.

"I didn't feel called to do so. I've expressed my feelings privately to her son, of course." Corrine took a sip of her cider.

"Oh, of course," Don said.

I looked from face to face. "So, who do you think killed Stella? You all knew her better than I did." I sipped my wine and waited.

"I'm putting money on some long-lost lover who came back to see her and knocked her off when she spurned him." Ed pursed his lips and nodded slowly, as if he'd given the matter great thought.

"Really?" Corrine dismissed that idea with a wave of her hand. "No, it's going to be someone local, mark my words."

"Come on," Ed said. "We all know she wasn't America's sweetheart, but a killer right here in South Lick? I don't think so."

Don swallowed and stood. "Excuse me, folks. I'm going to see if Roy is all right."

I watched where he headed, curious if that was only an excuse to avoid the topic, but, in fact, he beelined it for Roy, who stood alone, somehow in possession of a beer in each hand. Catching sight of Adele on the other side of the hall, I waved. She waved back and returned to her conversation with the couple she sat with. I still needed to talk with her about Roberto and Mom. Not here, though. And I was still hungry. But after I took a bite of the coleslaw, I wished I hadn't. The cabbage was limp and a little sour, and a greasy mayo overwhelmed any other flavors. I returned to the fish, not sure I should even try the potato salad.

Corrine looked up at Ed. "When are we going shooting next?" She winked as she pointed a finger gun at him.

Ed's gaze darted at Jim and then at me. "Fall's my busiest season; you know that, Corrine. Probably can't get out until next month sometime."

"It's ruffed grouse season right now. And quail opens November eighth. Your loss."

"You have fun without me, then." Ed eyed me. "You have any plans to serve catfish, Robbie?"

"Not with this delicious dish five miles away. I'll let you corner the market."

"Excellent plan," Ed said. He took a swig from his beer.

"People are loving my gourmet burgers, so that's a good niche for me." I smiled across the table at Ed. "And my breakfasts, of course."

He blinked a few times with an unpleasant pull to his mouth. "Of course."

I wiped my hands with a towel and used it to open the restroom door, then propped it open with my foot while I tossed the towel into the wastebasket. Working as a chef created clean-hand habits that endured even when I wasn't cooking. Letting the door shut behind me, I was about to head back to the reception when I paused in the deserted back hallway to examine a large black-and-white mosaic laid into the white-tiled floor. A black circle of tiny tiles held an ornate capital *E*, also in black, on a background of tiny white tiles, with a squished black ornate *C* written through the *E*. The hall wasn't heated and I rubbed my hands together to warm them as I examined the mosaic. I heard footsteps and turned.

"This used to be the Elite Club Casino back in the Roaring Twenties," Don said, also gazing at the mosaic.

"Don't sneak up on me like that," I said, fanning my face with one hand. My thudding heart wasn't only from my being surprised, though. I was alone with a man who'd known my father.

"Sorry." He moved to the other side of the circle. "Didn't mean to. I love this building. Built in the heyday of the spas, more than a hundred years ago." He'd removed his tie and unbuttoned his jacket, and his comb-over could have used freshening up.

"This mosaic is pretty cool. So the *E* with the *C* is for Elite Club?"

"It is. They gambled and drank and danced up a storm. There was another Elite Club down in French Lick, but this was the mother ship, the first one built." He pointed to the wall. "See that button?"

An old-style push button in a small frame was set into the wall at about my eye level. Somebody kept the fixture's brass polished and it, along with the tile, made me want to put on one of those dropped-waist flapper dresses with the fringe, add a forehead band, and sip a glass of moonshine.

"After Prohibition started in 1920, they'd sometimes get raided by the cops. If the police showed up, the receptionist would push the button, which set off a signal letting customers know they needed to split out the back door." He tapped his temple with one finger. "Quite the system."

I mustered my inner courageous being and took a deep breath. "Don, I have a question for you about what happened not a century ago, but a few decades ago."

He glanced at me for the first time since we'd been in the hallway. "You do, do you?" His eyes looked as worried as the first time I met him.

"You knew my father, Roberto Fracasso." I tried to keep my voice from wobbling. I shivered, whether from the chilly air or from nerves I couldn't tell, and clasped my left elbow with my right hand.

"I did." He stuck his hands in his jacket pockets. "You look just like him, you know."

"I saw a picture of you and my mom with him. I wished you'd said something to me about him. After I moved here, I mean."

"I figured your mother would have told you."

"She never did. And now I can't ask her." I swallowed and blinked away sudden moisture in my eyes. "I read about the quarry accident, and how you saved him."

"Yeah." Don looked down at the tiles again.

"How bad were his injuries? The news article said something about a possible spinal cord injury. Was he in the hospital long? Was he paralyzed?"

"He survived and then went back to Italy."

"That's all you know? Didn't you visit him when he was hospitalized?"

"I didn't." His mouth slid to the side like he was chewing the inside of his lip.

"Mom must have." I pictured her sitting at his side, holding his hand, stroking his brow.

"I guess she must have."

"Did Roberto know about me? Have you had any contact with him since then?" I asked.

"I don't know, and no. You're asking too many questions."

"Really? I find out after twenty-seven years who my father is. I discover you knew him, were friendly with him. Yeah, I have questions."

"Robbie, that was a long, long time ago. Your mom dumped me for him. You think I'd want to 'keep in touch,'" he said, surrounding the last words with finger quotes, "with this 'so-called friend'? With the handsome foreigner who stole my girl?"

Chapter 18

When I returned to the reception hall, after Don turned and strode in the opposite direction, after I'd recovered a semblance of calm, I was grateful to see people were leaving. I needed to be in the store before closing time at two-thirty, so I walked out with Jim, but declined a ride home. This was the kind of day my brain needed a bit of fresh air and exercise to recover from, even though my too-short stroll didn't do much to clear the mind. I was still rattled by my encounter in the hall with Don.

"How was lunch? Quiet?" I asked Phil ten minutes later, who was wiping down the tables. "Seemed like everybody in town was at Stella's service."

He shook his head. "Busy. A bus full of seniors came in, and I'm talking a full-sized bus. We were totally booked. Sold out of almost everything, and made a couple three cookware sales, too."

"Great news for the bottom line," I said.

"You need to order in for tomorrow, if it isn't too late," Danna added from the sink, where she was loading up the industrial dishwasher.

"I guess it's a good problem to have. We're heading into the weekend, so I'll contact the supplier right away." I put down my purse and tugged at the drawer in the antique desk, where I kept my tablet, but it wouldn't open. I whacked at it and jiggled it with no result.

"That drawer all whopperjawed?" Phil asked, moving toward the desk.

"What?"

"*Whopperjawed.* Out of alignment. Stuck."

I nodded and watched as he treated the drawer more gently, finally opening it.

I thanked him and retrieved my tablet. "So I need to order buns, salad stuff, cheese?" After Danna nodded, I tapped those in. "What else? I have plenty of frozen patties."

"Pickles. I think we're okay for breakfast tomorrow," Danna said. "But order more OJ, eggs, and bread for the weekend."

I entered those as Phil sang a song I didn't recognize, then I took the tablet into the walk-in and did a survey there.

"How do tuna burgers sound as a Friday special?" I asked as I emerged. "I saw a recipe that looked good, and I might try lamb burgers on the weekend, too."

"Sounds delish," Phil said.

I added a few more ingredients to my list. "Thanks, you guys. Go on home, I'll finish up," I said. "I owe you, Phil," I added.

He blew me a kiss. "I will exact an appropriate price from my friend," he sang to the tune of "Oklahoma."

After they left, I locked the door, turned the sign to CLOSED, and sank into a chair. So Don was still angry with Roberto all these years later. And with my mom,

I supposed. Damn. I forgot to ask him about her pen. If he owned one, they must have been in touch, so he couldn't have been all that mad at her. I doodled on the pad in front of me. *Bloomington Hospital. Will they give me my father's records? His Italian address at the time?*

A long, exhausting bike ride would calm me down and clear my brain. I could ride to Bloomington and find their records department. But that would take the rest of the afternoon and I had a business to run. I doodled for another minute, then I decided I could call them now and drive over once my ordering and prep were done. Oh, and take the day's till to the bank.

Two minutes later I disconnected in frustration. The woman in the records department, a Marie some-body, was distinctly unhelpful. She didn't care that I said Roberto was my father. More likely, she didn't believe me, pointing out the obvious that we had different last names, and that she could only release records to proven next of kin. *Damn it all to heck and gone.* I couldn't prove it if I couldn't find him. I wasn't sure I really wanted to talk to this man who had abandoned me—if he'd even known about me. At the same time, I longed to meet him, see the person I'd gotten half my genes from, especially now with Mom gone. Maybe Adele would sign a statement saying she believed he and I were related.

I returned to the tablet and jabbed in the order. I'd done fine without a father for twenty-seven years. Another few hours, days, or a lifetime wouldn't make any difference.

* * *

After I submitted my order, I made a hasty decision. The urge to find out about my father was too strong to put off. I locked the till in my little safe, instead of going to the bank, threw a load of napkins and aprons in the washer, and raced over to the IU Health Bloomington Hospital, the van bouncing on the bumpy road that led out of town to the state route. The Dodge complained on the uphills and rattled down the downs, but I shaved six minutes off the half-hour drive.

I cautiously approached the door labeled RECORDS. I needed to figure how to examine the records of Roberto's hospitalization. If I hadn't already called and been rejected, I might have been able to talk my way into it. Now what was I going to do? I peered at the hours listed next to the door. They closed at four-thirty, which was in ten minutes.

I glanced to my right as a woman strode down the hall toward me. Slim and fit, she wore purple jeans and a turquoise sweater. She carried a messenger bag slung across her chest, bandolier style, over a badge hanging from a red-and-white lanyard. She looked somehow familiar, but I couldn't place her. She extended her hand when she got close.

"Robbie, right? I'm Lou. We ate breakfast at your store on Sunday. We'd cycled out."

"Of course." I shook her hand. "Nice to see you again." I checked her badge, which read LOUISE PERL- MAN. An old-fashioned name and likely the reason she went by Lou. "Sorry for not recognizing you."

"No worries. Different clothes, different context." Lou cocked her head and smiled. "So, what are you doing here?"

"Oh." I gazed at the closed door. "It's kind of a long

story. But I need to see the records of a man who was hospitalized here about twenty-eight years ago. I think he's my father—the one I never met. Never even knew his name until yesterday."

Her dark eyebrows lifted and she whistled.

"Yeah, I know." I blew air out through my lips. "Anyway, the woman on the phone said I'd have to prove we were related before she'd let me see his file. But he's Italian, and—"

She held up a hand. "I love a good mystery. Come with me and don't say anything." She pulled open the door.

Since I had no choice but to follow her in, that's what I did.

"Hey, Marie," Lou said. "Breaking in a new student."

An older woman with a pinched face sat at a desk behind a counter, apparently the Marie who'd refused me access two hours earlier. She glanced up without speaking and then returned her gaze to her computer screen.

Lou beckoned to me with one finger. I kept following her until we passed through a door on the far side of the office and it closed behind us.

"I'm a new student, am I?" I said. "What kind of work do you do here?"

"I told you I was a grad student, right? I'm in medical sociology, and I'm researching the cultural effects of medical practices, specifically hospitalizations. Length, cost, and how it relates to social class, race, income levels, and stuff like that." She lifted her bag over her head before sitting at a long desk holding five desktop computers. "I spend half my life here lately." She tossed a long brown braid back over her shoulder.

"Wow." I gazed around the room. It was enormous, and looked like library stacks, except instead of books it was rows of floor-to-ceiling files.

"Here, sit down." She pointed with her elbow to the chair to her right even as she typed, staring at the screen.

"Is this going to get you in trouble?" I asked as I sat.

"Nah. I'm in here a lot. Our department chair got permission for me, and a couple of other students; that's why the gorgon out there believed the ruse."

I leaned closer to her. "Marie was the one on the phone who said I couldn't have access."

Lou lifted one shoulder and let it drop. "This is her fiefdom. Can't blame her, really. What other power does she have in her life? I bring her something from Nashville Fudge Kitchen once in a while to stay on her good side."

I laughed my relief. "Eating their fudge is like going to heaven without having to die first."

"You bet. Despite all these physical files"—Lou waved her head to indicate the rest of the room— "everything is online. And these days they only keep digital records." She glanced at me, hands ready on the keyboard. Her nut-brown fingers sported a half-dozen silver rings on both hands, one with a triangular hunk of turquoise surrounded by a heavy silver band, and unpainted nails evenly trimmed to a no-nonsense length. "Now, how specific can you get about this Italian of yours?"

I shut my eyes for a second, trying to remember the date, then opened them. "I think it was June fifteenth," and told her the year. "He dove into the Empire Quarry and hurt himself."

She tapped and waited and typed some more, examining the screen as she went. "Got it."

My heart was going triple time. My hands were cold and sweaty at once, and I felt woozy. I was about to find out if Roberto had been seriously hurt, and maybe even how to contact him.

Lou read aloud: "'Admitted with injuries consistent with diving into the reported body of water, blah, blah, concussion, broke his left tibia, contusions, lacerations . . .'"

"No spinal cord damage?"

"I don't see anything about that."

"Whew. I was worried he'd been paralyzed, or worse."

She stared at the screen.

"What?" I asked.

"There's something here about a contusion on the back of Roberto's head." She wrinkled her nose. "How'd he get that from diving?"

"From a submerged hazard, maybe? They're always warning people about old cars and underwater rocks you can't tell are there."

"Hmm. Interesting."

"What?" I was starting to sound like a CD that had been left in a hot car too many times.

"Some other guy was admitted at the same time—"

"Don O'Neill?"

"Yeah. All he suffered was a broken arm. Dove in to rescue Roberto, he said. A woman called the ambulance and came in with them."

"That must have been my mom. She was seeing Roberto. Or Don. Or both. I couldn't get a straight story from Don earlier today."

Lou looked sharply at me. "What's your last name again?"

"Jordan. Mom was Jeanine Jordan."

"Well, unless she was in the witness protection program or something, it wasn't her. The one who reported the accident was a Stella Rogers."

Chapter 19

I stared at her. "Are you sure?"

She pointed to the screen. "See?"

I leaned over and read the words. *Stella. Huh.* Could there be a connection between that line of a decades-old hospital admittance form and Stella's death?

"Who's Stella, anyway?" Lou asked, sitting back in her chair.

"She was a friend of Don's. But she was murdered on Saturday. Shot."

"She's the one? I saw that on the local news." She whistled again.

"She's the one. Bad news is, they found her with one of my biscuits stuffed in her mouth and one of my mom's pens on the floor." I hunched into my shoulders. "I didn't kill her, I promise you."

Lou's laugh was deep and rolling. "Don't worry, I didn't think you did."

"But the police do, or at least I'm one of those infamous 'persons of interest,' and they don't seem to be making much progress on finding who actually did the deed." I folded my arms. "It's weird I finally discover who my father was and he turns out to be somehow linked to the murder."

"That's weird, all right. Isn't it kind of a stretch, though, to say he's linked to the murder?"

"I just mean that he knew Stella, and that she was there when he was hurt," I said.

"What are you going to do now?"

"Heck if I know." I gazed at the files beyond us. "Wait, can you help me with one more thing? Does it give Roberto's Italian address anywhere there?"

"You want to contact him." She looked at me with surprisingly light blue eyes, or maybe they only looked light in her tanned face.

After I nodded, her fingers flew over the keyboard. I'd always been fascinated by watching people type. They all used their fingertips differently. Lou was touch-typing with all ten, but her pinkie flew up to the numbers row and even the function key row frequently, and she only pressed the SHIFT key with her left pinkie, never with her right. Others used two fingers and were surprisingly fast and accurate, while certain people laboriously pecked with only the thumb and first two fingers on each hand.

"Tuscany. A place called Montecatini Terme." The words rolled off her tongue like she wasn't an American. "No street address."

Tuscany. That made it real. Maybe I could find him now. If I wanted to. Maybe he could tell me what happened all those years ago.

Lou sat back again. "I've been there. Gorgeous corner of the universe. And the food? To die for."

"I've never been anywhere. California and here. That's it. When were you there?"

"I was on a cycling tour of Tuscany after college.

Montecatini Terme has hot springs and spas going back centuries. Perfect after a long day of riding. That's what '*terme*' means. 'Thermal,' you know, like *thermal baths*."

"Just like South Lick, except here they were mineral baths," I said. "Maybe that's why Roberto came here."

"That area of Tuscany is super hilly for biking, too. Also like Brown County. He must have felt right at home, except for the language."

I scrabbled in my purse for a minute. "Do you have a pen I can use? I can't find anything to write with."

"Hang on." Lou held up a hand and faced the computer again. A moment later a printer whirred to action at the end of the table. "Printed the whole record out for you. Just don't tell Marie." She snorted and then laughed again. "As if."

I'd just tucked the printout into my bag when the door to the office opened.

"I'm leaving, Louise," Marie called. "Make sure you check the doors when you go."

"I always do, Marie. Have a good evening," Lou said. After the door closed again, she continued, "Close one! Almost caught me red-handed." She examined her palms with a grin. "Nope, nothing there."

"You're sure. . . ."

"Hey, I'm here with permission. I'm only teasing. I print stuff out all the time. How does she know what it is?"

"Well, thank you, Louise." A giggle slipped out of me. This was like sneaking out back with a girlfriend in middle school and sharing an illicit cigarette.

"Hey!" She elbowed me. "Marie insists on calling me Louise. I can't train her out of it, even though nobody but my grandmother is allowed to call me that." She glanced at the time on the computer. "Oh, what the hell. Want to go for a beer at Nick's? I don't really need to work here today."

"Love to." I could use a new friend about now. And it was too late to call Italy, anyway.

I didn't make it home until seven. I'd stuck to only one beer, nursing it along as I got to know Lou better over a plate of onion rings and crispy fries, while she demolished a stromboli, with bits of sausage and pizza sauce leaking out of the bun onto her plate. As always, Nick's English Hut was hopping with students and professors, being a block from Indiana University. The local institution, getting on for a century old, served up beer in Mason jars, featured a decent pub menu, and employed a fleet of no-nonsense, fast-moving waitpeople. Adele had taken me there for lunch once when I was out visiting during high school. A short waitress named Ruthie, on the far side of sixty, wearing a halter top, almost threw our menus at us. These days Ruthie's photo hung on the wall next to her framed obituary.

Chatting with my new friend had been a fun break from work and worry. But now that I was home, it all flooded back. I worked in the restaurant, getting the biscuit dough ready and premixing the dry ingredients for apple-spice muffins. As I did, I went over and over what Lou and I learned from the report. Stella called in the accident. Roberto presented with a contusion on the back of his head, but no spinal cord injury. He hailed from a hilly place with therapeutic springs, just like Brown County.

I set up five tables, laying the bundles of silverware wrapped in cloth napkins at each place. I pictured the opening morning, with Corrine striding in here like she was queen of the town and owned the joint, too. She'd later told me Stella was blackmailing men in town. But which ones? What if she'd been blackmailing Corrine about something, too? That could be part of the reason the mayor detested her assistant. Stella certainly could have been blackmailing Ed about being a womanizer, especially if he was going after young, even underage women. And the report of the bump on the back of Roberto's head bugged me. Maybe Don whacked him on the head from behind, making him fall into the quarry, and then lied about Roberto diving in. Stella could have seen the whole thing. But why was she killed now?

I frowned at the basket of silverware bundles, which was now empty. I needed to roll more. But first I needed to put the laundry to dry. Using cloth napkins was a little overboard, and meant more labor, but I hated thin paper napkins. Plus I thought the blue cloth brought a touch of class to my rustic restaurant. Hey, it was more environmental, wasn't it? I headed over to the laundry closet, transferred the load, and pressed START. I glanced around the store. Everything else was ready. If I could find Roberto, maybe he'd tell me the truth about the quarry. But would he want to talk with his long-lost daughter? It was possible he didn't even know about me.

Only one way to find out. After I freshened up Birdy's dry food, doled out a dollop of canned treat into a small dish, and refilled the water bowl, I sat at my laptop. At least now I knew a town to pair with his name. This time when I typed in *Montecatini Terme*

after *Roberto Fracasso* and clicked *Images,* several versions
of the silver-haired man appeared. In one of the
photos, he beamed over the head of a tiny boy with
dark curly hair who perched on his lap. *A grandchild,
perhaps?* His hair was identical to mine at that age. I sat
back. *That would make him my nephew. And it would mean
I have a half sister or half brother out there. Maybe more than
one. Wow.* I was so used to not having any family except
Mom and Adele. And because Adele never had children, I didn't even have cousins.

I clicked on the picture to make it bigger and
leaned in, gazing at it. Roberto was handsome for an
older man. I liked the look around his dark eyes.
Smile lines radiated out, but I detected a hint of sad-
ness in there, too. Birdy jumped up on my lap and settled in, his head on his front paws. I stroked his soft
head as I looked at my father. Maybe I could look up
how to say "Dad" in Italian.

I went back to the Web tab. One link included the
word *"Professore"* in front of his name. Even I could
figure out that meant "professor." The link included
"Università di Pisa," too. Which must be University of
Pisa. *Gee, maybe he teaches next to the Leaning Tower.* I'd
always wanted to see that.

I clicked the university link and then swallowed
hard. I saw his e-mail address. *Damn.* It was too late to
call Italy—it must be around midnight or something.
But it was never too late to send an e-mail message.
Composing one could take the rest of the night,
though. If I was going to reach out to him, I needed
to word it exactly right. And I didn't particularly like
opening myself up to being hurt. What if he never

answered? What if he denied being my father? What if . . . what if I drove myself crazy with wondering? I told myself in no uncertain terms to cut it out. Either write the thing or don't.

Folding napkins with a couple fingers of Four Roses in a glass at my side should have been a nice, meditative way to calm my mind. Instead, the task was rote enough to let my crazy brain roam at will. I'd clicked SEND on the short e-mail twenty minutes earlier and immediately regretted it. After much stewing and deleting, all I'd typed was:

Roberto: My mother was Jeanine Jordan. She died earlier this year. If you are the Roberto Fracasso who was in Indiana twenty-eight years ago, please contact me. I'd like to talk with you about her.

I'd signed it, included my cell phone number, and attached the picture Phil took of me on opening morning, since his skill with a camera was on par with all his other talents, and it had come out halfway decent. I'd even taken my hat off for it, so my hair that matched Roberto's was evident. I figured framing the note to be about Mom and not my genetic connection to Roberto was safer. Once he took a look at my picture, he'd guess, anyway. I worked on the subject line longer than the actual message, finally settling with *Regarding Jeanine Jordan,* which ought to catch his attention and not look like junk mail.

But was it the right thing to do? What can of

wriggly night-crawling fish food was I opening, one twist of the can opener at a time? Maybe he wouldn't open the e-mail. Maybe he didn't read English. Maybe it would go straight into his SPAM folder, or whatever they called it in Italian, despite Mom's name in the subject line. *Oh, well. Too late now.*

I'd just brought the silverware tray to the table and started rolling bundles when my cell rang. My heart thudded to the floor and lay there beating up a storm. It couldn't be Roberto already, could it? If it was nine at night here, it must be dark o'clock in the morning over there. Did the man not sleep? Paralyzed, I stared at the phone. I always kept it on vibrate, and it jiggled its way over to a spoon on the varnished wooden table. I forced myself to check the display and then laughed with a nervous quaver as I picked it up and connected.

"Jim," I said, "I'm so glad it's you."

"Is something wrong?"

"No, no. Well, you know. It's not that everything is right, what with Stella and all. But . . ." I couldn't go on. I couldn't tell him on the phone that it appeared I'd found my father. So much had happened in such a short period of time, but it just wasn't phone conversation material.

"You're confusing me."

"I'm sorry. I thought someone else was calling me and I was glad it wasn't who I thought it was." *Or am I?*

He didn't speak for a moment. *Uh-oh, does he think I'm hanging out with another man?* I lined up a fork on a napkin and stacked a spoon on top of it.

He cleared his throat. "I called because I wondered

if I could make you dinner tomorrow night at my place. But if you're busy—"

"No, I'm not busy. Not at all. I'd love dinner at your place, Jim. I . . ." I couldn't say I had a lot to tell him, because then, for sure he'd ask what it was. "What time, and what can I bring?"

Chapter 20

"Robbie," Danna said, moving to my side as I flipped cakes during breakfast the next morning. We experienced our usual rush despite the weather having turned cold and stormy. The coatrack was full of dripping raincoats and the antique umbrella stand held a half-dozen soaked umbrellas.

I glanced up at her grim tone, one I'd never heard her use before. "What's going on?"

She tossed her head to indicate something behind her. "You have to trade places. I'm not talking to him." She grabbed a clean apron from the box, threw it on, and started the sink water running a little too hard, scrubbing her hands like she was punishing them.

I twisted to see Ed Kowalski examining the menu at a table by himself.

"Gotcha." I pointed to the orders. "The two specials platters are up next." I also ditched the grease-stained apron I'd been wearing for a fresh one. *Poor Danna.* No woman should have to put up with harassment. He'd better not try anything on me.

I adjusted my hat and grabbed the order pad and

pen. We could have gone hi-tech and used a digital ordering system, but a tablet for every table was expensive, and who needed a digital device mounted next to the grill? It'd be a wreck, full of grease splatters and flecks of batter in a week. Or a day, more likely.

I steered for Ed's table. "'Morning, Ed. Decided to eat out again today?"

"Thought I'd see how the competition was doing after a week." His mouth smiled, but his little eyes didn't.

"Things are going pretty well." I waved the order pad at the other nine tables, every one of them with at least two customers seated. A party of six men occupied the biggest table.

"Can you put together a small sample portion of everything you've got?" He frowned at the breakfast menu.

"Seriously?" I raised my eyebrows. "You *are* checking out the competition. You want five omelets?"

"No, of course not." He blinked and stabbed at the menu. "Give me the Kitchen Sink, but with only one egg. And a couple of pancakes, bacon and sausage, white toast, biscuits, meat gravy. Like I said, one of everything, but small-sized. When I came in on opening day, all I tried were the biscuits, gravy, and eggs."

"I can't do a Kitchen Sink omelet with one egg. It won't hold it." I set my hands on my hips.

"Whatever." Ed waved a hand. "And coffee, of course."

"Of course," I muttered as I headed toward the coffee station. "A 'please' would have been nice."

One of the white-haired men at the large table way-laid me with an "Oh, miss?" and a smile that could have lit up a dark night in January, so I changed course. Ed and his sampler breakfast would have to wait.

"How's everything?" I asked after introducing myself.

"Delicious." The man patted his nicely rounded midsection with both hands, a plate of half-demolished pancakes in front of him. "Super delicious. Miss Jordan, we wondered"—he glanced at his tablemates, several of whom bobbed their heads in agreement— "we're a men's breakfast and Bible club, and we wondered if we could reserve this table for eight o'clock every Friday morning. If it wouldn't be too much trouble."

"That sounds like a good idea to me." Several paperback New Testaments lay on the table, along with a couple of well-thumbed black Bibles. "It's no trouble at all."

He beckoned to me to lean in and lowered his voice. "We used to meet in Nashville at"—he tilted his head toward Ed across the room—"at another establishment, but we like it here better. Samuel recommended we give you a try." He pointed at one of the men.

"I'm glad you're pleased with Pans 'N Pancakes, and I'm happy to reserve the table for you all. I'll make up a special sign and put it out every week. How does that sound?"

"Perfect. We're much obliged."

"Are you always six, or are there more? The table seats up to eight."

"Never more than eight."

"Perfect, then. I'll be right back with more coffee, gentlemen. Anything else I can get you?"

One man held up his juice glass, and another asked for a refresher on his tea, thanking me for my trouble.

At the far end of the table, a slender man with dark skin and a full head of wiry grizzled hair waved me over.

"Is my grandson working today?" He smiled up at me. "You know, Philostrate?"

"Oh, Phil. No, he's not a regular employee, but he does make the desserts for lunch. And I'm sure you know he designed our logo and did a lot more to help me get started." I smiled back. "He's a good friend."

He extended his hand. "I'm Samuel MacDonald. I'm pleased to make your acquaintance. I'll tell Philostrate his recommendation was well-founded."

I shook his hand and thanked him before I bustled away. I sure wasn't about to turn away a weekly group of polite and hungry Christians, especially one including Phil's grandfather. Ed might not like it, but fair was fair in the free-market economy.

I handed Ed's order to Danna. When she frowned at it, I added, "He said he wants a small portion of everything on the menu. Not every omelet, just the Kitchen Sink."

"He'll never change his own menu, or the quality," she said, sliding the spatula under a cheese omelet and flipping it with care. "I don't know what he thinks he's going to accomplish by tasting your much better breakfasts."

"I don't, either. But he's a paying customer." I wrinkled my nose. "Or not. He comped my breakfast at his place the other day. I guess I'll have to return the favor." I leaned close to Danna. "Give him really small portions, okay?" A giggle slipped out.

She snorted. "You got it. He'll be lucky if I don't spit in it."

"I wouldn't blame you, but let's not get carried away. I don't want to get sued."

A few minutes later, after bringing Ed his coffee, topping up drinks at the Bible table, clearing another table, and making change for a third, I loaded up my arms with Ed's order.

"Here you go." I set the plates on the table. I carried over a jam and syrup caddy from the table that just vacated, then turned to go.

"Any news about the murder case?" Ed asked, his eyes on his food. "I heard you've been asking a lot of questions around."

"Not really. And I don't have any news." I gazed at him. "They're way past the forty-eight-hour window, though."

His gaze met mine for the first time.

"I read somewhere if they don't solve a crime in the first two days, they're unlikely to," I added.

"I'm surprised you're still out walking free after they found your pen at Stella's place." He forked a bite of omelet into his mouth.

"What? I sure didn't leave it there," I said. "If I killed her, you think I'd be stupid enough to leave my own pen at the scene of the crime?"

"Any murderer can't be too smart in the first place, don't you think?" He looked at me, speaking with his mouth open as he chewed.

I barely kept myself from squeezing my eyes shut. "Enjoy your breakfast, Ed. It's on the house."

I turned away and busied myself clearing dirty dishes and greeting a new group who walked in. The next time I heard the bell on the door jangle, I glanced over to see Ed's back passing through it. Talked with his mouth full and couldn't even be bothered to thank me after he shoveled in his samples. I strolled to the front window to see him climb into a shiny black car parked in the HANDICAPPED slot next to the ramp I'd built. I stared at the front license plate. Even through the downpour I could make out *KCSTOR*. That had to be for Kowalski's Country Store. The same plate and the same shiny black car that nearly ran me off the road on Sunday. Which had to be a coincidence. Because if it wasn't, trouble was seriously brewing right here in River City. Or Brown County, as the case may be.

I flipped through the e-mail in-box on my phone a couple of hours later. Nothing from Roberto, and refreshing the display didn't change the results. I'd checked first thing when I got up this morning—maybe he'd replied when he first checked his own e-mail—but my speeding pulse was disappointed when I couldn't see a single thing from Italy. My texts and voice mail were as empty then as they still were now.

The image of Ed's black car popped back into my brain like an evil jack-in-the-box. And about as creepy, too. He couldn't be so worried about his own restaurant he'd try to run me off the road. *Nah. Or could he?*

A pan clattered onto the floor with a bang, breaking my reverie. Danna bent over to retrieve it, calling out, "Sorry." One lone customer sat, nursing his coffee and paging through this week's *Sentinel,* which he must have brought in, since my copy still sat rolled up in a rubber band inside the plastic sleeve they used when it rained. I glanced at the big wall clock.

"Hey, we haven't gotten our delivery, have we?" I said, walking toward the desk. "It's already ten-thirty."

Danna shook her head. She focused on scrubbing the pan she'd dropped.

"Seems late. We're in trouble for lunch if it doesn't come, right?"

"Buns, salad, cheese."

"And the tuna I wanted. I'd better call them."

"Yeah."

I glanced at her. The delivery could wait a minute. I moved to her side and lowered my voice. "You okay?"

She gave a particularly vigorous swipe to the pan in the sudsy sink. "I wish there was a way to get back at Ed. He's abusive. He's an awful boss and he serves shi . . . um, garbage for food. He should be out of business. I hated having to even see him this morning."

I reached up and patted her back. "I'm sorry you had to work for him. And glad you're out of there. I can't really forbid him from coming in here, but I doubt he'll be around much, if that's any help."

She blew out a breath. "Thanks, Robbie." Her usual competent and slightly cocky expression returned as she looked down her shoulder at me, the topaz stud in her nose sparkling. "Now go call the supplier or we'll be serving garbage for lunch, too. Or at least orphaned burgers."

I laughed and headed for the desk. A minute later I said, "The truck's on its way, had to detour around a bridge that washed out in Beanblossom."

The man reading the paper paid his ticket, giving me a funny look as he did so, and departed, leaving the *Sentinel,* as well as a tip, on the table. I cleared and wiped his table, tucking the *Sentinel* under my arm, and put the money in the jar. I was caught up until the supplies came, so I sat and straightened out the paper. The top story was about Stella's murder, of course, since she was killed after the last edition of the paper came out. I read through the article, not expecting to learn anything new, but curious about how they would report it.

Holy bovine. No wonder that guy gave me a strange look. I squinted at the paper and reread the third paragraph:

> Police consider South Lick newcomer Roberta Jordan a person of extreme interest in the case. It was her biscuit in the victim's mouth. It was Jordan who'd had ongoing conflict with Stella Rogers. And Officer Bird has hinted at other evidence implicating Jordan that he said he's not at liberty to reveal. Jordan's newly opened restaurant, quaintly named Pans 'N Pancakes, might not be long for South Lick, after all.

This was a news story? I heard Mom's voice in my head: *"Consider the source, honey. Consider the source."* Biased reporting in a small-town weekly notwithstanding, everybody in town read it. If residents hadn't heard of my involvement in the murder before, they certainly knew about it now. Maybe there wouldn't be any more breakfast rushes or lunch rushes, either. I set my forehead in my hand, elbow on the table, and stared at the paper.

When the truck rumbled up to the service door at the side of the building a few minutes later, I folded

the paper so the sports section was on the outside and
rose to receive my order, almost missing hearing the
bell on the front door. I glanced over my shoulder,
groaned, and then kept right on going. Buck Bird was
the very last person in the universe I wanted to talk
to, because I sincerely doubted that he'd dropped by
only for a plate of pancakes.

By the time I put away the deliveries, Buck was settled
at a table, his legs stretched out to Kentucky, a breakfast platter in front of him already half eaten. Maybe
he was only here for food, after all. Fine with me.

After I waved to him, I washed my hands and rough
chopped scallions. Then I cut the half-frozen tuna
into cubes. Kind of unrealistic to expect fresh seafood
smack in the middle of the country. Heck, the middle
of the continent. But when tuna was flash frozen at
sea, it kept fine for something like fish cakes or tuna
burgers. I missed California red snapper fresh from
the pier, though, or a creamy halibut steak. I fed the
tuna into the institutional food processor, along with
the scallions, a couple of lemons' worth of juice,
mayo, capers, Dijon mustard, dried dill, and bread
crumbs.

Damn. I hadn't gotten a chance to check my e-mail
in a while. The more time that elapsed without an
answer from Roberto, the less likely it was I'd ever get
one. I pulsed the processor, whirring the mix together. His e-mail address could have been old.
Maybe he didn't teach at Pisa University anymore. Or
he was on sabbatical somewhere. Or he was married
to a jealous wife, who didn't want him to reply. Or he
just didn't care. I did want to know about Stella's in-

volvement with Don, but I imagined they'd simply been friends.

I pulsed a couple more times, merging the flavors, reducing the textures to an even mix, then stopped before it turned to mush. I could have used the meat grinder on the cookware shelves, but this was faster. A shadow fell over my work. A tall-enough shadow it could only be Buck. I twisted my head around and up.

"Yes?" I turned my whole self to face him before I got a crick in my neck.

"Guess you saw the story in the paper," he drawled.

"I sure did. Guess everybody else in town did, too. So you've been hinting at evidence, have you?"

"Of course not. You know how reporters are. They twist every cussed thing you say."

"Seems to me you'd better find the person who killed Stella, and soon, or I'm going to lose business faster than green grass through a goose."

"I sure wouldn't want you to have to close." His tongue swiped at a crumb of biscuit at the edge of his mouth before he wiped it off with a brush of his hand. "Your breakfasts bring me in mind of my grandmama's, God rest her soul. I used to spend summers with her down in Floyds Knobs. Just across the Ohio River from Louisville."

I might have acquired a few local expressions, but I sure as heck didn't say the name of the biggest city to the south as "LOW-uh-vull" with the *L* sound swallowed at the end. But then again, this part of Indiana was almost Kentucky, so it made sense Buck sounded more Southern than Midwestern.

"Are you making any progress on the murder?" I had the feeling there was something else I wanted to ask Buck, but I couldn't think of what it was. I lined a deep rectangular container with a length of plastic wrap and reached for a spatula. Scraping the fish mixture into a bowl, I began to form patties, laying them side by side in the container. "Maybe you should, you know, call in the state police or something." I filled the first layer and laid more wrap on top of it.

"Don't think we're going to need them. We're starting to get somewhere."

I glanced up from my work and rubbed the side of my forehead with the back of one hand. "Oh?" A caper fell off my hand to the floor.

"Had a eyewitness place someone going into Stella's house the afternoon she got herself killed."

"Who was it?" They needed to solve this case, and soon.

"Can't tell you."

"What about the DNA on my pen? Is that going to help?"

"Ah, that's a problem. State lab's all backed up." Buck shook his head. "Won't get results for quite some time. Could take longer than a visit from my mother-in-law."

"Didn't realize you were married." I checked his left hand. Sure enough, a gold band encircled his finger. "Stella was shot, so you must be looking into the gun. What kind it was, size of the bullets, stuff like that."

He laughed. "You sure don't know dang-all about firearms, do you?"

"No, I don't. Answer my question." I resumed working, but I formed the next patty with a little too much force and it squished out between my fingers. I swore and scraped the mix off my fingers and back into the bowl.

"Yes, Robbie, we're looking into the weapon."

I glanced across the room, where Danna moved from table to table. She hummed softly as she laid out fresh silverware packets and checked the salt and pepper shakers on each table, getting ready for lunch. Wires trailing out of her ears led to her apron pocket.

"Danna said Corrine goes shooting regularly," I said in a soft voice. "Sometimes with Ed Kowalski."

"Do you think Corrine killed Stella?" he asked softly. "It's the odd person who don't own a gun around here, you realize. Persons like you."

"Corrine sure as heck didn't like Stella. Told me she should have been able to pick her own assistant."

"Well, we're investigating all possibilities. I expect we'll make a arrest any day now."

Whether he meant it or not, I still had lunch to prep. An arrest would be great—as long as it wasn't my own. And from Buck's comment about how he wouldn't want me to have to close shop, I guessed he wasn't expecting to arrest me, either.

Chapter 21

By noon the place was bustling. Every table held customers, and a party of four browsed the cookware shelves, waiting for seats to open up.

"The sign must be doing the trick," I said to Danna when she delivered an order to the grill. I'd posted a sandwich board out front an hour earlier with a notice about the tuna burger special.

"You hooked that up," she answered, offering a high five.

I slapped her hand, but wrinkled my nose. "What does that mean?"

She laughed. "It means you did a good job with it. How old are you, anyway?" She turned back to the tables.

Twenty-seven, to be exact. But eight years made a big difference in knowing teenage slang. Plus I'd been working and supporting myself for a long time. Now that I owned a business, I felt a lot older than I might have if I were still in school, or out traveling and exploring the world, living carefree like there was no tomorrow.

I plated up three tuna, one veggie, and one turkey burger, added the specified sides, and hit the button on the round bell signaling they were ready. An hour later things calmed down enough for me to stuff a quick cheese sandwich into my mouth and use the restroom. When I emerged, Corrine held court at the table nearest the door. Don sat next to her, studying the menu, looking like he might have gotten over his antagonism toward her.

"Oh, Robbie," Corrine called, beckoning me over. "I have a wonderful proposal." When I passed Danna, she rolled her eyes. I continued toward the mayor.

I greeted her and Don. "What's up?"

"I want to hold a fund-raiser for the Brown County Animal Shelter. I think we should have it here Saturday night. I already have half the local merchants on board, right, Don?"

"Sort of."

"Eddie has a real soft spot for animals, too, and he's promised to sponsor the event in a big way," Corrine added.

"So a week from tomorrow?" I asked. "That should be doable."

"*No-o-o.*" Don drew out the word. "She means Saturday, like in tomorrow. I think it's too soon."

"Tomorrow night?" I tried not to screech.

"Are you busy?" Corrine demanded. "Think of all those poor kitties and doggies languishing in crowded little cells like common criminals." She widened her eyes at me. "We can't wait a minute longer."

"But what if people already have plans for tomorrow night?" I folded my arms. "It's pretty short notice."

"This town needs something to take our minds off the, you know"—she waved me in closer and lowered her voice—"the murder. And it will be great publicity for you and your restaurant, Robbie. Set yourself down, now. Let's make plans."

This woman was a force of nature. An answer of "no" was clearly out of the question. Don gave me a sympathetic look and raised one shoulder.

"I'll get banners made and strung up across Main Street," Corrine said. "You can hang one out front, too. We'll print up flyers and deliver them to every household."

"Who's *we*?" Don asked, rubbing his forehead.

"I snagged a intern from IU this week. He'll do it."

"You realize it's Friday afternoon?" Don asked.

Corrine tsk-tsked. "Turner's an eager beaver. He'll stay as long as I need him. Now, what about food, Robbie?" Corrine folded her hands in front of her and batted black fake eyelashes at me.

"You mean, what am I going to prepare with one day's notice? I hope you don't think I'm donating the cost. I can't afford to do that yet."

"We'll pay you back. Or, maybe you and another restaurant can work on it together."

I thought for a minute. "I could ask my friend Christina over at the Nashville Inn. She's the chef there now and they're much more well-established. They might donate the raw materials to get the publicity, and she and I can prepare the food together."

"Excellent. Just a bunch of appetizers is fine. Little meat pies and mini buffalo wings, you know, stuff you can eat with your fingers. And what's that Greek stuff called?"

"Spanakopita." She'd just described the most labor-intensive kind of food. Maybe Christina and I could make a trip to the Costco freezer section and pass their hors d'oeuvres off as homemade. I shook my mental head. *Nah.*

"That's it. Oh, Danna, take and bring us some coffee, baby, would you?" Corrine called, stirring the air with one lacquered hand.

"Are you sure you don't want to wait at least another week?" I asked. I'd been feeling tense before she showed up with her harebrained idea, and it sure wasn't helping to calm my stressed-out stomach.

"No, we need to do this now. I'll get a special liquor permit for you to serve wine and beer. Don, ask that cute brother of yours to bartend."

"You mean Abe?" Don looked at me. "Is he cute?"

"Actually, he is." I laughed at his bewildered reaction, the tension broken for a minute.

"Maybe we can auction stuff off, too." Corrine tapped her nails on the table. "You'll donate a gift card from the store, Don, and we'll get Ed to do the same."

Don nodded with a head made of lead, and the set to his mouth wasn't a happy one, either.

"Robbie, you ask Adele what she can give us for an auction," Corrine continued. "That wool of hers is getting pretty famous. I'll think on what else."

Danna set three mugs of coffee on the table without a word. I thanked her, but the words bounced off her back as she returned to the grill. She must figure she was getting roped into this crazy scheme, too. I imagined she was right.

Corrine drew out her phone and began tapping notes into it at what sounded like a hundred words a minute. If I tried that with fingernails like hers, it would be 100 percent typos, but she must have figured out how to make it work.

"All right, we're all set, then." She took a sip of coffee and plonked the mug down. "Come on, Don, we have work to do." She rose and sailed for the door. Don trailed behind her like an unhappy towed dinghy.

By the time I got over feeling like I'd been hit by a stun gun, they were gone. True, the event would be good exposure for Pans 'N Pancakes. If people didn't think a murderer was poisoning their spanakopita, that is. Speaking of a town's worth of food, I pulled out my own phone and hit Christina's number as I watched Danna at the grill.

After I greeted my friend, I said, "I need a big favor from you and the Nashville Inn."

"What's that?"

"Well, it's . . . Why do you sound like you're in stereo?"

"Because I'm right behind you."

I whirled to see her bent over, laughing. "Dude, quit laughing at me," I protested.

"You're funny." She disconnected the call and slid her phone into the back pocket of skinny jeans she wore with a simple yellow sweater. "Nice place you've made here. I like it." She gestured around the space.

"Thanks," I said, putting away my own phone. "I kind of like it, too. But what are you doing here? You don't work Fridays?"

"I needed to pick something up in Bloomington and dinner prep's all done. I thought I'd stop by, see what you've got going on, maybe wangle lunch, too. But what's this big favor you need?"

"Sit down and let me fix you a tuna burger, then we'll talk." I waved at a couple that was leaving and called out a thank-you.

"Ooh, sounds fab. I'm going to check out the pans while you cook."

It didn't take me long to grill her burger and crisp up the bun, then assemble it with the sauce I'd made, plus lettuce and a big tomato slice. I added a scoop of potato salad and a pickle to the plate and brought it to the table that Danna had prepped with a place mat and a napkin-wrapped packet.

"Soup's on," I called to Christina. I brought over two iced teas and sat down.

She sat opposite, saying, "I love those Swans Down hexagonal cake pans. I might need to buy a couple of those for home." She bit into the burger. *"Mmmm."*

"Thanks. So our new mayor got a total bug up her, um, rear end. She wants to hold a fund-raiser for the animal shelter here."

Christina swallowed. "Good idea. Good PR for you."

"Except it's tomorrow, and she only told me an hour ago." I filled Christina in on the details. "Do you think the inn would donate materials? You and I can make the apps in the afternoon, maybe?"

She finished another bite before she spoke. "Crazy timing. I'll have to ask the boss, but I do think the inn will make the donation. However, we have a two-hundred-person wedding reception scheduled for tomorrow night. I'm flat-out busy. Was just picking up the cake in Bloomington."

I frowned. "I'll never get it all done myself." I glanced at Danna. Maybe I could enlist her help with cooking.

"But listen. We have bunches of extra hors d'oeuvres in the freezer. Mini meatballs, little quiches, buffalo wingettes, that kind of thing. Somebody scheduled a function and then canceled at the last minute. The appetizers are taking up space and aren't going to keep much longer. How about we donate them? Save you all that time."

"Seriously? That would be perfect. When Corrine described a menu that takes more work than any other kind of food, I was wondering how I'd pull it off."

"Yeah, so you simply heat up ours. The work's already done, and the inn gets credit for homemade. You can add something of your own, like mini cheese biscuits, maybe. Or how about tiny tuna sliders? This is incredible. Sure beats White Castle." She pointed to the burger. "Capers, right?"

"Exactly. That's a really good idea about the appetizers. You've saved my bacon, girlfriend."

"Happy to help." She looked around and then leaned toward me. "I also came by because I heard a morsel of news about Ed Kowalski that you might be interested in."

"Gossip or hard fact?"

She tilted her head sideways a couple of times. "Some of both. Appears he's in trouble with the Board of Health. Had kitchen violations—grease, vermin, that kind of thing."

"Are they going to shut him down?"

"The little bird who told me said he only got a warning this time. But Board of Health violations are never a good thing—mainly for the customers. Who wants mouse droppings near their breakfast? And now the Board of Health will be breathing down his neck about everything."

* * *

By two o'clock the restaurant was empty and quiet. Outside the rain had blown through and sun streaming in through the windows warmed the old pine floor. I checked my e-mail, but there was nothing from Italy. I blew a breath out and set to wiping down the tables.

"What's up, Robbie? Seems like something's bugging you," Danna said over her shoulder from the sink.

I walked over to join her and leaned my back against the now-cool grill. I tossed the rag back and forth from one hand to the other.

"Kind of a long story." I kept tossing.

She raised an eyebrow. "You don't have to tell me."

"It's just that I never met my father. Mom and me, we didn't need him. But this week I found out who he was, and I dug up his e-mail address. And then I sent him an e-mail. In Italy."

"Italy? That's awesome." She turned her head to look at me. "You look Italian, now that I think about it. So, did he write back?"

I shook my head. "No. That's the problem. If I'd never found him, I wouldn't even care. But now, well, I guess I care."

"That sucks." She turned back to the sink. "If you can find his number, you could text him. E-mail's kind of old-fashioned, you know."

"I'll give him another day or two."

"I never knew my own dad, either," Danna said, her arms up to her elbows in the soapy water, her hands jostling the pots and pans as she scrubbed.

"Really?" A big old grabber on a crane pulled me

out of my own stupid swamp of dejection. "Did your mom want it that way?"

"She didn't have much choice. He died when I was a little baby."

"I'm so sorry to hear that, Danna." I stopped tossing my rag around and started to wipe down the counter next to the grill.

"It's okay." She rinsed a big pot and set it upside down on the drainboard. "One of my uncles used to take me to the father-daughter dances and stuff like that. Mom and I were cool by ourselves."

"That's how it was for my mom and me, too. Corrine's very attractive, though. I'm surprised she never found another partner." Come to think of it, my mom was a knockout, too, in her sun-bleached surfer way. I'd never thought about why she didn't find a man to love her.

"Mom dated some. She likes to be in control, though." Danna raised one eyebrow and grinned at me. "Maybe you've seen that."

I laughed. "Sure. Like this fund-raiser thing. If anybody can pull it off, I guess it's her."

"She's pretty bossy, but she can get business done, for sure."

I checked my e-mail one more time after Danna headed home at two-thirty, even though I'd looked at it less than an hour before. I saw the invoice from the delivery. A solicitation from the American Culinary Federation. A coupon from a restaurant supply company. But nothing from Italy, not even in my SPAM folder.

Stretching, I walked with leaden feet to the front

door to turn the sign to CLOSED. I opened the door, instead. A gust of wind blew a few dry leaves into a mini cyclone scudding down the street, the same wind that had blown the storm through and east to Ohio. Everything was washed clean by the rain, but the air held a taste of winter. A fox squirrel dug its brownish orange head in the golden leaves at the base of a beech tree across the road, then the critter hurried into the woods.

I took a deep breath. The week's puzzles would get solved one way or another. I knew I wasn't a murderer. Even if Buck arrested me on some kind of false evidence, the truth would come out sooner or later. And Roberto? Well, I'd lived without a father my whole life. I didn't need one now.

But I did have an aunt down the road I hadn't seen in a few days. I shut and locked the door, turned the sign to CLOSED, and tossed my apron in the laundry bin. I wasn't due at Jim's until six, and Danna and I had completed a bunch of the prep for tomorrow as we'd continued to talk, as well as cleaning up from today.

On my way to Adele's, which was out on Bean-blossom Road, I realized I was in front of Stella's house. I slowed to check it out. Her front garden already displayed a look of neglect. An oak leaf sat pasted to the top of a green gazing ball, which perched atop a three-foot-high dirty white pedestal with Grecian curlicues. Next to it, a garden decoration almost lay in the dirt, one of those boards cut and painted to look like the behind of a hefty aproned woman bending over to weed. Curled, dry leaves nestled behind the corner of a low picket fence, which needed a paint job.

I shuddered, speeding up again, and soon the van was clunking along the rutted gravel road to Adele's farm. The woods opened up to a peaceful vista of sheep grazing on a gentle slope beyond a fence. I pulled up next to her cottage, which looked like it belonged in an English village. The front garden, bounded by a low picket fence, held a riot of fall-tinted flowers still blooming in shouts of yellow, red, and gold. Vines trailed over the fence and the doorway, and a peach tree grew flattened and trained against the side of the house. A big pot overflowing with pink geraniums occupied the front stoop, since Adele never used that door. The garden featured her own gazing ball, as many Indiana gardens did, this one a blue-swirled globe held up by a whimsical pink metal flamingo.

A small Honda sat behind Adele's red pickup. *Oops.* She had company. Maybe I should have called first. Maybe I wouldn't be crying on the shoulder of my only relative, after all. When I climbed out of the van, her Border collie, Sloopy, ran up and yipped at me, then stuck his white snout into my offered hand. After I rubbed his black head, I reached back into the van for the container of biscuits I kept for him and handed him one. Adele had showed me how adept he was at rounding up the sheep and told me *"collie"* meant "sheep-herding dog" in Scottish.

I knocked on the side door and waited. I glanced down and groaned at the flecks of pancake batter mixed with grease spatters on my jeans, but I knew Adele wouldn't care. She still didn't come to the door. She could be out in the barn. I hadn't seen her in the fields anywhere and hoped she was okay. She was a tough cookie, but she wasn't a young one. I didn't recognize the car from anywhere and I shivered. *With a murderer skulking around free, what if . . .*

No. Don't go there. She was probably out in the barn. I pressed the doorbell and, after a minute, turned away.

The door opened behind me. "Robbie, come on in," Adele said.

I turned back. I started to greet her, but then stopped when I saw a man behind her. This was definitely not a dangerous situation, though. Adele's cheeks were suspiciously rosy and her oversized shirt was misbuttoned, one side of the collar sticking up into her neck and the shirttail on the opposite side flapping forlornly against her yoga-pants-clad thigh.

"I don't want to interrupt—"

"Nonsense. Come in and set with us. Do you know Samuel?" She stepped back to reveal a barefooted and smiling Samuel MacDonald next to her, also looking like he'd just pulled on his clothes.

"Phil's grandfather. We met, when, just this morning?" I greeted him and shook his hand when he extended it. I had no idea Adele had a love life. I wasn't so prudish or ignorant I didn't think people in their seventies couldn't enjoy a physical relationship, but I kind of wished she'd told me. I gave a mental shrug. Maybe it was new. Or maybe Adele wanted to keep her private life private.

"How about a mug of hot cider with Sorghrum to warm you up?" Adele asked after I followed them into a kitchen that smelled deliciously of freshly baked bread. "And I have sourdough in the oven. Should be done right about now." A timer dinged.

"I'd love some," I said.

A couple of minutes later, we were all seated at the table with steaming mugs of mulled cider in front of us, mugs fragrant with scents of cinnamon and cloves. The bread rested on a cutting board on the counter, smelling like heaven. Samuel set a squat, round-shouldered bottle of an amber liquid in the middle.

"What in heck is 'sorghrum'?" I asked. Despite being a chef in the area for the past three years, I'd never heard of it.

"Sorghum spirits. It's new," Samuel said. "A local guy distills it from an Amish farmer's sorghum. An Amish farmer with thirteen children. He doesn't even drink alcohol, himself." He laughed. "They wanted to call it sorghum rum, but the state wouldn't let them."

"Want to try a hit?" Adele asked, uncorking the bottle and pushing it in my direction.

"Why not?" I sniffed the spirits, its heady aroma hitting my sinuses. I poured a little into my cider, tasted it, and grimaced. "It's kind of molasses-y."

"Too sweet?" Adele asked.

"No, it's okay." I took another sip. "I guess it grows on you."

"So, what brings you over, honey?" Adele asked me as she laid a knobby, age-spotted hand on Samuel's wrinkled, darker one, his pale pink fingernails neatly trimmed. He gave her the sweetest smile I'd seen in a long time.

I outlined Corrine's harebrained scheme for the fund-raiser. "And she wants to do it tomorrow." I shook my head.

"Hey, she can pull it off," Adele said. "Corrine's competent. So she wants me to donate wool? I can do that. Long as it's tax deductible."

"She said it's for the animal shelter, so I guess it would be."

Adele eyed me. "I'll bet you really came over here to talk about your father."

"Maybe. But we'll do that later." I glanced at Samuel.

"I can leave you girls alone." He started to stand.

"No," I said, holding up my hand. "Sit down. There's nothing really to talk about. I mean, I found his e-mail address in Tuscany, Adele, but he hasn't answered. As I've been telling myself, I lived without a father this long, I can keep doing it." I blew air out through pursed lips, and then blinked hard as suddenly wet eyes threatened to make a liar out of me.

Adele stood and kneaded my shoulders for a minute, then she busied herself slicing the warm bread. She set the cutting board and a glass dish of butter on the table, along with knives and three small plates.

"Eat."

We all fell to buttering and savoring the chewy, crusty slices in silence.

"I chatted with Corrine's daughter, Danna, this afternoon," I finally said. "Turns out she's lived without a father most of her life, too. She said he died when she was a baby, so she never knew him."

"He was killed, when, dear?" Samuel said to Adele. "Sixteen, seventeen years ago? Danna must have been a li'l bit of a thing."

"He was killed?" I stared at him. "You mean, murdered?"

"No, no, nothing like that. He was killed in a hunting accident. Fool rifle went off wrong." Samuel made a tsking sound.

"There was some speculating at the time if Corrine had a hand in it. It was only the two of them out in the woods, you know."

"Why would she kill her own husband?" I asked.

"Rumors do fly. He was reputed to be a bully and a philanderer." Adele raised her eyebrows. "But we have something perfectly legal in this country called divorce. You don't need to kill a husband to get rid of him. Anyway, nothing came of it. She was never charged with being involved."

Chapter 22

It had turned into such a brilliant cool fall day I impulsively turned into the north entrance of Brown County State Park on my way home. My van clattered over the boards in the only double-tunnel covered bridge in the state. I flashed my yearly pass to the ranger at the gate booth, then parked near the Abe Martin Lodge and buttoned up my thigh-length black jacket, glad I'd worn sturdy sneakers. The parking lot was jammed, as it was every fall, but the park was big enough that I'd never found the trails too crowded, at least on weekdays. Sure, a murderer was still at large, but walking in a busy state park in broad daylight, with rangers and hikers aplenty, shouldn't be a risky proposition.

I could spare time for a brisk walk before I needed to get home and do tomorrow's prep. I set out on Trail One, inhaling the crisp air, gazing at sassafras trees turning from green to peachy orange, their lobe-like leaves hanging down as if sad they would soon lose their grip and become forest mulch. A gray, black, and white nuthatch scampered upside down on the smooth gray trunk of a beech, and a squirrel ran, cheek bulging, up the shaggy trunk of a shagbark hickory, depositing its winter dinner in a crevice and apparently ignoring the beauty of the tree's brilliant yellow foliage.

A white-haired couple strode toward me in their sensible hiking boots, walking sticks swinging, cheeks pink from exertion in cool air. As I stepped back to let them pass, I returned the blue-eyed woman's smile. But when I walked on, it stabbed me in the heart that my mom would never be a white-haired senior citizen. She wouldn't get the chance to find love late in life. She would not ever know of my life, of my successes and failures, whether in business or in love.

I admonished myself to enjoy where I was right now. Mom would have wanted me to take in this brightly colored day, not to stew about the unfair timing of her death. I trod on until I came to the sign for Trail Two, which was a two-mile loop I knew passed both the stone Lower Shelter and the North Lookout Tower up on the hill, a classic Lincoln Log cabin built on top of a smaller limestone-brick base. If I hustled, I could get back in time, and a dose of fast exercise was just what the doctor ordered, anyway. Or would have if I had signed up with a doctor, which I'd never bothered to find here in Indiana, since I was blessed with the healthiest constitution of anyone I'd ever met. I never got sick.

Setting out on the trail, I heard a noise and whipped my head to the right. Had I been followed? Catching a glimpse of the white tails of two deer bounding away from me through the underbrush, I laughed. I kept walking and my tension began to ebb. I breathed deeply and focused on putting one foot in front of the other. I'd nearly reached the tower when a loud, sharp report sounded. I froze, then I heard two more shots. *Hunting in the state park? That isn't allowed, is it?* I glanced down at my dark jacket and jeans. Great. I wasn't wearing a thread of bright color. Now what? Thoughts of Danna's father killed in a hunting accident crossed my mind.

Or maybe this wasn't an illicit hunter. Maybe it was Stella's murderer. I swore, turned around, and started to race back the way I'd come, patting my pocket for my phone as I ran. Except the only thing in there were the keys to my van. I swore again. The trail was empty of people. When I took a second to glance behind me, my toe caught on a root and I went sprawling, scraping my palm on a branch and whacking the other elbow on a stone hidden under the fallen leaves. I scrambled up, my heart beating so fast I could barely breathe, but I kept running until I switched back onto Trail One. I slowed to a fast, nervous stride until I was able to gulp a few deep breaths, and then I set to jogging again. I didn't stop until I emerged in the parking lot. I leaned over, hands on my knees, panting.

"Miss? You all right?" a man's voice asked.

I straightened to see a stocky, middle-aged park ranger walking toward me. Wiping the sweat from my forehead, I said, "I heard shots in the woods. Are people allowed to hunt here?"

"What trail were you on, miss?" He pursed his lips.

"Trail Two. I was getting close to the Lookout Tower."

"Oh, then it's no problem."

"Sure felt like a problem. Look at me. I'm not wearing orange. Shouldn't I be able to take a hike in a public park without some fool hunter nearby?" My voice had risen so high, it cracked. I swallowed hard.

"You can calm down, now. It wasn't no hunters. We have an after-school target practice class near there. Don't worry a bit about it. It's all controlled and there aren't no trails behind where the targets are set out."

Target practice. By children. I squeezed my eyes shut for a moment, then opened them and tried to smile at him. "Well, thanks, then."

"You have a good day, now."

After I arrived home, I parked by the side and let myself into my apartment. Birdy wove through my legs, chirping away, as I tried to walk down the hall. I finally picked him up, laid him on my shoulder, and stroked his head as I walked so I wouldn't trip over him and break my neck. I set him down in front of his empty bowl. No wonder he was being so cuddly. After I scooped a cupful of dry food into it, he fell to munching and I fell into a kitchen chair.

What a day of discovery. Realizing the black car was Ed's. Reading in the *Sentinel* that, in their eyes, I might as well be arrested for murder. Hearing from Buck about the eyewitness report of someone going into Stella's house. Agreeing to the fund-raiser and then learning of Ed's trouble with the Board of Health. Finding out Danna and I both grew up fatherless. And seeing firsthand evidence of Adele's boyfriend. The only thing I hadn't learned was how my father felt about me. Which couldn't have happened, I realized, since I hadn't told him I was his daughter. And now it was nighttime in Italy again.

I stood, planning to take a good long shower and

get ready for my dinner date. At least that made me smile. I hadn't had a chance to relax with Jim since Monday night. Maybe we could suspend all talk of murder and suspects and simply enjoy ourselves.

Halfway to the bathroom, I heard a noise from the direction of the store and froze. Nobody should be in my store. *Nobody.* I reversed tracks to the kitchen and retrieved my phone from my bag. Then I crept toward the connecting door, in which I'd installed a one-way mirror with the window on the side of my apartment. I hadn't really thought through why, but I had imagined I might have a need to observe what was going on in the restaurant without being seen. Other mirrors were installed around the store because I liked the way it reflected back light and I'd noticed customers liked to look in them, too.

I peered into the window, but I didn't see anyone skulking about. My view didn't reach to all the corners and behind shelves and counters, though. *Damn it. Should I call 911?* I wasn't about to go in there myself, not in a county where the majority of adults toted guns. My heart was a giant jackhammer in my chest. Good thing I hadn't poured more than a short shot of that liquor Adele had offered.

I got real close to the window and tilted my head, trying to see if I could spot anyone at the far edges of its view. Nothing. Maybe the noise was from the wind, which hadn't let up its gusting all day. Could be a false alarm. I still wasn't going in there until I thought it was safe. I retreated to the kitchen and grabbed my keys off the hook. I made my way quietly outside around to the front. I could check out the rest of the interior from the big windows facing the street. If I didn't see anybody, I'd go in that way.

An unfamiliar car was parked out front. *Huh?* If someone had broken in, would they leave their car sitting there for everyone in town to see? Speaking of that, a Jaguar rolled by, giving a beep as it passed. I cringed, but I gave a little wave to Corrine in the driver's seat. So much for sneaking up, unnoticed. I was still going to try. I tiptoed up the side stairs of the covered front porch running the width of the building and pressed my nose against the glass farthest from the door, my heart mimicking an Indy 500 race car revving up for the start of the race.

But I was peering right smack-dab into the back of the six-foot-high freestanding drinks cooler. I moved to the next window, which unfortunately was not as clean as it should have been, since I'd run out of time before the grand opening and never got around to washing all the outside glass. I rubbed a round spot clean, but I still couldn't spy anyone.

"Robbie? What are you doing?"

"Yikes!" I whipped my head to the right. "What in—"

The screen door slapped closed behind Phil, who stood with head atilt staring at me, two empty baking sheets in one hand.

"What in what?" he asked. "What are you doing out here?"

"Jeez, Phil. You about gave me a heart attack." I sank into the closest rocking chair, patting my chest. "I thought I heard a burglar in the store. Or worse, a murderer. I was trying to look in the window." I obviously needed to start paying more attention to my surroundings. He was the fourth person to sneak up on me in probably that many days, or fewer.

He snorted. "So now your dessert man is a thief?"

He held up the pans. "Just dropping off your order for the weekend, ma'am."

"But how did you get in?"

He jangled a bunch of keys with his other hand. "With the key you gave me months ago? You don't remember?"

I squinted and wrinkled my nose. "Oh. Maybe I do remember." I parceled out the words like I was a really slow person dealing cards.

He laughed and sat in the next chair over, which complained with a mighty creak.

"Thanks for bringing the desserts. Good thing I didn't call the cops, right?"

"You could say that." He rocked and creaked back and forth. "I phoned and texted you a bunch of times, but you didn't pick up."

I checked my phone, which I still clutched in one hand. Sure enough, the volume was completely off. The voice mail icon and the text icons were both lit up, though, and the tiny red light in the corner of the display blinked insistently.

"I was over at Adele's." I looked at him. "Did you know your grandfather and Adele were hanging out?"

"No, but he's been looking awfully cheerful lately. He even asked me to go clothes shopping with him in Bloomington. Said he needed to update his wardrobe."

"I apparently surprised them both at Adele's this afternoon. All rosy-cheeked and dressed kind of slapdash." I waved a hand at the car in front of the store. "But that's not your car, is it?"

He shook his head. "Swapped out with my mom. Mine's in the shop."

"Big to-do here tomorrow night, did you hear?"

"Corrine's fund-raiser?" he asked.

"Crazy. Got anything you want to donate? And will you come?"

"I can do up a certificate for a month of Friday desserts," he said. "Delivered with a song. How about that? And a couple extra trays of brownies for the event itself."

I laughed. "I like it. All of it."

Gazing down the street, he stopped rocking. "Speaking of the police." He pointed.

I let my eyes follow where his finger pointed. A South Lick police car drove toward us, although not with all the bells and whistles lit up. "This better not be what I'm afraid it is." I shivered.

"I read the *Sentinel* online today. Agree. It better not be," Phil said, his eyes glued to the cruiser.

But the car didn't slow at the store. We watched as it kept on going.

"Did you see that?" he asked, with a sudden turn of his head toward me.

I nodded, keeping my gaze on the police car until it turned the corner a few blocks into town, in the direction of the police station.

Wanda was driving, and Don O'Neill sat in the car. Not in the front seat, either.

Chapter 23

I locked my back door at two minutes before six o'clock and hustled down the drive, clutching a bottle of wine. It was only a ten-minute walk to Jim's condo downtown, but I hated to cut time close like this. Although, even if I was late, I doubted Jim would have a dog in that hunt. I wore a pair of jeans I thought flattered my posterior, tucked into knee-high leather boots, and finally decided on a tunic-length soft sweater in a deep rose after trying on and discarding nearly every sweater I owned. My hair, which I'd rearranged about sixteen times, now fell in loose curls on the shoulders of my jacket.

I'd never been to Jim's home before. His law office? Sure, a dozen times. He'd held the closing for the store there. Before then, we'd met to arrange the purchase details; and after that, to get all the permits sorted out, with no help from Stella. But I'd passed his building bunches of times, the one he'd pointed out on our way home from the roadhouse on our date that seemed like weeks ago instead of only six days. The downstairs of his building housed the consignment shop, as well as Wheelworks, the bike shop where I left my cycle for tune-ups.

I walked fast, even though I'd rather be cycling. I was overdue for a long ride. I got all kinds of itchy when I didn't get out on the roads for a few days in a row. I could have ridden to Adele's this afternoon, but I'd thought it might end up making me late for dinner. Tonight I didn't want to ride home in the dark with wine in my system. Not another soul was out, not even on this stretch of Main Street. South Lick shut up like a hermit crab at the end of the business day. There were only a couple of restaurants to draw people out, and the one bar was on the other side of town.

So it looked like Don was in custody. He must have been the person the eyewitness saw going into Stella's house before Stella was killed. I wished he weren't the murderer, but wishing didn't have any place in a crime investigation. At least the authorities focusing on him should take the pressure off me.

Cutting through a narrow path running alongside the bank, I took the shortcut down the alley behind the row of shops. The sun hadn't yet set, although clouds were blowing back in and the light was dim between the backs of the three-story buildings on either side. Glancing up, I saw lights on in a couple of windows up high, but there weren't any windows at street level, only locked metal doors.

I heard a rustling behind me and checked over my shoulder, but it was only dry leaves twirling in the wind. *Maybe walking alone in an alley with a murderer on the loose isn't such a hot idea. No,* I told myself, *Don is sitting safely in a jail cell. Or is he? But what if Buck was wrong? Maybe he'd only brought Don in for questioning and then let him go.* I scrabbled in my bag for the reassuring feel of my phone, extracting it and sliding it into my jacket pocket. Anyway, it wasn't a very long alley.

I'd almost reached Walnut, the cross street I was heading for, when a loud, high-pitched noise *zinged* past me. A puff of red dust popped out of the bricks in the wall to my left. I stared at it and swore as I broke into a run. Another shot landed in the pavement where my foot had rested a second before. Yelling, I didn't take the time to see where it came from. I ran as fast as my short legs could take me, not stopping until I was in the clear, smack in the middle of Walnut.

The shots stopped. I stared back at the alley, but no one emerged. If somebody was shooting at me, I was in big trouble. And this wasn't any after-school target practice, either.

A car honked and I levitated like a kangaroo, emitting a screech as I did so. I was standing in the middle of the street, after all. I gave a weak wave at the impatient SUV and made my way to the far sidewalk. My legs barely held me up, and my brain was as full of Jell-O as my legs.

I should call the police. And hurry to Jim's. No reason not to do both, I finally told myself. I pressed 911 and set off at the fastest stride I could muster.

"Dispatch. What's your emergency?"

My ears were ringing, but I could hear her through it. "Someone just took two shots at me. I was in the alley behind Main between Walnut and North Streets."

"Are you safe now?" she asked.

"Yes. I think so."

She asked for my name and address, which I supplied. "Where are you at now?" she asked.

"I'm walking to my friend's condo, 180 Walnut.

I'm almost there." My voice wobbled as I walked, but I didn't care. My legs wobbled, too.

"We'll send someone to check out the area. Did you see the shooter?"

"No."

"Any idea who it might be?"

"No!" How could I have an idea when I didn't even . . . *Oh. Stella was shot dead. Was I meant to be murder number two?* No, I wasn't about to get into a discussion of Stella's murder with a dispatcher. "At least one of the shots went into the brick wall, though."

"The officer will call you at this number with further questions. You're sure you're safe now, Ms. Jordan?"

"I'm not going into any more alleys, I'll tell you that much."

"Wise decision. Thank you for your call." She disconnected.

I'd never been so happy to see a building as when I arrived at number 180, although the two stores flanking the lit entrance were closed and dark, of course. I located Jim's buzzer on the panel in the doorway and pressed it, leaning my shoulder against the wall.

His tinny voice crept out of the speaker. "Robbie?"

"Yep."

"I'll buzz you in. Third floor, back."

A buzzer rasped and the door clicked. I pulled it open and hurried down a hallway with black-and-white tiles in a diagonal pattern on the floor. A large potted plant sat at the base of a well-lit marble stairway leading up. The walls were a clean white and the whole thing projected an airy, spacious feel, which helped me finally breathe again. When I hit the landing on the second floor, I glanced up to see Jim hanging over the railing one floor up.

"Welcome to Hollywood," he called.

I kept climbing, my boots clacking on the marble. I hung on to the banister in case my legs gave way. When I reached the third and top floor, I said, "It does kind of remind me of Hollywood." I handed him the wine, which miraculously I didn't drop in my desperation to escape the shooter.

"It's the Art Deco period, the new modernism. This building was constructed in 1939 and I love it." He took my hand, padded along the hall in his socks to an open doorway, and extended his other arm. *Mi casa.*

I walked in ahead of him, letting go of his hand. When I spied a leather couch, I sank down onto it and let out a big breath.

"Are you all right?" Jim hurried to my side. He peered down at me. "You look pale. Did something happen?"

"Somebody took a couple of shots at me."

"What?" He plopped down next to me. "Are you hurt? Did you call the police? Where were you?" He stroked my forehead and ran his hand along the back of my head. That should have been a heavenly sensation, but I could barely feel it.

"Hey, one question at a time. I'm not hurt. If they were aiming for me, they missed. Not by much, but that's all that counts, right?" I smiled, but it didn't have much strength behind it. "Yes, I reported it to a dispatcher. An officer might call me back."

"Was it at the store?" His pale eyebrows drew so close in the middle they almost merged.

"No, the alley. I was cutting over to Walnut, behind Main. Not the best idea after hours, I realize."

"Oh, Robbie. If you'd been hurt, I—" He extended

an arm behind me and wrapped the other one around me, hugging so tight I could hardly breathe.

I finally managed to wriggle free. "But I wasn't hurt. I sure want to know who took aim at me, though."

Forty minutes later I sat catty-corner from Jim at a small dining table near the window with the last, weak rays of daylight slanting through the trees above South Lick Creek. Candlelight reflected off our wineglasses as we dug into salmon steaks he'd gas grilled on the small deck cantilevered out from the building. A dish of roasted sweet potatoes with a curry treatment sat in the middle of the table next to a wooden bowl filled with salad. Goat cheese and dried cranberries peeked out of the greens. The beige place mats and forest-green napkins matched the simple masculine decor of the room.

"This is super, Jim. Thank you." I lifted my glass of Pinot Grigio.

"Makes me nervous cooking for a chef, but I gave it my best effort." He laughed as he matched my lift. "Here's to you, Robbie."

"Here's to not getting shot at." I took a sip and set the glass down. I was recovering from the wobblies, but I couldn't shake the shock of being someone's target. "The shots angled downward and there aren't any windows on the street level. Whoever it was must have been on one of the upper floors."

"I wonder who it was. The top floors of those buildings have flats in them."

"Any idea who lives there?" I savored a bite of the sweet potato. I'd never thought to use Indian flavors on the deep orange root, but it was a perfect match.

For a moment the food took my thoughts away from the alley.

"Well, they're not fancy penthouses, I can tell you. More like bare-bones low rent." He pushed his glasses back up his nose.

"More so, the question is, who would want to aim a gun at me? And then fire it." I glanced at my phone, which lay still and dark on the far side of the table. "I'm surprised the police haven't called me back yet."

"Could take them a while to check things out."

"Yeah, they might be busy with something else. I forgot to tell you I saw Wanda driving Don in a cruiser earlier today. And he was in the back. Does that mean they arrested him?"

"Interesting. Yes, it might. I'm assuming it's in connection to the murder." He gazed at the now-dark window, running the thumb of his left hand over his fingernails.

"If they arrested Don for the murder, then it wasn't Stella's murderer who shot at me."

"Unless . . ." He cocked his head.

"Unless they got the wrong guy, I know. This afternoon I thought I was getting shot at, too."

"Really?"

"I took a quick walk in the state park, and all of a sudden, I heard shots. I was out in the woods and I didn't know if it was hunters or some lunatic aiming at me. My walk turned into a run trying to get back to my van. And then a ranger said it was only a youth target practice I heard. I felt pretty stupid."

"You couldn't have known it was target practice."

"Too bad what happened on my way here wasn't as innocent." My phone lit up and vibrated, so I grabbed it and connected. I said "hello" and heard

Buck's voice in return. "Did you find my shooter?" I kept my gaze on Jim.

"Nope. We checked out the apartments above the bank, though, and didn't pick up any suspects, although a couple of the apartments are either empty or nobody answered the door. Did you get a sense of what kind of firearm they used?"

"What? How would I know that? I don't know the first thing about guns, remember? Can't you, like, figure it out from the bullet hole in the wall?"

"What bullet hole?"

I slumped a little. "You didn't look at the walls of the alley? I told the dispatcher one shot went into the brick wall."

"It's a pretty long alley." Static crept around the edge of his voice.

"No, it isn't. It's only one block long. And I was down near Walnut. Maybe twenty yards away." I tapped my fork against the side of my plate.

"We'll take a look in the morning."

"In the morning." I rolled my eyes at Jim.

"Yup. If you think of anything else you might have seen or heard, you call the station."

"I will. Hey, I saw Wanda driving Don O'Neill in a cruiser today. Did you arrest him for the murder?"

Jim leaned forward, forearms folded on the table.

Buck didn't speak for a minute. When he did, it was in a mournful tone. "Can you imagine for just a little minute why I can't talk to you about that, Robbie?"

"I have a valid reason for asking. If he's the killer, then I'm not, right? I can put a sign on my door that says, 'Okay to Eat Here. She's Not Going to Murder

You.' I've been losing customers because I was a person of interest, at least according to the *Sentinel*."

He blew out a big, noisy breath. "Yes. We're holding Don for the murder. But we have a long ways to go."

"Was he the person reported to have gone into Stella's the day she was killed?"

"That's right. He says he didn't kill her, of course."

"Of course."

"That he simply went over to visit her." Background noise flowed out of the phone. "Gotta go. We'll look into your shooter as we can, Robbie. I'd advise—"

"Staying out of alleys. I promise."

He disconnected and I filled Jim in on what Buck told me.

"So they're holding Don," Jim said. "Interesting."

I gazed at the remnants of my interrupted dinner. "You wouldn't even believe what Corrine cooked up for tomorrow." I told him about the fund-raiser.

"Poor timing," Jim said. "I can't believe she's going to get much of a turnout."

"There was no stopping her. I don't mind hosting the event. It'll be good publicity." I finished my last bite of salad and gazed at him. "Do you think Don would kill Stella?"

"No idea. It's hard to imagine why anyone would kill another being—you know me, I don't even believe in killing animals for food—but we all know murder happens. I wonder if she was threatening him somehow."

I tapped my fork on the side of my plate and narrowed my eyes.

Jim reached out and waved a hand in front of my face. "Earth to Robbie, come in, please."

I looked at him. "I found out something very interesting this week. Well, yesterday and the day before. Remember when I said I was going to the library? Well, I found a picture of Mom and Don, all right. And I think I also found my father."

His eyes went as wide as the Ohio River. "No kidding."

"No kidding." I shook my head. "He's an Italian named Roberto Fracasso. I look exactly like him. He was a Rotary scholar who stayed with Don's family the spring before my mom moved to Santa Barbara— the year before I was born. And then I read about an accident at a quarry, where he was injured. A news article said Don jumped in and saved him."

"Amazing. This Roberto survived the accident, though? Quarries are awfully dangerous."

"He did. I kept digging, and found out he's a professor in Tuscany. I sent him an e-mail, but he hasn't responded." I raised a shoulder and let it drop. "Last night when you called me? I thought it might have been him. Believe me, I wasn't disappointed you called." I laid my hand on Jim's.

"You were disappointed it wasn't him."

I swallowed hard. I nodded, then took a sip of wine. "But back to the murder for a minute. I went over to the hospital in Bloomington and ran into a friend who works in the records department. She and I searched online until we found the information about his admission. I was sure it would have been Mom who called for help, but I was wrong. It was Stella. She's the one who called the ambulance and came in with Roberto and Don."

He cocked his head. "I don't get how that connects to Stella's murder."

"I'm not sure. What if there was something fishy about the quarry accident? I think Don was dating Mom. Then this handsome Italian blows into town and she falls in love with him. Maybe Don pushed him in or whacked him on the back of the head. And Stella saw him do it. And she was blackmailing him all this time."

"That's a lot of *ifs* and *maybes*, Robbie."

"You got that right. And it was all so long ago. I'm not sure how I'll ever find out."

He turned his hand so our palms were facing and squeezed. "Do you have to?"

"I guess not. None of my business, right? Buck has Don. Presumably, he has evidence. And it's starting to look like Roberto doesn't want to talk to me." I blew out air. "I'll just get back to what I'm supposed to be doing. Which is running a business. And speaking of that, tomorrow's breakfast customers are going to be pretty unhappy unless I get home and get stuff ready."

Jim looked down. He pursed his lips and tapped the table, then he looked out into the dark, avoiding my eyes.

Now I'd put a big old damper on his hopes for the evening. "I'm sorry. I'm not much of a dinner guest, talking about murder and the past the whole time. Plus I'm going to turn into a pumpkin any night when I have to open the next day. I think Sunday's going to be a better date night, all things considered."

He looked back up and raised his eyebrows. "Did you just invite me out for Sunday?"

"If you're free." I raised my eyebrows and smiled.

"I believe I am. But I did make my special super-creamy coffee ice cream for you tonight. Sure you can't stay a few more minutes? Then I'll drive you home."

"Oh, twist my Santa Barbara arm." I smiled back. At least something was right in the world.

Jim pulled up his Prius in front of the store and reached his right hand over to rub my shoulder. "Let me come in with you and make sure everything is okay."

"'Okay,' as in no murderers lying in wait? Or snipers?" I gave a little laugh, then frowned. "You don't think . . ." I gazed at the dark building, lit from within only by the red glow from the EXIT sign that was always on and the pale light from the drinks cooler. I gave a quick glance at the street behind me, too.

"No, I don't think. But let's make sure."

After I switched on the lights, we checked out the cooler, the restrooms, and my apartment.

"Thank you," I said as we walked back to the front door. "You were right. That does make me feel better."

"Good. You might think about motion-activated lights for the porch, too, and even one inside."

"That's a great idea. I'll put it on my to-do list." We moved out onto the porch. "So, will you be coming to this crazy fund-raiser tomorrow?"

"Why not? As long as Corrine doesn't make me donate a day of lawyering or anything. How about I come over early and help out?"

"I'd love that. Five o'clock?"

He nodded, then he planted a long, delicious kiss on me before clattering down the steps.

Smiling to myself, I locked up tight and puttered around the store, getting things ready. I set the tables, mixed up the perennial biscuit dough, and rummaged in the cooler. The tuna burgers hadn't sold out, so I wiped the Specials chalkboard clean. I wrote: *Spicy Tuna Hash*. I could mix the fish with sautéed onions and garlic, use the potatoes that were getting soft, and add a bit of jalapeño. Not too much, though. This part of the country wasn't known for a love of peppers, unlike where I'd grown up. I smiled, remembering when I'd challenged my friend Mike, a guy almost twice my size, to a pickled jalapeño contest in college. We sat across from each other, with a half-gallon jar of the pickled peppers between us. I looked him in the eyes, fished one out, and ate it. He returned the look and ate one. I ate one. Back and forth, until he finally caved right before I was about to. Then we went out for huge bowls of cool, soothing ice cream.

I set my hands on my waist and looked around the store. If Corrine thought she was going to draw in a big crowd tomorrow, we'd have to make an open space where people could mingle. Jim and I could push all the tables to the periphery and serve the food on them. Or maybe Corrine would need them for the donations. The cabinet held a supply of white-and-blue paper tablecloths I'd ordered, just in case. Speaking of donations, I should donate a Pans 'N Pancakes gift certificate. Whoever bid on it could use it either to buy cookware or a meal. I moseyed over to my office corner and fired up the computer and the printer. I'd created a gift certificate with our logo and a fancy border before the store opened, so now all I needed to do was print it out on half-sheet card stock.

As the printer *zoo-zooed* its print heads, I took a deep breath and opened my e-mail. I stared at the in-box. Right up top was *Regarding Jeanine Jordan,* the subject line of the e-mail I'd sent to Roberto. But this one included a *RE:* in front of it.

"Be still, my heart," I said out loud, and patted my chest. I clicked open the message.

> *Ms. Robbie Jordan.*
> *My father is Roberto Fracasso. He was in Indiana many years ago, yes. I do not know anything about your mother. My father is quite ill in hospital now with infection. We do not know if he gets better. He told to me if you want to call him he will talk with you. Write back to me for the number if you will telephone.*
> *Graciela Fracasso Molteni*

Graciela. My half sister. I read the message over and over, my eyes filling with hot tears, my heart thudding. My father ill with an infection in the hospital, an illness he might not survive. I'd just found him and now I might lose him. But he said he would talk with me. The words blurred on the screen until I tore my sleeve across my eyes. I stood and paced around the store. I wanted to get in my van, drive to Indianapolis, buy a plane ticket (no matter the cost), and fly to that hospital in Tuscany. Or get Scotty to beam me up and plop me down there now, right now. Infections were bad. And hospitals could make them worse. What if I never got to meet him?

Instead, I sat and read the message again. And again. Finally, fumbling with the keys, I typed a short reply: *Please send me the hospital name and number. And his room number. As soon as possible.*

I went back and added *Thank you, Graciela* to the beginning. I wanted to stay on this woman's good side. On a new line I started to type, *And tell him,* but then I shook my head and erased it.

Tell him what? That he was my father? That I love him? I've never even met him. Graciela would think I was crazy and I'd never get his phone number. The time in the corner of the monitor read 10:10. She'd sent it at six, late at night in Italy. And right after I'd left for Jim's.

I added to the bottom: *Thank you so much, Robbie* and pressed SEND. Then I sat there, stunned. I was sure I wouldn't hear back until the morning, and then I'd be in the breakfast rush. *Wait. If it's ten o'clock here, it's three in the morning over there. If she got up at seven, maybe she'd write back at two in the morning my time. Or three?* I could get up extra early and check. If I could even sleep.

My agitation made me doubt that. I got up and poured a little bourbon in a glass; then I found the playlist I'd labeled "Mom" on the computer. I'd never known why she loved to listen to opera so much, until now. I started the Bocelli album playing, the one where he sings arias from a number of operas, which I'd listened to dozens of times since I lost my mom. I set it to play *"Che Gelida Manina"* from *La Bohème,* one of her favorites. As the tenor sang, I found Roberto's picture again and gazed at his face. At the end of the song, I knew the words translated to: "Now that you know me, speak, tell me who you are! Will you say?"

"Will you tell me who you are, Roberto Fracasso?" I asked the image. "Will you say?"

Chapter 24

With a big yawn I slapped the BREW button. That alarm going off at five-thirty, after I finally got to sleep at eleven, was getting old. Neither my hundred sit-ups nor my shower did little to lighten my heavy eyelids. Finding no new e-mail from Italy kept my heart heavy, too. Birdy swishing around my legs was the only spot of light in the dark of predawn. I'd filled his bowl and sat down on the floor, stroking his back as he ate, hearing him chirp with what sounded a lot like happiness.

I pulled the biscuit dough out of the cooler to warm, along with eggs and milk, and began to assemble the pancake batter. I'd set it aside and was dicing potatoes when the bell on the door jangled. I'd unlocked it for Danna and didn't look up.

"'Morning, Danna," I called. When she didn't answer, I glanced toward the door. My eyes widened. Roy stood there, watching me, the still-dark morning behind him. He was dressed in green-and-tan camouflage gear, a matching blotchy cap on his head. Some kind of a long gray-and-silver gun was slung over his shoulder by a strap. A gun I didn't want to have any part of.

I turned toward him and mustered a smile. "Hi there, Roy. We're not open yet." I pointed to the sign in the window and then to the wall clock, which read six-thirty.

He looked around and narrowed his eyes. "Abe here yet?"

"Abe?"

"Abe O'Neill."

"No, he's not." I sensed flour on my cheek and swiped at it with one hand. "We're really not open, you know, not until seven. The hours are posted."

"Damn. Was supposed to go grouse hunting with him. Told him to meet me here. Can I get a cup of coffee while I wait?"

I blew out a breath. "Okay. But you'll have to put your gun in your car first."

"It's legal. Open carry law." He glowered. "Got a license for it."

"I'm sure it's legal." I spoke slowly and clearly. "But I'm uncomfortable with a gun in my store, so please lock it in your vehicle. If you want coffee, that is."

He grumbled to himself, but he left. When he came back in, his hands were empty, and he sat at a table for two. As I carried a full mug to him, Danna strode in. She wrinkled her nose at seeing Roy, but she simply waved at me and went straight to the box of clean aprons.

"What's he doing here?" she said in a low voice when I joined her in the cooking area.

"Dunno. Said he's meeting someone to go hunting and asked for coffee. I made him stash his rifle or whatever it was in his car first."

"Good." She glanced at the Specials board. "Want me to take over the hash?"

"Sure." I told her my rough idea for a recipe, then I walked over to my computer and set the Bocelli to playing again. So what if Roy glared at me? We could use a little mood in the place. I dolloped out a pan of biscuits, slid them into the oven, and started sausages cooking.

"Heard Don was arrested for Stella's murder," Danna said, still speaking softly as she chopped. "And you got shot at."

"All true."

"You okay?"

"Yeah. I don't suppose they'll find who was using me as target practice, though. Seems like everybody in the state has a gun." I shot my eyebrows in Roy's direction.

"Even my mom. Who is on a super rampage with this event of hers. She never shut up last night, on the phone with literally the whole town."

We worked side by side until seven. I turned the sign to OPEN and on my way back asked Roy if he wanted a refill.

"No. Don't want a shaky hand for shooting."

"Want to see a menu?"

"I ate at home, but that bacon smells awful good. Gimme a side of that and a couple three biscuits with gravy."

I didn't budge.

"Please," he added.

"Meat gravy or miso gravy on your biscuits?"

"Me so what?" He shook his head in bewilderment. "No idea what you just said. Meat gravy, of course."

I welcomed a party of four men dressed in orange

vests and pants like Roy's. I gave Roy's order to Danna, surprised he'd actually eat cooking from my restaurant, from *me* whom he'd accused of stealing his property. I poured coffee for the newcomers and distributed menus. Abe might be late because of dealing with Don. Maybe he was posting bail or something, if they even did that on weekends. Roy could have a long wait.

At about seven-thirty Corrine flew through the door like a whirling dervish. A young man trailed in her wake, carrying a sheaf of bright yellow paper.

"Robbie, I have flyers," she announced in a loud voice, making everyone but Danna look up. "We'll put one up on the door and you can hand them out to all your customers." She waved at the dude she'd brought, likely her intern, who set a stack of the papers on a table and then went back outside. Through the glass I saw him taping a flyer to the door.

"Okay, Corrine," I said. "Not a problem."

"Fabulous fund-raiser tonight, folks!" She smiled at the hunters. "For a excellent cause—our poor, neglected, abandoned animals."

"What time, ma'am?" one of the hunters asked. By the way he snickered and elbowed his buddy, it didn't look like he was asking so he could put it in his day planner.

"Seven to ten," Corrine answered proudly.

I clenched my jaw. Sunday morning was going to be a blast. "The chef at the Nashville Inn donated appetizers, by the way," I said to her. "I'll heat them up here."

"Splendid. Too bad we lost Don's efforts for the event, but justice will be served."

Leave it to Corrine to give her event higher priority than an arrest for murder. "Do you think he killed Stella?" I asked in a low voice.

"Search me. If the authorities think he did, then he likely did." She raised one eyebrow. "Oh, hello, Roy." She called over to him as she gave a little wave, then she whispered to me, "That boy's two sandwiches shy of a picnic."

Roy glanced up, but didn't reply to her greeting. He then fell to eating from the plate Danna delivered.

"You aren't going to need my daughter all day long, are you?" Corrine asked me.

"I work until two-thirty, Mom," Danna said. "Of course Robbie's going to need me."

"Fine, fine. Nashville Vintners wines and Big Woods Brewing beer are being delivered at five-thirty, Robbie. Call me"—she extended her pinkie and thumb, tucking the middle three fingers near her ear—"if you need anything." She sailed back out the door.

"Whew," I said under my breath. But then business picked up too much to think about it. Customers streamed in until they occupied all the tables. Five hungry men stood waiting for tables and three women browsed the cookware shelves as they waited. I'd have to install a bench near the door. I glanced at Roy, who sat alone in front of his empty plate, thumbing a smartphone. I could put his table to a lot better use.

"Roy," I said as I approached, "it's awfully busy this morning. If you don't want anything else, I'd appreciate your table." I handed him his check.

He frowned but stood, dropping a couple bills on the table. "Don't know where O'Neill is. Now we missed the best shooting time, too." He looked over my shoulder at the door, where the bell hardly stopped ringing. "Speak of the devil."

Abe let the door shut behind him and stood in place, his eyes searching the space. I watched as he caught sight of Roy, who then strode toward Abe. They conferred in low voices. Roy gesticulated. Abe threw his palms up. Roy left. Abe saw me and slid past the line of customers, one of whom frowned at his back.

"'Morning, Robbie. Hope Roy didn't give you a hard time about waiting." He shook his head, glancing back at the door. "He's kind of a loose cannon."

"It's okay, least it was after I made him put his gun in his car."

"He brought his shotgun in here?" Abe's voice rose in disbelief. "That's nuts."

I looked around in alarm, but nobody seemed to have heard. I pumped my flat hand in a lower-the-volume gesture to Abe and lowered my own, too. "He said it was legal to carry that thing in here, and I said I didn't care. I wouldn't give him coffee until he took it back to his vehicle. Anyway, he ate, and he paid." I stacked up Roy's dishes, slipping the money and ticket into my apron pocket. I swiped the table with a rag, then waved for the couple at the front of the line to come on over. After I carried the dishes to the sink, I greeted the couple and handed them menus. Then I gestured to Abe to follow me to the office corner.

"Looks like you're not dressed for hunting, anyway," I said.

Abe looked down at his brown street shoes, clean jeans, dress shirt, and dark blazer and laughed. "Not exactly."

"I was sorry to hear about Don being arrested."

His expression turned fierce. "They don't have a lick of real evidence against him. Our lawyer's out of town, so I was just down there trying to talk reason into Buck, but he's not hearing it. And now it looks like Donny has to stay in their crappy little jail all weekend. It's just not right."

Even at ten o'clock the place was still going strong. Tourists, hunters, birders, locals, academics, cyclists—some of which overlapped—they all wanted to check out both pancakes and pans. My bank account was going to be some kind of happy, but my feet hurt, the rehabbed dishwasher I'd bought broke down at eight-thirty, leaving piles of plates in the sink, and we'd run clean out of bacon. It brought to mind a children's book Mom used to read to me, about a couple who ran a pizza parlor a century earlier. After people stopped wearing hats and the hat factory next door closed down, Frank and Zelda lost most of their customers. A funny little man came in and granted their wish for more customers. Soon they were run ragged by all the business, including a busload of basketball players who demanded pizza for breakfast. Eventually they closed the restaurant and opened a little food truck on the beach, at last getting their true wishes.

I was only a week into my own wish coming true, and was as positive as a battery terminal I'd find a way to manage—as long as I didn't have to add pizza to the breakfast menu. Still, I was going to have to fork over for another dishwasher, and fast. And, for sure, we were using paper and plastic *everything* at the event tonight, whether Corrine liked it or not.

After about half an hour, almost all the tables were

empty. I washed my hands, grabbed a cold breakfast sausage link, and, munching, pulled out my phone. I called the place where I'd bought the used industrial dishwasher and told them what had happened.

"I need a new one and fast. There was a guarantee on it, remember."

The guy said he needed to check the records and put me on hold. I tapped the desk as I waited.

"Yep," he drawled. "I'll take and bring you a new one. Be around later today?"

"You can install it today?" My eyes bugged out, even though I wasn't looking at him.

"Yep," came the reply. "About two, two-thirty?"

"I think I love you."

"Well, now, let's not get carried away, ma'am," he said with a chuckle.

When we were done, I pressed the number for the police station and asked for Buck, but I was informed he wasn't in.

"Could you please ask him to contact Robbie Jordan? I was shot at last night and I'd like to know what he has found out about it."

When the dispatcher said she would have him call me, I disconnected and sank into the chair at my computer as Danna valiantly tried to catch up with the dishes. My eyes widened when I saw another e-mail message from Graciela. I stabbed at the message three times with a shaking mouse before I managed to click it open. All it said was Roberto's room number and the name and number of the hospital. I looked around. I couldn't make the call now, not with Danna working on overdrive, customers still eating, and someone else walking up the front steps by the looks of it.

I stood and was heading over to scrub the grill when I saw that the person walking through the door was none other than Buck, all six feet a hundred of him. I veered in his direction.

"I just called you," I said. "Did you already get the message?"

"What a co-inkydink." He pulled out a chair at an empty table. "No, I didn't. But best I have something to eat as we talk."

I handed him a menu. "Did you manage to find time to check for bullets in the wall?" I folded my arms, tapping my right hand on my left elbow.

He looked up. "I'd like the pancake platter, please, with bacon and biscuits." If his drawl were any slower, it'd end up in the next century.

"I'm out of bacon."

"Then give me ham, please, and coffee." He glanced at the Specials board. "And a scoop of the hash, if you have some."

I scribbled on my pad and strode toward Danna. "Sorry, but Buck wants a truckload of food and I need to talk to him about last night. Can you—"

"No worries, Robbie." She pulled down the big sprayer and rinsed the plate in her hand, then grabbed a hand towel. "Really." She took the ticket.

"How do you stay so calm all the time?" I asked.

"Hey, growing up with my mom? You kind of have to figure how to keep cool, you know?"

I set a mug of coffee down in front of Buck with a tad too much force. It sloshed over the top and dribbled a dark line toward the vintage sugar shaker in the middle of the table. I sat myself down across from him, making myself fold my hands so I wouldn't show my impatience.

"The answer is, yes, we found the time. And we found the slug right where you described it." He sipped the coffee, watching me over the top of it.

"Do you know what kind of gun it came from?"

"Twenty-gauge shotgun, looked like."

"What about the angle and all that? Were you able to figure out maybe where the shooter was?"

"You been watching too many cop shows, Robbie." He chuckled. "That thang blasted into the brick wall and made a big old hole. We couldn't calculate the trajectory, just too messy."

"There were two shots." I set my chin on my hand.

"Didn't find the other one." He looked up as Danna brought over his order. "Thank you, miss."

She smiled and sauntered back to the sink.

"So, who would have a shotgun?" I asked. "How are you going to figure out who shot at me?"

Buck swallowed a mouthful of pancakes before he answered. "You know everybody around here hunts, carries, you name it. We're in the process of questioning the residents of the apartments down there, try to get them to tell us if they own a firearm. It's going to take a little while, though."

I stood. "Let me know when you find out anything." I strode back to the counter next to the grill and began scrubbing it with somewhat more force than necessary. As I did, the image of Roy popped into my head. Roy standing in the doorway with his gun this morning. A gun Abe called a shotgun. Me, I didn't know anything about guns, except there were long ones and short ones. I'd have to find a minute to call Abe sometime soon, see if he knew what gauge Roy's hunting gun was.

And I needed to help Danna with dishes. Get the Sloppy Joe sauce ready for the lunch hot dogs. Hopefully, I'd find a quiet minute to call Italy. And then host pretty near the whole town tonight. Living my dream was turning out to be a lot more complicated than I'd expected.

Chapter 25

I'd just delivered a turkey burger and two Sloppy Joe dogs to a clutch of birders when the entrance bell jangled once again in its steady medley of welcoming hungry lunch customers and bidding satisfied ones farewell. I glanced over to see Lou and her cycling friends from last week. After I smiled and waved them to an empty table, they clacked over in their cycling shoes, pulling off gloves, fluffing up helmet hair.

"Back for more, are you?" I smiled wistfully at their green-and-yellow jerseys. "I sure wish I could join you out on the road."

Lou threw her braid back over her shoulder. "Why don't you?" She stayed standing as the others sat.

I gestured around the store. "Way too busy. Dishwasher broke, too. And we're hosting a big fund-raiser tonight"—I pointed at the poster—"or I'd go out for a ride after we close." I raised a shoulder and dropped it. "What can you do?" I handed them all menus.

"Question for you," Lou said. She pointed at the restroom door, so I followed her over. She paused in front of it.

"Were you able to contact Roberto?" she said in a soft voice.

"I tried. Heard back from his daughter that he's quite ill. In a hospital over there." My throat thickened.

"Oh, no." She reached out and patted my arm.

"She sent me his room number and the hospital name a while ago, but I've been too busy to call. I'll try him after the store closes."

At the grill Danna stuck her hand in the air and twirled her index finger, our sign to each other an order was up. "Gotta run," I said.

"Hey, good luck. Let me know how it goes, okay?" She pushed open the restroom door.

I told her I would and headed toward Danna. The next hour got crazy—cooking, delivering, making change, wiping down, and trying to keep up with the dishes. I might have to start serving on paper soon, myself. I gave a quick call to Adele to see if she could come by to rescue us, but she didn't pick up. When I tried Phil, he said he was too busy, that Corrine had roped him into baking dozens of desserts for the fund-raiser. And that was the extent of my emergency help list.

But we made it through alive. I sold more corn fritter pans, managed to calm down a couple of hunters whose orders we mixed up, and nearly sold out of Phil's Kahlúa brownies. By one-thirty my stomach was complaining something fierce, as usual, and only a couple of tables were occupied.

"Danna, take a break and eat, why don't you?" I tried to elbow her away from the sink.

"Nah, I'm good. I ate during the lull, and I'm playing volleyball this afternoon. Don't want to have a full stomach." She adjusted the yellow bandana she wore tied in back under her dreads, which today she'd braided into a fat plait.

"You're going to play volleyball after working like a maniac since before the sun came up?"

"Sure. My friends and me? We play every Saturday."

I whistled and threw a turkey patty onto the grill. "Well, I'm going to eat. And I'm not playing volleyball at two-thirty, I'll tell you. Although, I wish I could get out for a long ride one of these afternoons."

"See? Same thing. We both need to stretch it out, get the heart rate up. We just do it in different ways."

"You got that right." A couple minutes later I sank into a chair with my lunch. I was halfway through it, munching on a crispy pickle, when Abe appeared in the doorway, this time wearing old jeans and a plaid shirt. I waved at him and he approached my table.

"Corrine roped me into hanging a banner across Main Street." He shook his head.

"For the fund-raiser?"

"With the company's cherry picker. Seems a little late, seeing as how it's tonight."

"No kidding. Right here in this restaurant, too." I yawned. "I have work to do later. Will you be there?"

"Of course. It's for a good cause, right? Hey, got any of those left?" He sat across from me and pointed at my burger.

"Sure. Turkey, beef, or veggie?"

"Beef, of course, with cheese on top. Where do I look like I'm from, California?" He laughed.

I laughed, too. He looked every bit the picture of a healthy Midwestern man, especially with that dimple going on.

"Back in a flash." I grabbed one more bite of my

burger, ignoring his plea as I walked away for me to sit and finish my own lunch first. It didn't take long to fry up a beef patty, melt a slice of cheddar, and assemble the plate. After I laid on a dill, and scooped hot fries out of the fryer, I carried it over to him.

He thanked me and tucked in. I sat and did the same. When I finished my lunch, I said, "Can I ask you a question? You said something about Roy's shotgun this morning. That's what you use to go hunting with?"

"Sure is, at least for grouse. For deer you use a rifle."

"What kind of gauge is the shotgun? Or maybe that's the wrong way to say it."

"His is twenty. So's mine. So are most grouse shotguns." He looked at me sideways, neatly wiping a drip of ketchup from the corner of his mouth with his napkin. "Why are you asking?"

"Somebody shot at me last night in an alley downtown."

"That sucks. You're all right, I assume, since you're working and all." Abe gazed at me.

"I'm fine. They missed. But Buck recovered what he called a slug from the wall. Said it came from a twenty-gauge shotgun."

"Not a grouse gun, then. Those spray out shot pellets."

"Oh. But another kind of shotgun would shoot slugs?"

"That's right. You're thinking Roy might have shot at you?"

I nodded as if molasses had a hold of my head. "When I saw him standing in the doorway this morning before we were even open, with a big old gun hanging from his shoulder, it did not give me a warm and fuzzy feeling, I'll tell you."

"He's a bit odd, but I think he's harmless. He's been expressing a few unhappy thoughts about you, for sure, with regard to the store and all." Abe narrowed his eyes. "An alley. Was it the alley behind the bank, the one near Walnut?"

"That's it. Did you hear about it at the station this morning?"

"No, afraid not." He selected a fry and slowly swished it in a figure eight through his ketchup.

"Then how did you know where I was shot at?"

He pointed the fry at me. Drops of red dripped one by one onto the table. "Those flats above the bank? That's where Roy lives."

Chapter 26

After Abe finished eating and left, I took a minute to call Buck. At least this time he was at the station.

"You have to find Roy Rogers," I said.

"And why would that be?" he drawled.

"Abe told me Roy lives in one of the apartments over the alley. And he was in here this morning with a shotgun."

"I'm actually way ahead of you. We know where he lives, and everybody knows he hunts. Has three more guns where that one came from, probably." His tongue smoothed over the middle syllable, making it sound like "prahlly."

"So, are you going to question him?" I cleared my throat to try to settle myself.

"We will, when we can find him."

"Oh, that's just awesome. So a guy who might have shot at me last night is out wandering around with one of his many guns. Maybe he shot his own mother, too. He was the one who found her. Maybe he shot her himself and then claimed somebody else did."

"Robbie, we're looking for him, okay? You just calm down there. You're safe. I'll try to send a patrol by the store every hour or so. That help?"

"I guess." *Not really.*

"Don't rightly think he killed his own mother, though."

I rolled my eyes.

"You take care now. Thanks for being an alert citizen." He disconnected.

ROBERTA JORDAN, ALERT CITIZEN. Maybe I should add that to the sign out front. I glanced over when the cowbell jangled.

"Yoo-hoo," Adele called with a wave. Vera followed her in.

I walked over to greet them, giving Adele a hug, and when Vera held out her arms, her too.

"I just couldn't stay away," Vera said, "from the food or the pots and the pans. When I was home, I realized I needed a couple four additions to my kitchen." She gestured to the cookware shelves.

"Hungry?" I smiled at this welcome change in my world. Things couldn't be all bad when two cheery, healthy, energetic senior citizens came to call.

"Boy, howdy, are we ever," Adele said. "I made Vera help me on the farm after she drove down this morning."

Vera whistled. "Those sheep are something. Stupid as all get-out."

"I was almost forced to use one of them kicks we learned when the ram wouldn't leave me alone," Adele said. At Vera's look of confusion, she went on to explain. "Robbie and I took a self-defense class together last year. Learned how to break out of a hold, hit the eyes and the kneecap, and run fast."

"We sure did," I said. "Hope I'll never have to use what I learned, though."

"Always better to be prepared," Vera said.

"Well, sit down and tell me what you want." I pointed to the board. "Danna whipped up an Asian soba-noodle salad as a special if you want that. With veggies and tofu."

"I want a big juicy turkey burger with all the fixings," Adele said, patting her stomach. "Got any beer to go with?"

I laughed. "I wish." I checked the clock and the rest of the tables, which were empty, and it was almost closing time. "Oh, heck, I have beer in my personal fridge. Vera, you too?"

"Why not? And I'll take the Asian noodle salad. Sounds yummy."

"Deal." I walked over to Danna and gave her the orders, thanking her. Then I fetched three beers from my apartment. When I was back in the restaurant, I poured them into the heavy plastic glasses we used for pop. Danna looked at me with a raised eyebrow pierced with a tiny silver ring.

"Don't tell anybody." I gave her a mock frown before carrying the drinks to the table. "Cheers." I sat and lifted my beer. We clinked, although it was more like a dull tap, then I took a long swig. That first one always tasted the best.

"Any news about Roberto?" Adele asked. "And yes, I took the liberty of telling Vera about your history."

Vera nodded encouragingly.

"I heard from his daughter." I told them about his hospitalization. "I haven't had a free minute to call yet. Hoping to this afternoon. Like between now and when this crazy fund-raiser gets under way."

"Shee-it, I hope he's okay." Adele pulled her eyebrows together. "After all that."

"Me too." I swallowed, more to get rid of the lump in my throat than the beer in my mouth. "So, are you both supporting Corrine tonight and coming for this gala?"

They looked at each other. "Of course," Vera said at the same time as Adele said, "I guess."

I laughed. I told them about the arrangements for the Nashville Inn appetizers and how Jim was going to help set up. Danna brought over the plates, Adele's burger sending up little heat waves, and Vera's light brown noodles glistening in their sesame-soy dressing with carrot and pea pod slivers mixed in.

"Take a load off, honey," Adele said to her.

"Okay," Danna said, and pulled out the fourth chair.

"Good for you for taking a break," I said. "I wish I could give you tomorrow off, but judging from today and last Sunday, I'm afraid I'm going to need you."

"No probs." Danna waved her hand. "I like the work. And if I hadn't been here today, you know my mom would have roped me into doing her errands for tonight."

The place was finally empty. I almost had to push Danna out the door, telling her I'd finish the cleanup after Adele and Vera left. Vera bought the meat grinder and a couple of tin pie pans stamped with MRS. WAGNER'S PIES. She was looking longingly at a pastry wheel and a vintage lemon press, but said her husband would kill her if she brought anything else home. I'd turned the sign to CLOSED, making sure the door was securely locked, trying it three times to make sure. Then the appliance truck pulled up to the wide service door and I needed to postpone calling Italy even longer while two burly guys disconnected and carted away the old dishwasher, then hooked up the new one.

When they'd tested the connections by starting a cycle and nothing leaked, I about hugged them for showing up so soon. I gave them each a tip, instead, along with my thanks. This time I made sure the service door was securely locked before heading to my computer. And my father's telephone number.

Instead of my brain, it was now my heart clacking as fast as the *Wabash Cannonball* coming down the tracks. I stared at Graciela's last message on the laptop and drew my phone out. I pressed the numbers as carefully as my shaking finger would let me. A three-part tone rang, however, telling me it was necessary to add the country code to dial outside the United States.

I swore, then sank into the desk chair. After a minute of searching yielded up 39 for Italy, I dialed again.

It rang. And rang. I wasn't going to give up, not now. I kept listening.

"Pronto." The man's voice was faint.

I opened my mouth to speak, but nothing came out. "Alo?"

"Is this Roberto Fracasso?" I managed to get out.

"Yes."

"My name is Robbie Jordan." I couldn't go on.

"You are Jeanine's daughter?" His speech sounded Italian, whatever that meant.

"I am." *Now what?*

"And she is dead. I am very sorry." He cleared his throat. "May I ask, what is your father's name?"

Ahh. "I never knew him. Or his name."

"Ahh." He laughed, but it was a weak sound. "You look like me. Your mother and I, we were sweethearts."

"I saw your picture."

"Jeanine, she didn't tell to you about me?"

"No. I wish she had."

"I think maybe I am that father of yours. But she never wrote to me about you."

I squeezed my eyes shut. My breath rushed in and out, heavy and fast.

"Robbie, you are there?"

I sniffed away the tears. "I'm here. I wondered if it was true, that you might be my father."

"I wish she'd let me know. So you are twenty-seven?"

"Yes. I wish she had told you about me, too."

"I have missed all these years of knowing you."

"We both have. Your daughter told me you're sick, in the hospital. I'm sorry to hear that. Are you improving?"

"I hope so, but they are not sure. It's a bad infection in my foot. They might have to cut it off."

I cringed and sucked a breath in. "I hope not."

"Tell me, Robbie, how did you find me?"

"I was looking for information on my mom and a man named Don O'Neill. I think you lived with his family?"

He said something in Italian that sounded a lot like a person swearing. "He did something very bad to me."

I waited. Sounded like my guess was true. I finally spoke. "Did it have to do with the accident at the quarry?"

"It was not an accident, *cara*. Donald was angry I was loving your mother, Jeanine. He hit me on the head and pushed me in. I was lucky I did not die or become *paralizzato*."

"Paralyzed. Was my mom there?"

"No, no. It was that Stella. She's a bad one, too. She must have seen him do it. Or convinced him to push me."

"She was killed last week. Murdered." I heard his quick intake of breath.

"I am not surprised. You ask Donald what happened. I make a bet he still lies about it." I heard a noise in the background, and Roberto conversed in Italian with someone. He came back on the line. "Robbie, I must go. More examinations."

"Okay. Please get better."

"I will do my best. I am full in my heart to talk with you. When I am better, you will come to visit me, yes?"

"Yes." He disconnected. I stared at the computer in front of me, not seeing it. My heart quieted as I stroked the edge of the desk with one finger. I had a father. He wanted to see me. I had a half sister and nephew, too, and maybe other siblings. I hoped they'd want to get to know me.

And Don O'Neill was a lying bastard.

A knock on the door startled me out of my reverie. Who in the world? The knock became more insistent. I turned my head. *Oh. Christina. Appetizers. Fund-raiser.* The real world raised its insistent head, but somehow I knew I could handle whatever it threw my way. I had a father.

Chapter 27

"How about a glass of wine?" I asked after I helped Christina unload the boxes of frozen appetizers.

She gave me a wistful look. "I wish. But it is Saturday, after all. And that wedding is coming right up. I expect I've messed up the schedule even bringing these by. Rain check?"

"Of course. Thanks bunches for taking the time. And tell the management we'll give them full credit."

"Way ahead of you, girlfriend. That envelope"—she pointed with her car keys—"contains stand-up labels with the name of each appetizer, ingredients in microscopic print for the allergic and paranoid, and 'Donated by the Nashville Inn' in bigger letters than the name of the food. The boss does not mess around when it comes to publicity."

I laughed. "Do I ever know that. I should take a lesson from her."

She headed for the door. "See you soon." The bell clanged and she was gone.

I laid the boxes out in a single layer and checked them. Dozens and dozens of finger foods, exactly as

Christina had described them. Mini quiches. Buffalo
mini drumsticks. Tiny, spicy meatballs. All I needed to
do was heat them up and arrange them on serving
trays. But I figured I really ought to contribute something from my kitchen, too, for my own reputation, if
nothing else. Christina had suggested mini tuna sliders. I didn't have any more tuna, but I could whip up
tiny hamburgers and turkey burgers, and that would
connect with my lunch menu. The vegetarians in the
crowd, if there were any others besides Jim, would just
have to settle for mini quiches.

What to use for slider buns, though? Biscuits would
likely crumble. I checked the clock, which read three
forty-five, and ran a couple cups of warm water into a
stainless-steel mixing bowl. In five minutes I'd assembled a simple yeasted dough, with olive oil and a few
snips of fresh rosemary, which came from the pot out
front, added for smoothness and flavor. I gave the
dough a quick knead until it was shiny and slid it back
into the bowl, which I'd rubbed with oil. After I turned
the soft, warm mass over, leaving a sheen of oil on top,
I covered the bowl with a clean, damp tea towel. The
dough wouldn't need more than an hour to rise, and
less to bake. If I baked the buns in muffin tins, they'd
be uniform little puffs, perfect for slicing and throwing
a slider into.

In the name of saving time later, I decided to cook
the small patties now. I could keep them in the
warmer and assemble the sliders right before the guests
arrived. Which was supposed to be when? I glanced at
the poster that Corrine's flunky—I mean, intern—
had taped to the wall, and groaned. In three hours is
when. Nothing for it but to knuckle down, even
though what I longed to do was return to my *Stella*

Murder puzzle and see what else I could figure out. Instead, I switched on the opera, jacked up the volume, and began to roll golf balls of meat between my hands, pressing them flat onto a baking sheet.

But you can't keep a puzzler's brain down on the farm for long. *Ed. Don. Roy. Corrine.* Their images popped up and down in my brain like an old-fashioned arcade game, and *Stella* was the name written in bright neon lights on top, the unifying force. Ed, who'd been friendly with her in the past, but denied it, and was now having trouble with his own restaurant on a bunch of fronts. Don, who'd tried to kill my own father—with Stella looking on. The same Don, now arrested for the murder he claimed he didn't commit. Corrine, who owned guns. Corrine, who'd been investigated for killing her own husband and admitted to hating her difficult administrative assistant. And Roy. Was he off-balance enough to shoot his own mother? Why, to get her house? And if it was he who shot at me in the alley, why in the world? Did he really think knocking me off would finally get him my store? There was no way he'd be able to organize himself to run a place like this, I was pretty sure, unless he wanted to turn it into a gun shop or something.

When the timer for the rising bread dinged, I was almost surprised to see six dozen puffy round burgers resting lightly grilled on pans—three dozen of beef, three dozen of ground turkey, each no more than two inches in diameter. I didn't think my mind had produced anywhere near what my hands had during the same time. No clear answers came through. So I covered the pans of patties with foil and slid them into the warmer on its lowest temperature. Hot enough to fend off salmonella, low enough not to toughen them.

So my hands now fell to oiling six vintage muffin tins, their metal blackened by decades, perhaps centuries, of women wiping butter or lard around the insides of the cups and then baking mini spice cakes, savory corn muffins, delectable cream puffs, sweet blueberry muffins, decadent chocolate cupcakes. And today I'd follow in their hallowed footsteps by adding to the patina with yeasted slider buns. A couple of the pans featured different designs pressed into the metal of the cup bottoms: a star, a swirl, curvy lines, concentric circles.

I plucked off golf balls of dough and pressed each into its indentation in the pan, flattening the orb with the backs of my fingers. I'd just finished the last pan, miraculously coming out even with dough and cups, when the bell jangled. I looked up with a start, then relaxed.

"Welcome to the crazy house," I called to Jim. "Is it already five?"

In a sky-blue T-shirt and faded jeans, he looked as delicious as the rising buns, but he was obviously prepared for the evening's activities, too, since he carried slacks folded on a hanger, with a black dress shirt draped over the top.

"Hear ye, hear ye. Let the record show it is five o'clock in the court. All rise. Ms. Jordan, what do you have to say in your defense?"

I laughed louder than I'd laughed in what seemed like months. "Mr. Lawyer, sir, I plead guilty to being hoodwinked and cajoled into hosting a community fund-raiser for which I am little prepared. Sir."

He hung his hanger over a hook on the coatrack, aiming a mock frown in my direction. "Be forewarned,

Ms. Jordan. You are in for a severe disciplinary action." In four long strides he enveloped me in his arms.

I looked up into those emerald eyes and attacked him with a hungry kiss. We only surfaced when my phone set up a racket of ringing, amplified by the stainless-steel counter it rested on. I extricated myself, heart racing with lust, and reached behind him to answer it. I kept my gaze on his flushed cheeks and now tousled hair. He leaned back against the counter with a sexy smile and folded his arms.

I greeted Corrine. "Yep. The food is all set, and we're just about to arrange the space."

"The lieutenant governor is a old friend of mine. She's going to stop by during the evening, so I've alerted the press," Corrine said.

I whistled. "You have connections."

"That I do. The drinks should be there any minute. Danna's going to help out, should be there by six-thirty. Anything else you need?"

"Who's bringing paperware? You know, cups, napkins, that kind of thing? And what about nonalcoholic drinks?"

"All covered. I ordered bottles of sweet tea and water. Gotta run, hon." With that, she disconnected.

I stared at the phone in hand.

"What was that all about?" Jim asked.

"Oh, only Corrine bringing an old friend from Indy. Who happens to be the lieutenant governor." I shook my head. "And the press, whoever that means. What do you think, the *Sentinel*, the *Democrat*, the *Indianapolis Star*, or the *New York Times*? That woman is a force of nature."

"Oh, yeah. That's putting it mildly. Now, what do we have to do here?"

* * *

By the time the drink truck arrived, Jim and I had pushed all the tables to the periphery, stacking the larger ones double high in the corner to make more room. The smaller tables we arranged with chairs around them, and lined the rest of the chairs around the walls. We placed one long table in front of the drinks cooler so guests wouldn't feel they could help themselves to my inventory. Another table we arranged catty-corner for the food, and a third on the opposite side of the room for the silent-auction items. I laid my blue-and-white paper tablecloths on all three.

But the truck came late. It was already six and I hadn't started heating up anything besides baking the buns. When the timer rang, I pulled the rolls out of the big oven, and they looked awesome, all lightly browned and puffy. I set them on cooling racks as Jim helped the delivery guy haul in cases of beer, nonalcoholic drinks, and a dozen boxes of wine.

"How you doing?" I asked the burly man, whose thinning blond hair was pulled back into a skinny ponytail at the nape of his neck.

"*A-l-l r-ight*," he drew out into near about five lazy syllables. "Smells good in here," he drawled with a smile.

I handed him a hot roll in a paper napkin and thanked him. "We need to keep the cold drinks cold," I said to Jim after the man left, setting my hands on my hips. "Red wine's the only thing doesn't have to be served chilled."

Jim fell to lining up boxes of Nashville Vintner's red on the far end of the drinks table, digging out the spigot on the first two. "Ice?" he asked, without looking up.

I snapped my fingers and strode to the shed out back, returning with a big old shallow galvanized-steel tub. "This'll be just the ticket." I dusted it off, set it on the table, then started bringing big scoops of ice from the ice bin until it was half full.

When I began opening cases of beer, Jim elbowed me aside. "You must have cooking to do. Let me do this. And I'm assuming you're going to change, too? Not that you don't look great just like you are."

"Huh." I looked down at my black T-shirt and jeans, which I'd been working in all day. "No kidding. Back in a flash." I hurried to my apartment, splashed water on my face, and peered into my closet. Where was my personal dresser when I needed one? Finally I grabbed a cap-sleeved black jersey dress I knew flattered my curves, pulled on black tights, added a chunky necklace in the colors of the rainbow with matching earrings, slid on a half-dozen silver bracelets, and ran a brush through my hair. I was cooking, so I couldn't wear it long. Instead, I twisted it up in a knot, securing it with a multicolored clip, and slipped on black ankle boots with heels.

Almost through the door to the restaurant, I heard a plaintive meow. "Oh, poor kitty cat. I have been neglecting you something fierce." I bent to stroke Birdy, then made sure his food and water dishes were full and fresh before I headed back to the event at hand.

Jim emerged from the restroom, all spruced up, too, in his gray slacks and black shirt, his hair tamed with water and fingers, I wagered. I glanced at his feet, which were clad in the same running shoes he'd worn with his jeans.

"Nice choice of footwear, Counselor."

"Forgot my dress shoes. Hey, people know me. It's not a job interview, then, is it?" He laughed. "You look awful nice, Robbie."

I twirled for him and struck a model pose for a second.

"Got an apron I can wear to complete my outfit?" he asked.

I threw him a clean one and pulled one on myself. I glanced at the wall clock as I crossed the apron strings behind my back and tied them in the front.

"Help me out?" Jim was struggling to tie his apron in back. "I'm terrible when I can't see what I'm doing."

"You're funny." I moved behind him and took the ties in my hands. I resisted the sudden urge to pull him close to me, ignored the imperative to press my body against his and wrap my arms around him. He smelled alluring up close, and the smooth black cloth of his shirt would have made a silky pillow for my cheek. Instead, I tied a bow and gave him a little pat on the fanny.

"Let's get this show on the road," I declared. "Folks are going to be here in half an hour."

"Or sooner." He pointed at the door, which opened to Corrine, Danna, and Turner, the intern, the last two with arms full of bags and boxes.

"Isn't this just a thrill?" Resplendent in a V-necked black dress with sliced sleeves above four-inch red-and-white Manolo Blahniks, Corrine waved as she sailed toward us. So far, it looked like we were all complying with a black-clothing dress code.

Danna, wearing a turquoise long-sleeved top and print peasant skirt over flat leather boots, only rolled her eyes. *So much for the dress code.* "Where do you want the plates and all?" she asked. She'd wrapped her dreads with a turquoise band into a long flow down her back.

"You can put plates and napkins on the food table and cups where the drinks are going," I told her as I indicated the tables I meant. "I thought we'd put silent-auction items over there," I told Corrine, pointing at the far table.

"Good, good."

"I made up a Pans 'N Pancakes gift certificate to donate." I headed for my desk. "Let me go get that. Then I've got to get the food ready."

"I'll help," Danna said.

Jim returned to stuffing beer, water, boxes of white wine, and tea bottles into the ice, clinking and crunching as he worked. Meanwhile, the skinny intern with a head full of thick, dark hair stood near the door looking as bewildered as a lost lamb, his arms barely reaching around whatever it was Corrine had stuffed into them.

"Turner, you set up the auction table," Corrine directed him. "He's got the sign-up sheets, pens, the rest," she said to me.

After he unloaded his burdens, I handed the young man my gift certificate for forty dollars, told him the minimum bid should be twenty, and turned to the appetizers. After Danna slipped an apron over her head, I asked her to assemble the sliders.

"You'll need to cut open all the buns first. They should be cool enough now." I slid one out of its cup and tossed it from hand to hand.

"I'll make up a savory mayo for the turkey burgers. You know, with Thanksgiving seasonings," she said. "Sage, rosemary, thyme. A little fresh parsley."

"Great idea. Think we should add a slice of cheese to the beef sliders?"

She cocked her head. "Nah, too much work. Fresh black pepper and a squirt of ketchup should be enough. Or maybe I'll mix a few drops of hot sauce into the ketchup." Her eyes sparkled with mischief. "Hoosiers need a little livening up, you know?"

"I like the way you think." *What a godsend.* I only hoped her mom realized Danna's talents lay in a restaurant, not a college, or at least not a conventional liberal-arts degree.

I set to transferring the now-thawed appetizers to baking sheets, then cursed. What was I going to serve them on when they were ready? It wasn't particularly elegant to leave them on the pans with years of hot temperatures having baked sugars and fats into the metal, and my kitchen wasn't equipped for catering. I glanced at the shelves of cookware across the room. Turner moved down the long table in front of the shelves, setting out sheets and pens for the donations (still nonexistent except for mine). My gaze traveled upward. Yes! I popped two full pans in the hot oven and strode toward him.

"Hey, Turner." I tapped him on the shoulder. "I'm Robbie Jordan. I own this joint."

"Turner Rao." He extended his right hand. "Nice to meet you, Robbie."

The cool, smooth skin of a hand that hadn't yet encountered many rough surfaces met mine. "Same here. So I need to get those trays down from up there." I pointed to the half-dozen flat tin trays standing on end against the wall on the top shelf. The disks were about fifteen inches across with an inch-high rim, and each featured different old-fashioned soda products:

Nesbitt's Orange, Brownie Root Beer, Dr. Wells. And, of course, the Coca-Cola checkerboard tray, which interspersed the red company logo with white squares. Its printed motto: *Delicious and Refreshing*. The trays would be perfect, once I got them cleaned up.

"Can you help me get them down?" I asked.

"Sure." He laid down his papers and squinted up at the shelf. He was a beanpole of a guy, but not quite tall enough to reach up there.

I grabbed a long-handled popcorn popper off a shelf and handed it to him. "See if you can use this to bring the tray forward enough to make it fall."

He stretched the tool up, and in a second the Nesbitt's tray came flying down. I reached out my hands, but missed. The tray hit the blue-and-white tablecloth on its way down, leaving a smudge of rust and orange paint, and then clattered onto the floor.

"Turner, can't you do anything right?" Corrine called in a sharp voice from the chair where she'd perched, looking up from her phone.

Turner didn't respond, instead picking up the tray and brushing it off. Corrine's response was totally uncalled for. *Poor kid. And good for him for not rising to the bait.*

"It's okay. I asked him to help," I answered her. She sniffed and looked back at her phone, her long red fingernail tapping out something or other.

Working together, we managed to get the rest down without mishap.

"I'll clean them for you," Turner said. His deep brown eyes bore into mine.

I saw both more sensitivity and more resolve than earlier. I realized I hadn't ever really looked at him and now thought he looked at least part Indian, from

India. That would explain the last name. I was willing to place a bet his mother's maiden name was Turner, though.

"That'd be a huge help. Thank you." We stacked up the trays. "If you can't scrub off the rust, I'll line them with foil or a napkin." As we carried the trays to the deep sink, I added in a low voice, "I appreciate your help, even if she doesn't."

By seven o'clock the door never shut. As soon as one or two people entered, somebody else showed up right behind them. Turner was now stationed at a small table next to the door, collecting everybody's suggested entrance donation. He was even set up with a Square reader on an iPad so he could swipe credit cards—a smart move, for sure. Wanda, dressed in street clothes, sauntered in with another woman, and handed him some cash. Roy, dressed in a brown blazer and slacks, followed the women in, with no gun in sight, to my great relief. Buck must have found him, questioned him, and let him go. Georgia, the library aide, was next to enter, followed by two men. While it was intriguing to watch everybody arrive, my to-do list wasn't empty.

A few minutes later I glanced up from arranging buffalo wingettes on the root beer tray to see Adele, Vera, Samuel, and Phil making their way toward the donation table. Adele set down a rough-woven basket full of skeins of yarn in lovely pastel shades and conferred with Turner for a moment. Phil placed his event brownies on a table. Then he caught my eye and raised up a colorful sheet of paper that looked from this distance like it held color pictures of an assortment of his desserts, plus a few stylized musical notes, before handing it to Turner. I headed toward Phil to bring the brownies to the kitchen area.

"I'll do it." Phil held up a hand. "I brought a few serving trays to use." He also wore a black shirt, with skinny black pants and a tie in the bright blue of the restaurant logo.

"You're an angel."

"Yeah," he said, then fell to cutting and arranging the desserts on two so-called "throwaway" round aluminum trays, the kind I always wash and reuse. After he finished and cleaned his hands, he headed for the old piano in the corner, sat, and began to beat out a ragtime tune, which made me smile, despite the few out-of-tune keys. The tuner I'd brought in months earlier said it wasn't really worth paying to get it up to primo playing quality.

Corrine posed next to Turner's table and greeted all newcomers, arms outstretched, schmoozing. Her red-painted mouth held a permanent welcoming smile. Various townspeople drifted in, in twos and threes and fours. Several added items to the donation table, while others headed straight for the cold drinks tub or the boxes of red wine. Corrine sure called that one right, ordering wine boxes so nobody needed to struggle with corkscrews.

At a commotion near the door, I looked up from the mini quiches I was arranging. Corrine was in the process of giving Don O'Neill a bear hug. He extricated himself, glancing around. She gave him a big old slap on the back.

Wait. Don? So he's out of jail. Huh. What's that about? I glanced around. Buck wasn't here or I would have asked him. If I got a chance, I'd ask Don himself. I was pretty sure Wanda wouldn't tell me a thing if I inquired of her.

"So they let you free, did they?" Corrine asked in her usual booming voice. "I didn't think they caught the right person."

As I recalled, she'd expressed an entirely different opinion earlier in the day.

Don smiled wanly and swallowed. "Told them all along it wadn't me." He sidled toward the beer tub like a man in the desert.

Danna and I worked together to set out the appetizers and sliders, along with the labels Christine had included. I'd taken a minute earlier to print up a couple of similar ones for the sliders and for Phil's brownies. Jim finished cooling the drinks, shed his apron, and now held a bottle of beer. I'd never gotten a chance to tell him about either Roberto's or Don's involvement in the accident. Well, life was going to settle down one of these days, wasn't it? Jim headed toward Don, who was now talking with Barb from the hardware store and Georgia. Maybe Jim would get the story from Don. Or not.

Abe strolled in next, wearing a tuxedo with green suede sneakers and no tie. This guy had style. He saw me and headed my way, a small brightly colored piece of cardboard in his hand.

"Thanks for coming," I said. "What's that?" I pointed to the cardboard, which looked a lot like a banjo.

"My donation." He raised one eyebrow.

"It's a pretty neat cardboard banjo." What was I supposed to say?

He pointed to a printed label on the round part. "Two introductory lessons in the fine art of banjo picking."

I peered at it, then straightened. "'Donated by Abraham O'Neill,'" I read. "You teach music?"

"I've been playing banjo since I was eight. Been in a few bands." He held out a CD in his other hand. "Cut a couple of records."

"I'm impressed." What other levels of depth did he have?

He laughed. "Don't be. It's only down-homey music, what my dad used to call hillbilly picking. Where do you want these?"

I pointed to Turner and the donation table. "Thanks," I called after him, watching as he wove through the crowd. I turned back to Danna, who was squirting little circles of ketchup on top of hamburger patties already sitting on their bottom buns, a tiny leaf of lettuce in between. These occupied the Nesbitt's tray, which, in fact, needed a layer of foil to protect the food from the rust. At least the outside of the rim was still mostly a shiny black with bright orange soda bottles lying on their sides, so it looked pretty.

"Did they come out even, the patties and the buns?" I asked her.

"Short one bun."

"That's right, I gave it to the drinks man. Nice job thinking to add lettuce."

"Gives it a little crunch." She squirted the last one, and I helped her top them all up.

"Hey, everybody."

At a raised voice from the doorway, I whipped my

head around. The buzz of the room quieted as Ed pushed through the door.

"Eddie's here," he announced in a big sloppy voice. "To support those poor little animals." He raised a fifth of Jim Beam in one hand and swigged from it. "It's BYOB, right?"

Chapter 28

Don rushed to Ed's side, relieving him of the bottle. I watched as he strong-armed Ed to the food table and made sure his friend filled a plate.

"I ain't hungry, Don," Ed protested. His ruddy skin was even more flushed than usual, but his hair was neatly combed. He wore a plaid three-piece suit, wide lapels and all, like an outfit on a 1970s TV rerun. "And what're you doing out of jail, anyway?"

Heads turned at that, but all Don said was, "Eat."

The buzz in the room resumed, with several townsfolk shaking their heads and turning their backs like they'd seen this sideshow before. A couple held hands and walked slowly the length of the donation table, pointing and picking things up, sometimes signing the bid sheet. Three men stood talking near the sliders, beers in hand, feet set apart. Wanda chatted with the friend she'd come in with, but she kept her gaze on Don. A woman swept in the door, followed by a harried-looking younger woman and a man with a big camera on his shoulder. Our lieutenant governor, no doubt, and the reputed press presence. Adele, holding a half cup of white wine, made her way toward me as I set out the last trays of mini quiches and tiny meatballs. I lifted my apron off before giving her a hug.

"What do you think?" I gestured at the spread of food, which was rapidly shrinking.

"It's all yummy. I think this is going to be a big success, despite the short notice."

I took a good look at her. "That's some outfit. Looks good on you." Adele, whom I'd rarely seen out of a pair of sensible trousers and either a T-shirt or a sweater, wore a dress-length top slit up the sides over baggy pants angling in slim at the ankles. The cloth was a subdued print in soft shades of yellows and blues, which made her blue eyes more vivid, and wide rows of embroidery decorated the neckline and cuffs. A silver necklace studded with blue stones nestled against the tanned skin covering her collarbones.

"It's from India. Samuel brought it from his latest trip there." Adele's cheeks pinkened.

"What does he do in India?"

"Mission work at an orphanage. They've been building a library and improving the schoolroom."

"That's a labor of love," I said.

"'Labor of love'?" Samuel appeared at Adele's elbow, dapper in a light gray suit and a tie that matched the buttery yellow in Adele's outfit.

"Your good work overseas," I said.

"It's not much." He shrugged. "The kids in the orphanage are regular dolls, and grateful like children in this country haven't been in a long time."

"I'd like to go with you one day, if I can ever find anybody to watch my animals," Adele said.

Phil still played at the piano, now taking requests.

"What about Phil?" I asked. "I bet he'd stay at your place as caretaker. His talents seem endless."

"Possible," Adele agreed. "He's a good boy."

"That he is, that he is." Samuel wandered off toward the piano.

Adele lowered her voice and fixed her gaze on my face. "Any more word from Roberto?"

I smiled. "I talked to him. Adele, he wants to meet me. He said Mom never told him about me."

She put an arm around me and squeezed. "I'm glad for you, honey. Real glad."

"He's in the hospital, though. Has a bad infection in his foot."

"Is he going to be all right?"

"I hope so." My throat tightened like somebody was closing up a C-clamp on it.

Corrine stood next to the donation table across the room. It now looked well populated with certificates, a gift basket of wine and jars of local picnic foods, a selection of books wrapped up in a ribbon, as well as the yarn, the banjo, and other items I couldn't get a good glimpse of. I hadn't had a chance to peruse it carefully and hadn't bid on a single thing.

Corrine clapped her hands. "Everybody?" she called out. When nobody but the folks right near her quieted, she put two fingers to her lips and let loose with a piercing playground whistle. It definitely got people's attention.

"As your mayor I'd like to thank you all for showing up during this difficult time in our small town. And as lovers of defenseless animals, the shelter and I thank you for your generosity, too." She gestured to a trim woman, with a tidy cap of puffy blond hair, next to her, the one who'd been followed in by the camera.

"We're honored to have the lieutenant governor of our lovely state here to say a few words." After the applause ebbed, Corrine introduced her, and the suit-clad woman spoke three pro forma sentences to the effect of how glad she was to be here and what wonderful services the shelter offered, while the cameraman recorded it.

As nearly half the attendees held up phones to snap a picture, a black-and-white blur streaked by. Birdy leapt past the official to the donation table and, with one more mighty leap, ended up on the top shelf of the cookware.

"There's one right there," I said in the ensuing silence. "His name's Birdy, but he's not exactly defenseless anymore. And he's not supposed to be in the store, either." The real question was how he had escaped from my apartment. I was sure I hadn't left the door open. But did I lock it?

People laughed and pointed as Birdy proceeded to bathe in view of everyone. I didn't join in the laughter, imagining who might have left the party and gone poking around in my private living space. And with Don released, it meant the true killer was still on the loose. Perhaps right here in this crowd. I hugged my suddenly goose-pimpled arms.

Corrine went on. "We're all grateful to our newest businesswoman here, Robbie Jordan, for hosting us on short notice and for providing such delicious food. Welcome to South Lick, Robbie!" She gestured at me and clapped, making sure everybody else did, too. The camera now pointed in my direction.

I tried to wave down the applause and mustered a smile. The show must go on. "I'm glad my store and restaurant is open, finally, and happy you all could join in this great cause. I was lucky to have lots of assistants tonight. Jim Shermer helped set up, Phil MacDonald baked the delicious brownies, and Danna Beedle, here, is my new right-hand woman." I pointed to each of them in turn. "The Nashville Inn donated all the appetizers—except our sliders—so be sure to stop on over there and thank them if you can. Most of all, thanks to Corrine for her superb organizing."

Corrine bowed her head in acknowledgment. "Now, we have lots of fabulous items for the silent auction, so be sure you don't let yourself get outbid. You only have a half hour left." She swept her arm toward the donation table. "A big round of applause to all our donors. The auction closes at eight sharp, hear?"

The state official left minutes after Corrine's introduction, but not before Corrine made sure I'd met her and shaken her cool hand. She seemed to me like a person with higher ambitions, one whom this little town might never see again in person. Spying Jim near my apartment, I headed in his direction.

"Come with me?" I beckoned when I got near. He raised his eyebrows, but he followed me to the door, which, sure enough, wasn't locked. It wasn't even latched. I looked at Jim, turning as cold as the bottom water in a quarry pit. "I wondered how Birdy got out. I didn't leave this door open, I'm sure."

He tested the handle and the door opened easily. "You didn't lock it?"

"I guess not. Remember, you reminded me to change? And time was getting short. I maybe didn't lock up after myself." I smacked my forehead. "Dumb. But not so dumb as to leave it ajar. Pretty sure that cat can't open a latched door. And speaking of the cat . . ." I scanned the shelves where I'd seen him last. Sure enough, he slept curled up on top of a rusty vintage American Cutlery Company scale on the top shelf, weighing in at seven and a half pounds. Conversation had picked up where it left off. Bottles clinked, a woman laughed, and music emanated from the piano.

"Hang on a sec," I said, striding toward my kitty. "Birdy, come on down," I called when I stood in front of him. He perked up his head, yawned, and jumped down onto one of the donation sheets on the table.

"Ain't she the cutest thing around?" Georgia said in delight.

I wasn't in the mood for chitchat, so I only said, "He's a he," but I softened it with a smile. I picked him up by his scruff and carried him in my arms to the apartment door.

"Ready?" Jim asked.

I pushed open the door. When Birdy scrambled in my arms, I set him down and watched him streak toward the kitchen and his bowls. Jim stepped in, too, his eyes scanning the living room.

"I want to check out the apartment," I said as I shut the door behind us.

"Let's walk through the rooms together, if that's okay," I said. "I could do it alone, but—"

"With what's been going down around here, I'd feel more comfortable making sure nobody's lying in wait for you." He took my arm and we systematically checked the apartment.

I blushed a little at my bedroom. I'd never gotten around to making the bed and today's work clothes, including a black bra, lay on a heap on the bedroom floor, right where I'd left them. But no one lurked in the closet. As we moved through the apartment, nobody jumped out from behind the couch and the back door was securely locked. My laptop sat in its place on the little desk. Everything in the kitchen seemed in order, or at least as I'd left it, which was kind of messy. At least it looked like my mess.

I shook my head. "Huh. Maybe I didn't latch the door after I got dressed, after all."

"One more closet?" Jim tilted his head toward the space where I stashed coats, brooms, and charcoal off the back hall.

"Oh, yeah." I headed over there and pulled open the door. And shrieked. Jim rushed to my side.

"Hey, Robbie." Roy pushed aside my raincoat and stepped into the hall, wearing an abashed grin.

"Roy, what in hell are you doing in Robbie's apartment?" Jim's voice was stern.

My heart once again beat faster than a turbocharged engine on Memorial Day weekend. "Yeah."

"Oh, you know. I thought the door was to one of the bathrooms, had to take a leak." Roy's breath smelled of alcohol and his diction was too relaxed— even for a native of the county.

"It's clearly labeled 'Private.'" I folded my arms, my heart slowing back to something resembling normal.

"Guess I done missed that."

"And why were you in my coat closet?" I pointed. "You couldn't possibly have missed that this was my apartment and not the restaurant's restroom." I wanted to shake a portion of sense into this man, or at least shake the truth out of him. Was he that dense? Was he looking for something of mine? Or what?

He grinned again. "I confess." He held up his palms.

"I just wanted to look around, see what you done with the place. I was going to live here, you know." His grin gone, he lifted his chin. "This was all s'posta be mine."

"Well, it isn't yours. You could be charged with trespassing, you know," Jim said in his best lawyer voice. "Even if the door wasn't closed, it is posted 'Private.'"

"Don't get your panties in a twist, Shermer. I'm leaving, okay?" Roy pushed past us into the kitchen, then he turned back.

"Listen, you want to charge somebody, you charge Mayor Corrine out there." He pronounced the name as Corrine herself did, as "Co-reen." "She killed her husband, you know, long time ago. My mom knowed all about it. She'd been taking money from Corrine for years."

"Blackmailing her?" So the story was true. Corrine herself had mentioned Stella blackmailing men. But cleverly failed to mention her own case.

"Call it whatever you want. My mom had the goods on her. And on a bunch of others in town, too. Did she share the proceeds with me? She did not."

Stunned, I watched him disappear into the living room. Jim followed and I heard the door close with a firm click. He returned a moment later.

"Want me to get Wanda to charge Roy?" Jim asked, gazing at me with eyebrows pulled together. "She's still there, in the restaurant."

"Damn." I shut my mouth and stared at the doorway to the living room. "I don't know. Should I?"

"It's your call. Seems like a pretty clear case to me."

I nodded slowly. "Please. I'm also going to check the place more carefully. Who knows what he made off with?"

Chapter 29

Jim went out to talk with Wanda, having said he'd keep an eye on the door to make sure nobody else got in. I made another, even closer sweep of my apartment, but I still didn't find anything missing. I headed back to the party, this time making sure I locked the door after I closed it. Jim waved to me from across the room, where he stood with Wanda and Roy. By the time I waded through the crowd to them, Wanda held Roy firmly by the elbow.

"Robbie, are you willing to make a statement Roy Rogers unlawfully entered your apartment and took up a position of concealment?"

"Yes," I said.

"Are you missing anything? I can add charges of larceny." Wanda looked almost excited about the prospect.

"Nothing's missing. Not that I can tell, at least."

Roy struggled. "The door to her apartment was open. I was only curious."

Wanda strong-armed him and gave him the stink

eye. "Roy, do I have to cuff you right here in front of the whole town?"

He glared at me, but he stopped resisting Wanda's hold. She walked him out the door.

The place was still bustling with partygoers, although the food was pretty much decimated. I snagged a forlorn quiche and downed it, then grabbed one of the last brownies. Luckily, the wine was still flowing. I poured out a cup of red and took a blessed sip, savoring the warming feeling as it went down. I gathered up a couple of plates and took the food refuse to the compost bucket, which was full.

Setting down my wine, I carried the bucket out the service door, letting it swing closed behind me, relieved to get out of the hubbub for a brief moment. I stopped when I sniffed cigarette smoke. Don's voice followed. Glancing over my shoulder, I realized he stood directly on the other side of the six-foot-high fence, which shielded the service area from the street.

"I saw you. I saw you drive up that afternoon."

"So what? It's a public street." Ed's voice, no longer sounding drunk.

"I kept watching. You went into her house."

My eyes sprang open so far, I thought my eyeballs would pop out. Don was talking about Stella. Silence for a moment, and then a noisy inhale, followed by another waft of smoke.

"We used to go out, long time ago."

"That's not why you visited her, and you know it. Did you kill her?"

"Of course not. For alls I know, you knocked her off."

Don made a tsking sound. "Of course I didn't. Why would I?"

"Well, why would I?" Ed said with scorn.

"'Cause she was blackmailing you, just like she was soaking half the rest of town. What'd she have on you, huh? That you cheat on health inspections? That you molest girls?"

"Don't you even say it!" Ed was almost growling now. "You're the one who attempted murder some years back."

My nose tickled with a sneeze coming on. There could be murder attempted on me if I didn't get back inside—and quick. The compost could wait. I slipped back into the kitchen and managed to wait until the door closed before letting loose with a major *"Achoo!"*

I scanned the room for Wanda, until I remembered she'd taken Roy away. I stepped back into my apartment and left a message for Buck about what I overheard, then I headed back into the fray.

At ten before eight, Corrine whistled again. "Ten minutes to outbid your rivals, people," she announced in a voice that overrode the murmur of conversation, the clinking of beer bottles, even the Beatles songs Georgia was picking out on the piano with a small cohort of fans gathered around her, singing along.

Almost everybody in the room dutifully wandered over to the donation table. I was intrigued by the prospect of banjo lessons with Abe. On my way to the table to see what the bidding was up to, I passed Ed, who was slouched in a chair alone at the table, a bottle of water having replaced the one of whiskey. He wore the pawprint pin on his wide lapel.

"Not bidding on anything, Ed?" I asked.

He gazed up at me. "I don't got any extra money, unlike some of you. I help the animals out in person."

I kept my mouth shut on that one and kept on going. Resting on the donation table, Abe's cardboard banjo listed a couple dozen names on its sheet of paper. The last amount scribbled down was *$290*. I whistled. I didn't want banjo lessons that much. I found Jim writing on the sheet next to Adele's basket of yarn and gently elbowed him.

"I didn't know you were a knitter," I murmured.

He chuckled as he finished writing his name and jotted down *$160* next to it. "I'm an amazingly well-rounded and brilliant Renaissance man. I do not, however, count knitting among my talents. My mom, on the other hand, runs through yarn like a machine." He looked up and winked. "She's going to love this. I can give it to her for her birthday next month."

"It don't matter none if I outbid you," Barb said with a smile, sliding in next to him. "Your mama's not going to see no yarn." She grabbed the pen and upped his amount by twenty dollars, writing *$180*. She glanced up at the big clock and then took her time writing her name in slow, deliberate movements, one letter at a time.

"Hey," Jim said. He looked at his watch. "Nice try, but there's still two minutes." He took the pen back.

I let them go at their friendly competition, all in a good cause, and moved down the line. It was gratifying to see the gift certificate for Pans 'N Pancakes had been bid up to $150. These small-town Hoosiers possessed deeper pockets than I'd expected. Although, when I took a closer look, I saw it was only Vera and one other person who vied for the privilege of either a couple of hearty breakfasts or a few pieces of cookware. I stepped away to let serious bidders use their last moments, and turned back to check the food table.

Danna was moving about the room, clearing detritus from the tables. She held a stack of paper plates and crumpled napkins in one hand and several half-full drink cups suspended from the fingers of the other hand. As she went by where Ed sat, she gave him a wide berth. But it wasn't wide enough. I watched him lean out of his chair and squeeze her buttock. Danna whirled toward him as Corrine whistled again to signal the end of bidding.

"Don't you touch me, you dirty old lech," Danna snarled. She threw the drink cups, red wine and all, in his face, then she delivered a fierce backhand slap across that same, shocked face.

Ed's eyes widened as he slid off his chair with a yell. The sound of his head hitting the floor wasn't a pleasant one. After that, you could have heard a pin drop. Heck, you could have heard a flea land. Everyone in the room stared.

"Danna Beedle, what-all are you doing?" Corrine called out.

Danna gave an angry glance at Ed, threw a defiant look at her mother, and ripped her apron off. She strode for the door.

"Sorry about that, Robbie. The filthy bastard *so* had it coming to him," she muttered as she passed me.

I laid a hand on her arm until she paused. "You go, girl," I murmured.

She threw me a sideways smile and kept on going. The door slammed shut behind her, but the bell kept jangling like a reminder not to mess with her.

Abe rushed to Ed's side, with Don close behind him. Ed didn't move. As Don stood, rubbing his thumbs and fingers together on each hand in an ineffectual gesture, Abe laid two fingers on Ed's neck.

"Get your hands off me, O'Neill," Ed shouted, pushing Abe away and struggling to sit up.

Abe sat back on his heels. "Just wanted to be sure you weren't passed out, Ed," he said in a calm voice. "That you didn't get a concussion."

"I'd be fine if that little bi . . ." He glanced around him. "If that girl didn't haul off and whack me. Hey, Corrine," he called across the room from where he sat, "what aren't you teaching that daughter of yours?"

"I'm teaching her to respect herself, that's what," Corrine yelled at him, then turned her back. Somebody in the crowd gave a hoot of approval. I wasn't sure, but thought it might have been Adele.

Ed shook his head, his hands on his splayed-out legs. He grimaced as he felt the back of his head.

I walked over to Abe, who'd moved a couple yards away from Ed. I lowered my voice and said, "You sure Ed's going to be okay?"

"I was a navy medic. I think he's gonna be diagnosed as tipsy and stupid."

"He hit his head pretty hard. I heard it thud."

"Yeah. And it's his own damn fault." Abe moved close to Ed again. "Does your head hurt?"

"Darn right it hurts. But it ain't bleeding." He took his hand off his head and showed it to Abe, then glanced at me. "What are you looking at?"

I held my hands up, palms out. "I want to be sure you're all right."

"Huh. Oughta discipline that so-called employee of yours," he muttered. "Assaulting me like that."

I took four steps until I stood above him. I tried to keep my voice level. "You're the one who groped her, Ed Kowalski. That's illegal, in case you didn't know."

Chapter 30

Jim walked toward me a few minutes later as I kept busy tidying up the kitchen area, avoiding even looking at Ed.

"Ed left. A friend of his offered to drive him, which is good. He'll be okay." He pursed his lips and shook his head. "Do you know if Danna has ever let the police know about Ed harassing her?"

"I don't know, but I'm going to encourage her to." I exhaled and leaned into him. "I can't believe this day isn't over yet," I said, then gazed around the room. I motioned Jim to bring his head closer to mine. "I'm going to go ask Don what happened, why they set him loose. Want to come?" I made a little motion with my index finger toward Don, who now sat slumped and alone at the same table where Ed had been.

"Why not?"

I took his hand and we meandered on over. Before we got there, though, Corrine split the air with her whistle yet again. She began to read out loud from each bid sheet, announcing the winners. Happy townsfolk high-fived each other when they won, but I also glimpsed a few disappointed looks. When she was done, she moved next to Turner at the table where he'd been taking donations.

"Ladies and gentlemen," she called out, then waited until the space quieted again, "I have great news. My able intern, Turner, is going to tell you how much we raised tonight for the shelter." She glanced at Turner, who checked a slip of paper and then stood.

"We brought in a total of three thousand four hundred thirty-five dollars."

A surge of applause filled the room. Corrine smiled and went on. "The Brown County Animal Shelter is going to be tickled pink. Thank you all for your generous tax-deductible donations. You can pay Turner for your bid and then pick up your item. If anyone needs a receipt, he'll be happy to fill one out for you."

The "able" Turner *just barely* didn't roll his eyes, but instead nodded.

"Enjoy the rest of your evening. Our generous hostess has said she'll stay open until ten o'clock."

Not exactly. I'd been *told* I would. As conversation resumed, I pulled out a chair at Don's table and Jim followed suit.

"Hey, Don," I said. "Glad you could make it tonight."

"Didn't much want to, but it's awful hard to say 'no' to Corrine," he said, worrying the label on his beer with his thumb.

"We heard they were holding you at the station."

"Yeah. Somebody saw me go in Stella's door that afternoon."

"What made Buck change his mind and let you go?" I asked.

Don let out a whoosh of breath. He rubbed at the

label for another moment. "I didn't kill Stella. I kept telling them that."

"Buck must have collected evidence that made him think you did," Jim said, but he kept his tone casual and didn't try to make Don look at him.

"I was over there that afternoon, all right? Stella had been . . ." His voice trailed off.

I smiled in what I hoped was a sympathetic look. And waited, as did Jim. Smart man.

"She was blackmailing me," Don finally said. "It was messing up my life. I went over there to tell her she needed to stop. That I didn't care anymore if she told the world." He straightened and looked me directly in the eyes. In my Italian eyes.

"About Roberto?" I said in a soft voice.

Don nodded, and out of the corner of my eye I saw Jim give me an understanding nod.

"I talked to him in Italy on the phone this afternoon. So . . . what he said happened *is* true." I watched Don's face.

Don spoke after a long pause. "It was a stupid thing to do, and I've regretted it the rest of my life. I repented and became a Christian after that." He buried his face in his hands. "But it don't change what I done," he said in a muffled voice.

"Don, can we get back to why Buck released you?" Jim asked after a few moments.

"I have an alibi for the time Stella was killed." An unhappy Don looked up. "I didn't want to tell him, but I finally had to. I was with a woman. A married woman." He rubbed his forehead. "And I call myself a Christian."

* * *

Don downed his beer, stood, and stumped toward the exit with slumped shoulders. Georgia hurried toward him and touched his sleeve. After she spoke, Don shook his head and walked out the door. Georgia watched him go with the saddest expression on her face.

Jim squeezed my hand. "So you talked with your father?"

"I did. For the first time in my life." I squeezed back. "He said, among other things, that Don hit him on the head and then pushed him into the quarry, with Stella standing right there."

"Incredible."

"But I'll fill you in later on the details, okay? I need to be on duty here, especially since Danna left."

"Sure."

I wandered around, picking up discarded plates and cups, removing beer bottles from the trash and setting them aside to recycle. I moved past Phil and Abe, where they stood with a couple of other men.

"How do you know the toothbrush was invented in Kentucky?" Abe said. He grinned at me.

I stopped my cleanup, smiling at the state pastime of bashing the state to the south, and waited for the punch line.

"If it was invented anywhere else, it would have been called a teethbrush," Phil answered. "Did you hear the governor's mansion in Kentucky burned down?"

"Almost done took out the whole trailer park," one of the other men said, then guffawed.

"You guys are hot," I said. "I shouldn't, but what about this one? What are the best four years of a Kentucky Wildcat's life?"

"Third grade." Abe threw back his head and joined the others in laughter.

A uniformed Buck walked in. I waved at him, excused myself from the jokesters, and headed his way.

"Just the person I wanted to talk to," he said when we met in the middle of the room. "Heared about your intruder." He shook his head in exasperation.

"It was pretty freaky, finding him in my closet like that. At least he didn't seem to be armed."

"Actually, he was carrying concealed."

"Good thing he didn't shoot me." I dumped the trash I'd been holding on the nearest table and dusted off my hands. "It's just crazy this state even allows regular people to carry guns like that."

"That's the way of it. Folks'd get all riled up if you told them they couldn't defend themselves. But Roy has never been quite all there, you know."

"All the more reason he shouldn't be owning guns. Are you still holding him?"

"Had to let him go on bail."

"He'd better not come back here," I said. "Say, can you sit down for a minute? I want to tell you about a piece of the puzzle."

Buck looked wistfully at the food table.

"Go clean it out." I laughed. "I'll be right here."

In a minute he was back and chowing down on a few buffalo wings, the last turkey slider, all three of the remaining brownies, and a bottle of tea.

"Have you checked Stella's bank accounts?" I asked.

With his mouth full, he shook his head. "Need a warrant for that," he mumbled through his dinner.

"Roy said his mother was blackmailing Corrine.

Don told us a few minutes ago she was blackmailing him, too."

He swallowed. "Interesting. Kept Don in for almost twenty-four hours and he never told us that. Just kept saying he didn't kill her, and he had a alibi. It was like coughing up nails when he finally said he'd been with Georgia LaRue later on."

"Georgia from the library?"

"Right."

"All he told me was she was a married woman," I said.

"In name only." Buck snorted. "Her husband's older and has dementia." He tapped his temple, leaving a trace of buffalo sauce behind. "Lives in a nursing home. She's married, all right. But these days, only an overly moral guy like Don would think spending private time with her would present a problem. Anywho, I can check with the bank tomorrow after I get the warrant. Not invading Stella's privacy, seeing as how she's dead and all."

"I know why Stella was blackmailing Don."

Buck narrowed his eyes even as he bit off half the turkey slider and chewed as slowly as he talked.

I swallowed and looked around the restaurant. The numbers were dwindling. Jim leaned against a wall across the room and talked with Turner, who finally held a beer. Corrine sat at a table with Adele and Samuel and was laughing at something Samuel said. Phil and Georgia sat together on the piano bench, playing a four-handed tune, with Abe looking on.

"And?" Buck asked. "You going to tell me sometime in this decade?"

I gazed at him and told him the whole story. Of searching for news about my mom. Seeing her in the picture with Don and a man I resembled. Finding the news article about the quarry accident, and then the hospital records showing Stella called in the accident.

"Huh," Buck said. "I remember my pop talking about that Eye-talian's accident. I was ten or so. He musta wanted to warn me off swimming in the quarries. How does all that relate to blackmail, though?"

"It wasn't an accident." I watched as his eyes popped. "I tracked Roberto down in Italy. Just spoke to him this afternoon, in fact. He said Don whacked him upside the head and then pushed him in."

"Now, why in God's green earth would Don O'Neill act all violent like that?"

"He was jealous. Don was in love with my mom, but she'd left him for this handsome foreigner who'd swept into town. Who happens to be my father."

Buck whistled. He leaned in to peer at me. "It's true, you don't look much like the average Hoosier with all your dark hair and eyes."

Phil and Georgia finished a tune with a flourish to the applause of several people gathered around them.

"Not all Hoosiers are blond, you know," I said, pointing my chin in the direction of Phil and Samuel, who sat not far from him.

"I know, I know. Can we get back to the story?"

"Well, that's about it. Don, Stella, and Roberto were at the Empire Quarry. Don hit Roberto, pushed him in, and then jumped in himself, claiming it was to rescue Roberto. Stella saw the whole thing. Apparently, she'd been threatening to tell Don's secret ever since." I tapped the table with one finger.

"So that's what he wouldn't tell me. He kept saying he had business with Stella, and that he left her alive and well."

"If he's not the murderer, do you have any other suspects?"

Buck let out the longest sigh I'd ever heard. "Wanda told me what you overheard. I guess we'll be getting Ed in for questioning tomorrow." He cocked his head. "What did you say before . . . that Roy said Stella was blackmailing . . ." He glanced around the room until he spotted Corrine. When he spoke again, it was almost in a whisper. "Our fair mayor?"

"He sure did. Said she'd killed her husband."

"Thought that was a hunting accident."

"That's what Samuel MacDonald told me," I said. "But Adele said there was talk at the time that it wasn't an accident, after all. And she was never charged."

He whistled. "Guess I'd better be checking into her alibi for the approximate time of death."

Chapter 31

I called out a good night to Adele and Samuel at the door at a few minutes past ten, then turned back to the remnants of an all-community party. And I let out a big groan—Corrine, madam organizer, had left the mess to me. Well, and whoever I could corral of those few who remained. Phil and Turner sat playing cards at one of the tables, open beer bottles at the ready. Abe perused the cookware shelves, while Jim held his cell phone to his ear with a look of alarm on his face. He pressed a button and strode toward me.

"What's the matter?" I asked.

"It's my mom. She's taken a fall. I've got to get up there."

"Oh, no. To Chicago?"

He nodded, the corners of his eyes drawn down. "Well, Oak Park. I'm sorry I can't help out here. It's at least a four-hour drive."

"Don't worry about helping. But are you okay to drive that far? It's so late."

"I know. I'll be okay. I only drank two beers." He

looked at the kitchen area. "Can you make me a cup of coffee to go?"

"Of course I'll make coffee."

"I wish I could wait until the morning, but my dad is one of those helpless males without my mom at his side. And they're not young—they didn't have me until my mom was forty."

I hurried to the machine and set a pot on. Others might want a cup before they drove, too. By the time I fetched a traveling mug and a couple of hastily assembled cheese sandwiches from my apartment, the coffee was brewed.

Jim paced near the door, coat on. I brought him the mug and one of the sandwiches, which I'd slipped into a plastic bag. "Here's a sandwich to nosh on as you drive. I'll walk you out."

On the porch I took his face in my hands and pulled him down for a quick kiss.

"I hope your mom's all right. She's going to be really happy you're there."

"Thanks." He sucked air in through his teeth. "I hate to leave you with Stella's killer still out there."

"Don't even think about it. I'll be fine."

"I'll call you tomorrow. When I can."

"Good. Now go. And drive safe." I gave him a little push and watched, arms wrapped around myself, until he drove off. The night air was crisp, and the breeze brought smells of dew and wood smoke mixed with a touch of death—the death of all things green and fresh until spring. I shivered and went back in.

"All right, gentlemen, party's over," I called out. "Who's up for restoring this joint to its usual beautiful order? Help me out and your next breakfast here is on the house."

The poker players looked up, and Abe strolled toward me, a hand-cranked beater in his hand.

"Can I buy this?" he asked. "It's got a very cool mechanism."

"Of course." We completed the transaction, and then I walked over to the chalkboard and began to write, announcing the tasks as I went.

"We have to gather all the trash. Separate the recycling. Wash any pans. Sweep and mop the floor—I noticed more than one drink got spilled. Put all the tables and chairs back. And if anyone wants to help me set up for tomorrow, I'll foot you two free breakfasts."

Phil marched to the CD player and rummaged until he found what he was looking for. In a moment the music of the Alabama Shakes was rocking the airspace. Phil headed for the sink. Turner grabbed a broom, and Abe a trash bag.

During the next half hour, Turner unself-consciously danced with the broom and then the mop as he worked. Abe sorted and stowed all the trash. I wolfed down my own sandwich and then scrubbed the sink. In no time the place was spotless and restored to restaurant status. Phil set the last napkin roll on a table and let out a mighty yawn.

"Great teamwork, guys," I said, stretching my arms to the ceiling.

"Need a ride, dude?" Phil asked Turner.

The intern nodded. "That would help, since it didn't occur to Ms. Beedle that she drove me here."

"'Night, Robbie. Nice job," Phil said.

"Thanks to you both." I waved at them as they left. "You all set, or is there more I can help you with?"

Abe asked. "You know, second free breakfast and all."
His dimple went extra deep when he smiled like that.

I laughed. "Sure. How are you with a knife? There're melons to cut up for tomorrow, and I have to prep biscuit dough."

"I'm the best." He made a pretend show of tossing knives in the air in front of his face and did a soft whistle, which almost sounded like it, too.

"Follow me, Ginsu master." I beckoned to the walk-in. We both carried melons out; then I set him up with a good knife, a wide cutting board, a big stainless-steel bowl for the fruit, and a smaller one for the compostable parts.

After I washed my hands, I said, "A little whiskey to go with the job?" I grabbed the bourbon from my cupboard. When he nodded, I poured us each a couple of fingers, then I went back into the cooler for butter, milk, cheese, and eggs, leaving him washing his hands at the sink.

We worked in silence for a moment, me mixing baking powder and salt into flour, him slicing the skin off wedges of melon. I glanced over at him, feeling a touch guilty Jim was driving north alone in the dark toward a family emergency and I was here drinking bourbon with a man equally as handsome as Jim, but in an entirely different way.

"Good news your brother was released," I finally said.

"He's one messed-up man, I'll tell you."

"Was he ever married? Does he have kids?" I asked, cutting the butter into the flour mixture.

"No to both. I don't think he ever got over not succeeding with your mom. And now he's all upset word's getting out about him seeing Georgia. That church of his does a number on his head. Nobody but him really cares."

I dumped a bag of grated cheddar into the bowl and mixed it in. "Did he tell you about why he went over to Stella's?"

"To tell her he wasn't putting up with her soaking him dry? I wish he'd come to me for help a lot earlier."

"You didn't know about the incident at the quarry, then."

"No," Abe said as he sliced open another melon. "He's the oldest in the family, and I would have been a toddler at the time. He only told me about it when they let me visit him in jail. It's funny, he was my awesome big brother for so long. Now it's almost like I'm the older one."

"His store seems to be doing well."

"That he can do. He knows the stock, manages the staff. Yeah, that's a good gig for him. It's on the personal side where he doesn't do so well." He looked up. "You want these in bite-sized cubes?"

"Perfect, thanks. So you said you were a navy medic. Where did you serve?" I cracked six eggs into a well in the middle of the biscuit mix and broke them up with a fork, stirring lightly.

"A few years after 9/11, I thought I ought to volunteer. I figured they'd send me to Afghanistan or somewhere. Instead, I spent two pretty quiet years in Japan." He looked up and smiled. "I studied teppanyaki—"

"Where the chef cooks on a hot iron plate right in front of you."

"Exactly. The kind of chef who flashes knives around." He set a melon in front of him and sliced it open in a clean, fluid movement. "When I got back, I went to college on the government's dime, but I decided to be an electrician."

"Ed sure seemed like he'd had a couple when he walked in here tonight. You know anything about him?" After I took a sip of whiskey, I stirred two cups of milk into the dough with the same fork.

Abe frowned at the golden fruit in front of him, scooping the seeds and pulp with a spoon into the bowl. "He and Donnie are old friends, grew up here together. But unlike my big brother, Ed isn't good at business."

"Or keeping his hands to himself, apparently."

"That too."

"Is he married?" I kneaded the dough gently in the bowl, then turned it onto the marble, which I'd sprinkled flour on.

"Used to be. Nasty divorce. His wife soaked him pretty bad, but I'll bet he deserved it."

"Question for you. Do you think Stella had anything on Ed? Like a juicy tidbit she'd be blackmailing him about?"

He stared at me. "You think he might have killed her to shut her up?"

"I don't know what I think. She was apparently blackmailing lots of folks. Don and Corrine included." After shaping the dough into a thick disk ready to roll out and cut biscuits out of in the morning, I slipped it into a plastic bag.

"You know, that doesn't surprise me. Not a bit." He sipped from his own glass. "I didn't know Stella well, but she seemed a real bitch."

"That was my experience of her, for sure." After I deposited the dough in the walk-in, I scrubbed off the marble and tidied up. I needed to be way careful I didn't leave food out to attract vermin. I was sure this old building featured cracks and leaks aplenty where a mouse could sneak in.

"Done," he said. "Where does the compost go?"

"There's a bin right outside the side door there." I pointed to the service door. "Thanks a ton for helping." I stretched plastic wrap over the fruit bowl and set it in the cooler.

When Abe came back in, he washed the bowl and his hands, drying them on a paper towel. I was kneeling, sweeping up spilled flour with the hand brush and dustpan. I glanced up, sensing his eyes on me. He cleared his throat.

"This was a lot of fun, Robbie."

I swept the little pile of flour and bits of cheese into the pan and stood. "Agreed."

"I like spending time with you." He shoved his hands into his pockets. "Would you want to maybe go out for a drink one of these days? Or a meal you don't have to cook?" There was that dimple again.

Wow. I could hear Adele's voice in my head, saying, *"It don't rain, but it pours."* Abe must not have noticed that Jim and I were becoming an item. But how could he have?

He shifted from one foot to the other. He blinked and his smile faded. I needed to answer him.

"I . . ." *I what? I'm taken? Am I? Huh, Jim won't be back for several days. Nothing wrong with a free meal, is there?* "I'd love to. Tomorrow night? Store's closed Mondays, so I can actually relax on Sundays."

"It's a date." His smile was back in full force. "Pick you up at six?" He headed for the door.

When he glanced back, still smiling, I waved, then I watched him disappear. *Years in the dating desert and now two hot guys are interested in me.* I locked the door he'd left through, and did a little dance with the door handle on the drinks cooler as I passed by.

After making sure the restaurant was spotless and all the doors locked, I headed to my apartment, securing the door after me. I'd be in a sticky spot if Danna didn't show up in the morning, but I figured she would. Letting a creep like Ed rob her of her job would only satisfy him and screw her royally. Turning the tables was the best plan. I hoped Danna thought so, too.

Birdy wove through my legs, purring with all his avian overtones. Tired and wired at the same time, I sank into my desk chair. Birdy leapt into my lap and lay there purring as I stroked him. *What an evening. What a day.*

I'd spoken with my father for the first time. He'd not only not rebuffed me, but he'd welcomed me. A soused Ed let his inner harasser out of the closet, and Danna stood up to him with distinction. Roy, who might well have been the person who shot at me, snuck into this very apartment and not only got himself found, but also got arrested for trespassing. Don admitted his guilt in the quarry assault, as well as his victim status in the blackmail. And Abe asked me out on a date.

I glanced at the *Stella Murder* puzzle, which lay in front of me unfinished, unsolved. I could add a couple more blackmail victims—Don and Corrine—and proof of Ed's harassing. Picking up the pencil, producing the effect of losing my lap pillow as Birdy jumped to the floor, I also jotted down Roy's behavior. And frowned. What did he think he'd gain by snooping in my apartment, and then hiding instead of pretending he'd only picked the wrong door? Several people had mentioned Roy wasn't all there, like he had a developmental delay or another problem. In my dealings with him, he seemed okay. Ill-tempered, surely, and maybe not dealing with as full a deck as some, but his speech was fine and he didn't seem particularly slow. I thought again how horrific it would be if he killed his own mother. Maybe he wasn't right mentally, after all. Who was it, psychopaths, who didn't experience emotion like the rest of us? Or was that sociopaths? Roy certainly knew guns. But then, who in South Lick didn't, besides me?

Corrine was sure on the money when she said Stella had been blackmailing half the men in town. She just hadn't added "and me, too." I wondered if Buck would be successful in getting into Stella's bank records. A good hacker could, if the bank didn't cooperate. But I wasn't one, and the only one I knew was off on a vacation in Thailand.

I looked up when I heard a noise and cocked my head to listen better. I heard Birdy crunching his dry food, but the wind must have picked up, too. A branch scratched at the window like a scene from a horror movie. I shuddered a little. But I was safe in a sturdy building that had endured over 150 years. Wind wasn't going to get me. Opening my e-mail, I smiled at a message from Roberto's address. When I opened it, the smile faded like the wallpaper on a sunsplashed wall. It was from his daughter again:

Father much worse. In surgery for amputation.
Please pray. Graciela

My heart cried out its refusal. I couldn't lose my
father right when I'd found him. But I didn't know
how to pray, really, or whom to pray to. I sensed a
spirit greater than any of us existed in a dimension we
couldn't know, but it was not an entity I could entreat
for a favor. I closed my eyes and simply pictured the
dark-eyed, curly-haired man named Roberto trans-
planted to our Santa Barbara beach: whole, smiling,
healthy. That would have to do.

Chapter 32

Another late night, another eyelids-of-lead morning. My thoughts about Roberto had woken me up too early, and I'd decided to get a head start on the day. I stood in the shower for too long, hoping the water would wake me up. Instead, the warm flow threatened to put me back to sleep right there on my feet. When I switched it to cold for a moment, I shrieked, but at least my eyes were finally open.

As I dressed in jeans and a long-sleeved blue top, grateful the week was coming to a close, my gaze fell on the picture of Mom and me on my dresser. I was ten and we'd gone camping in Sequoia with a friend of mine and my friend's mom. The other mother snapped this picture of us in our hiking shorts and boots, Mom's arm around my shoulders, me giggling.

"Aw, Mommy. You could have told me about Roberto. He wouldn't have spoiled our lives, I'm sure of it. We could have taken trips to Italy. Maybe I'd have spent a couple of summers with him there. Or, he might have moved to California. Imagine if we'd been a family of three instead of two." I truly had never missed being an ordinary nuclear family until right this minute. *No use crying over spilled milk,* I scolded myself. *Or lost Italians, either.*

After I sat at my laptop and composed a quick message to Graciela asking how Roberto's surgery went, I tied my hair up wet, cranked through my sit-ups, and fed Birdy. I'd have to start spending more time playing with him. This afternoon, I promised him before I headed to work. I started coffee—first things first, and it was already six o'clock—then made for the walk-in to get the biscuit dough and the supplies for pancakes. I passed the closest table. And froze.

The square wooden top, the rolled-up blue napkins, even the sugar shaker—all were littered with inch-long black torpedoes. I gasped, bending down to look. Torpedoes they weren't. Droppings now covered the table I knew was pristine clean when I left. Panicked, I glanced around the room. Feces covered all the tables, the floor, the cooking countertops, and they were bigger than mouse pellets. My stomach roiled even as my brain raced. *Rats? How did they get in here, and in such number?* I shuddered in revulsion, bile rising in my throat. This wasn't a random rodent who happened to find a hole in the foundation. This was an invasion. Although, where were the animals now?

And if anyone saw it, my business would be shut down as tight as a stubborn clam the minute the health inspector caught word. Forget the biscuits—I needed to clean, and fast. But first an apron and rubber gloves. Once those were on, I grabbed the galvanized-steel basin, which sat upside down near the sink, and the hand broom. Table by table, countertop by countertop, I swept turds, napkin rolls, even the salt, pepper, and sugar shakers into the tub. I could sort it out later and I had extras. Once the tables were clear, I carried the tub to the service door and set it down. When I reached for the doorknob, my fingers sat on it, motionless. It wasn't locked. I'd checked all the locks last night. How had that happened? This was getting worse by the minute. At least the door was latched. That wasn't how the rats got in. I opened it and set the tub behind the trash cans in the enclosure. I locked the door after I went back in.

I was busy vacuuming when I heard a drumming on the front door that was loud enough to override the machine's thrum. My heart about leapt out the top of my head. I turned to see Danna pressing her nose against the glass. I let out a breath, dropped the vacuum, and let her in.

I faced her, my hands fluttering. "Um, I . . . There was . . ." The hum of the vacuum filled the air and I smelled the coffee for the first time.

"What's the matter, Robbie? Why are you vacuuming? It's already seven. Shouldn't you be cooking?" She wrinkled her nose and sniffed. "What's that smell?" Today her dreads were neatly covered by a brilliant green bandana.

"The worst thing happened. But you have to swear not to tell anyone. Promise?"

"Sure. What is it?"

"Last night a few of the guys helped me clean up. You could have eaten off the tables—they were that clean. This morning? Rat droppings everywhere! Every surface. It was totally revolting."

"*Eww.*" She opened her mouth like she'd tasted a vile dish. "Where'd they come from?"

"No idea. But if I don't get the rest cleaned up, we won't have to worry because I'll be out of business."

She set her mouth in a determined line. "What can I do?"

"Disinfect the tables and chairs. And countertops. Lysol spray and rubber gloves. Under the sink. I'll join you when I've finished cleaning the floor."

"Got it, General." She saluted and beelined for the sink. She bent down and opened the lower cabinet doors. "Hey, there aren't any droppings under here. Isn't that where mice and rats usually start, under the sink?"

I detoured from getting back to the vacuum. "You're right," I said, peering in. "Clean as a whistle. That's really odd." I opened a few more lower cabinets—all clean. Very odd. "Do you think somebody could have set this up on purpose? To sabotage me?"

"Maybe. But for right now, we don't have time to figure out who."

By seven-thirty we'd finished the cleaning, just. My brain usually worked on puzzling while I worked physically, but the stress of getting this place clean again overrode anything else. It was just a blessing we opened an hour later on Sundays. I started sausage frying to take the smell of Lysol out of the air, and I decided to make drop biscuits so I didn't have to use the marble pastry top. I wanted to scrub it about six more times before that happened. I took a second to pour myself a cup of coffee so I could keep going.

I hurried to get a pan of three dozen biscuits in the oven as Danna set up the tables with unrolled napkins and the minimum of silver.

"Extra salt and pepper shakers and sugar jars are

on that shelf." I pointed. "And if we don't have enough, people can share." I assembled the pancake batter and pulled the fruit out to take the chill off, grateful Abe had cut it all up last night.

The doorbell jangled at a couple minutes before eight and the first customer popped his head in.

"We're open. Come on in," I called, and gestured to him. I hustled over, turning the sign to OPEN, then handed him and two young boys menus, plus a couple miniature boxes of crayons for the kids. I might survive this rat threat, after all.

Danna and I had our hands full with customers all morning. The breakfast business never let up until almost lunchtime. We barely had time to hit the head or eat anything, ourselves. I made her sit down at eleven and eat while I made patties, then we switched. A few times I glimpsed a stray turd on the floor I'd missed, but I always managed to swipe it up with a paper towel. I lost track of how often I scrubbed my hands. Before lunch really picked up, I took a few moments in the restroom to splash water on my face. I took off my hat, tightened up my ponytail, then tucked it back through the hole in the back of the cap. I was living my dream, but it was exhausting. I couldn't wait to relax this afternoon, get out on my bike, inhale lungfuls of fresh air, and anticipate dinner with Abe. And figure out how in heck rats got into my store.

During lunch I recognized a few faces I'd seen for the first time last night. All that work to host the fundraiser had been worth it if it brought the store more visibility and interest from the local hungries. I was busy doling out three full hamburger platters when the bell jangled. I glanced up to see a uniformed Wanda hold the door for a woman in a dark blazer and a short, sensible haircut, who carried a thick briefcase. They paused inside the door, the woman's eyes scanning the floor, checking every corner of the restaurant. I did not have a good feeling about this. I knew that woman. She was Elizabeth Lake, county health inspector, and I was willing to bet a river of nickels she wasn't here for a turkey burger.

"Robbie," an unsmiling Wanda called, beckoning me over. She stood with feet apart.

I made sure the customers I'd just delivered to were all set before I headed her way. My guts lurched.

"Roberta Jordan?" the woman asked when I approached.

I glanced at Wanda and back at the woman. "Yes, I'm Robbie. Would you like to see a menu?"

"No. I believe we met when I approved the opening of your restaurant. Elizabeth Lake, health inspector for the county." She held her hand out, so I shook it. Then she laid her briefcase on the bench and opened it, drawing out a couple of sheets of paper.

"I am closing this establishment on the orders of the Board of Health. We have evidence vermin have recently occupied the premises."

I stared at her. How in blazes could she know? I mustered my inner warrior. "There are no vermin here. Never have been. Check for yourself." Then I remembered the tub full of evidence outside I hadn't had time to deal with. I was dead in the water if they found that.

She proffered one of the sheets of paper. I stared

again, but this time at a picture of rats . . . on top of my tables.

"Where did you get this?"

"We have our sources."

"Let me see that." I grabbed it out of her hand and carried it three steps to the front window, where light streamed in. It had been taken through that very window and the only illumination was from the drinks cooler and the red EXIT sign. But it sure as heck looked like rats standing here and there on the tables. On the rolled napkins. On the counters.

Elizabeth followed me and handed me another, this one of the cooking spaces, also covered with rats. It was a fuzzy shot, must have been taken with the zoom on. I glanced up at her. "What can I say? I admit I noticed a few bits of feces on the floor this morning." Figured I might as well tell the truth, sort of, so I wouldn't get charged with lying. "And I'll call an exterminator first thing in the morning. But we scrubbed everything with Lysol—"

"We?"

"My employee and me." I pointed at Danna, poor thing, who was hustling double time while I stood talking with a threat to my existence. "Danna Beedle."

"I'll need to interview her, too. But it doesn't matter if you scrubbed down. We need to run another full inspection and that can't start until tomorrow, since today's Sunday. For today, and until further notice, you're closed."

"I want a copy of those pictures." I set my hands on my hips. "And I want to know who took them."

"I'll send you a copy. To the store's e-mail address, right?" She checked a tablet she'd pulled out.

"Yes."

"But I can't reveal who sent them to us. We always encourage the public to report infractions, and if we gave out names, that might discourage Joe Citizen."

I knew what I wanted to do with Joe Citizen, but I kept it to myself. "What about these customers?" I said in a rasping whisper, gesturing around the store. "You're just going to kick them out?" My hands clenched into fists.

Wanda took a step toward me. I held up my hand to her. "Relax, Wanda. I'm not going to hurt anyone." No matter how much I wanted to.

"They can stay. We don't want to damage you un-necessarily. But I need you to turn your sign to CLOSED and not admit anyone else. After the current diners leave, we'll post our notices."

I squeezed my eyes shut for a minute. There was no worse disaster for a restaurant owner except food poisoning. I opened them and said, "All right. But I'm not happy about it."

Elizabeth pursed her lips and raised one eyebrow. "No one ever is."

Chapter 33

Danna and I sat at a table at two o'clock in an empty restaurant with a big orange sign on the front door: BY ORDER OF THE BROWN COUNTY HEALTH COMMISSIONER THIS ESTABLISHMENT IS HEREBY CLOSED TO PROTECT PUBLIC HEALTH AND SAFETY. There was more, but that was the really visible part. Visible to anyone who walked up the steps. To any car that drove by, any leaf-peeping tourist or vintage cookware fan. To any of my budding customer base.

"At least they didn't go snooping around and find the tub full of turds," Danna said.

"I know. I've got to get rid of all of it before tomorrow, though, so the inspection committee won't find it."

"I'll help."

"You don't have to." I traced one of the lines of wood grain in the tabletop.

"I want to. Come on, let's get it over with." She stood and rummaged under the sink to find two new pairs of rubber gloves. She tossed me a set and pulled on her own.

I blew air out, then rose and found a trash bag and three big nesting bowls. "We'll need to sort the laundry from the dispensers from the silverware." I followed her out the service door and stopped, stunned.

"Look at this day," I said. Golden and brilliant red leaves fluttered against a perfect blue sky. A balmy breeze caressed my cheek. The scent of freshly cut grass tickled my nose as the lazy drone of a small plane receded into the distance. A yellow leaf zigzagged its way through the air in front of me, landing on my foot.

"How can I be in such big trouble on such a perfect day?" I frowned. "I remember reading, after the attacks on 9/11, how people on the East Coast couldn't put together all that destruction and chaos with the clear, beautiful day it was." Not that this compared to that event, of course. But it was still jarring.

"I know what you mean." Danna opened the enclosure and dragged the tub out, but kept it behind the open gate, hidden from view to anyone passing by on the street. I separated the bowls and pointed.

"Salt, pepper, and sugar dispensers in that one. Silverware here. Napkins there. When we're done, we can empty out the dispensers and sterilize them along with the silver. I'll launder the napkins in super hot water."

We set to work, unrolling the napkin rolls, weeding through the disgusting pile, tossing the dispensers into their bowl.

"I still don't get how there were no traces of rats

under the cabinets," Danna said, throwing a fork into the silverware bowl. "That literally never happens."

"I know. And don't you think I would have seen droppings before now?" I shook my head and tossed an antique sugar dispenser a little too forcefully on top of the others. It crashed against the other dispensers, but blessedly didn't break, the old glass was that thick. "The other thing is, you should have seen the pictures. There were rats everywhere. It was like the Pied Piper had lured them all in. I had no idea this town even had rats. I've never seen a single one."

When the basin was empty of all but feces, Danna reached for the trash bag and stretched it wide open. "Dump it all in here," she instructed.

I hoisted the tub and let the turds slide in. I set it down, picking out the last two and dropping them in the bag, then I scooped up a few that dropped on the ground and added them.

"Be right back." Danna grinned and headed into the little patch of woods behind the barn.

I hosed out the basin and checked the enclosure. No evidence. Good. Curious, I lifted the trash cans. No rodent feces anywhere. Wouldn't rats first be out checking the trash for free food before squeezing into a restaurant? I didn't get it. The thought of someone doing it deliberately popped up again. But who? And why?

Danna came back, wadded the empty trash bag into a little ball, and stuffed it way down in one of the cans.

"Where'd you dump the evidence?" I asked.

"Let's just say I fertilized a few redbud trees." She hoisted two of the bowls. "We're not done yet. Get the door?"

* * *

Danna left to the accompaniment of the dishwasher running at its highest temperature, bless the heart of the small-town appliance guy yesterday. I never would have gotten a replacement dishwasher so fast if my restaurant was in California. I carried the soiled napkins into my apartment and started a load of laundry, also on the hottest water the machine offered, setting the load on HEAVY DUTY despite its small size. Even though the napkins were blue, I wanted to·add bleach, but I restrained myself. That oxy clean stuff and a good dose of detergent would have to do. Plus an extra rinse at the end. I'd do today's napkins, towels, and aprons separately.

I took a moment to check my e-mail, but there was no news from Italy. Sighing, I pushed open the back door. Birdy came at a gallop and streaked out.

"I really ought to get you a cat door," I said to his disappearing tail. It was still a drop-dead gorgeous day, even though the radio forecast a possible frost for overnight. I turned around and a minute later was back out juggling my laptop, a bowl of chips, a small bowl of salsa, and a beer. I set the stuff on the patio table and sank into a chair, stretching out my legs. I took a long swig of beer, then closed my eyes, letting the warm sun bleach my troubles away. A girl could wish, anyway.

I began to drop off into dreamland—that in-between state where you know you're still awake, but you start seeing pictures on the insides of your eyelids. When the pictures turned to rats, though, I popped my eyes open and sat up straight. I had real rats to look at. I opened the laptop, turning the brightness up to high, and found the e-mail from Inspector Lake. The sun was still too bright to see the screen well, so I moved my chair into the shade and peered at the first picture. What seemed wrong? I saved the image and opened it in a picture viewer where I could enlarge it. I blinked and looked again. Every single red-eyed rat was in the same position. All the tails curved around to the right. Exactly the same whiskers stuck out from each snout. Their heads angled in the same positions. I sat back and swore.

Somebody had staged fake rats in my restaurant. Either that, or they'd used Photoshop to alter a picture. The droppings were real—I knew that for a fact. So that was why there weren't any feces inside the cupboards. Whoever it was had scattered the evidence and the plastic animals about, gone outside, taken pictures, and then removed the rats. I jumped to my feet, knocking into the table and grabbing the beer just in time before it watered the flowerpot below it. I strode out to the edge of the woods and back. Who in hell would do a destructive, disgusting thing like that? Someone who wanted to put me out of business, that's who.

Elizabeth seemed like an intelligent person. Wouldn't she have noticed they were fake rats? I shook my head. If I hadn't enlarged the picture, I wouldn't have, either. I found the inspector's number on the bottom of her e-mail, dug my phone out of my back pocket, and called her. It went to voice mail, though, with her message saying the office was closed, to please call back during regular business hours, and to leave a message of any urgent health infractions. I left a message describing my suspicions and saying I needed that sign taken down as soon as possible. I doubted the inspector would think this was urgent. Although, whoever sent her the fake pictures sure hadn't waited for regular business hours. I munched a chip and opened the second picture. Same rats. Same problem.

Birdy sidled back. He settled into a spot on a warm flagstone and began to bathe, lifting his leg above his head in a pose worthy of a lifelong yogi. I thought again about getting better locks.

"Birdman, who left those rats in my restaurant?" I slid my phone back into my pocket.

He ignored me, then assumed the Sphinx pose, looking equally as inscrutable with his eyes half closed.

"And how did they unlock a locked door?"

I stared at Birdy and narrowed my eyes right back at him. Whoever did it must have picked the lock, which was a simple one in the doorknob itself. I'd heard a noise while I sat at my desk, hadn't I? I'd chalked it up to wind, even though a murderer was on the loose. What an idiot I was. It was past time to invest in some dead bolts. And see how much an alarm system cost. I stood again and gathered up all the stuff. If I didn't get a bike ride in, I was going to explode. Or go crazy. Or both.

I changed into my hot pink long-sleeved cycling shirt and socks, slipped off my jeans, and pulled on my black stretchy shorts, with the gel-filled padded seat that always felt a little like wearing a diaper until I mounted the bike. Then it provided exactly the cushion and protection my lady parts needed.

The pocket of my jeans rang. I hesitated a minute, listening, longing only to be out on the road, when I remembered Jim was going to call. Reluctantly, I pulled it out. Sure enough, the readout read *James Shermer*. I connected and walked back into the sun in my socks.

"Hey, how's your mom?" I asked.

"She broke her hip, but she's stable." He yawned. "Sorry, I didn't get in until about three."

"I'm glad she's okay and you arrived there alive. I was worried about you driving so far."

"I'm worse driving in the afternoon when I'm tired. When it's dark, I often get a second wind. And the coffee and sandwich helped. Thanks, Robbie."

"Any time. How's your father holding up?"

"Dad needs a lot of attention. I'm afraid he's in early Alzheimer's. I see it now I'm here. I haven't visited him in a while."

"Aw, too bad." When he didn't go on, I decided to tell him my news. "Had a little excitement here today, and not the fun kind, either." I told him about finding the droppings and getting shut down, and about the pictures. "I swear they're plastic rats, or rubber ones. Fake, anyway. I'm really steamed."

"Whoa. That's a lot to handle. I'm sorry I'm not there to help."

"What could you do? I'll talk to the inspector to-morrow. She's gotta see they're all identical."

He spoke away from the phone, then said, "I'm sorry, Robbie. I have to go. The doctor just showed up to speak with us. I wish . . ." His voice sounded wistful.

"You do what you have to do. I'll be fine. It's a stun-ning day and I'm headed out on my bike to blow off a load of steam."

"Good. Be careful, okay?"

I promised him I would and disconnected. I'd been careful cleaning up last night and look where it got me. With a cease-and-desist-to-cook order. Perfect.

Chapter 34

This was more like it. I'd headed up North Bean-blossom Road, the sun warming my back. Fresh, cool air cycled through my lungs as my legs pumped along the country road. I cut west over to Morgantown, one of the many sleepy little towns in the area, and rolled through at a slow pace. In the center of town, the senior citizens sat outside on a porch next door to Frenchy's Pub, which sat next to the Olde Vault Building Gift Shop, with a tiny single-story building squeezed in between, all three built of bumpy limestone bricks quarried in the early 1800s. Across the street was Kathy's Cafe, the hanging sign featuring a vintage Pepsi display bigger than the store's name below it. The menu proudly announced *Fresh Home-made Pies Made Daily,* and the window showed a *National Register of Historic Places* certificate.

Turning south on Route 135, I cycled past woods, cornfields, and a yellow poster inviting me to a fish fry, Saturday 11/7, sponsored by the Fruitdale Volunteer Fire Department. Plenty of cars full of leaf-peeping tourists passed me, but these were polite Hoosiers

who gave my bike and me a wide berth. I passed the
Mennonite church again, wondering if they were expecting a stranger in hot pink cycling togs, and then
spied the Bill Monroe Music Park. I'd never gotten
to one of the big bluegrass festivals the famous man-
dolinist had organized, and which were still continued every year in his memory, but I wanted to one of
these days. I'd been flat-out busy with renovations in
June when the festival happened. If I advertised in
the program next year, though, with any luck a
bunch of the business might head to my restaurant.
If I still owned a restaurant.

I glanced over at the big outdoor stage nestled next
to a wooded hill and pushed on. The harder I rode,
the less I thought about my troubles and could just
be present in this beautiful fall day. Semi present, that
is. Thinking of troubles reminded me of Roberto.
Maybe Graciela had sent an update on Roberto's
surgery after I'd set out on my ride. *Please, please let him
be all right.* I would check the second I got home.

I coasted slowly down into Nashville and locked my
bike outside the visitor center. After I used the facili-
ties, I headed for Miller's Ice Cream House. A big
creamy Double Dutch Brownie Nut cone was just the
ticket after all those miles. I licked it and meandered
through the streets. Since it was October, most of the
shops featured fall decor and Halloween decorations.
I paused in front of one store, with a grinning iconic
witch stirring a cauldron in the window and another
perched on a broom, waving. I stared, my eyes wide.
A clump of ice cream slid onto my hand and I licked
it off without tasting it.

Scampering on the shelf around the bottom of the

cauldron were plastic rats. The same rats I'd seen in Inspector's Lake's pictures. I headed through the open door.

"No food inside, please." A robust woman pointed to a sign above the door: NO FOOD OR DRINK ALLOWED, written in a curvy vintage-looking font.

"Sorry." I backed out and wolfed down the small remaining bit of ice cream, munching the cone as fast as I could. I strode back in. "Can I see those rats in the window?"

The proprietor, in a brightly colored apron with happy dancing leaves all over it, pointed to a basket near the register. "You got your rats right there."

I picked one up. The same red eyes. The tail curving the same way. "I'll take one." I reached around to the back of my shirt and grabbed my cycling wallet from the zippered pocket.

"Only one? Whole mess of cute snakes in that other basket." She pointed.

"I'll take just the one rat for now." After I paid her and took the small handled bag, I asked, "Have you sold many of these this fall?"

"A local man came in and bought up a couple dozen the other day. They're right popular this time of year."

How could I ask her without asking her? I thought furiously. "I'm supposed to bring decorations to a party, but I don't want to copy anybody else. Who was it who bought the rats?"

"Oh, it was Eddie. Ed Kowalski. You know, who runs that nice country store restaurant down the road?"

Chapter 35

I peered into the glass door of Kowalski's a few minutes later, furious, then I rattled the knob. I'd hurried back to my bike and ridden over here as soon as I left the store. But this place was closed for the day, and it seemed to be locked up tighter than bark on a tree. I banged on the door, anyway, but it didn't get me anywhere. Why was he closed on such a gorgeous day right in the middle of tourist season?

Ed had a lot of nerve, planting fake rats and real droppings in my store and then reporting it to the health inspector. That is, I assumed it was Ed. Somehow I doubted he bought those rats for a Halloween party, like I had made up in my story to the shopkeeper.

"Ed," I called. "You in there?" I knocked again. Silence was the only response. I cursed him silently, too. I clattered back down the stairs, the hard soles of the biking shoes making as much noise as a clog dancer, except with a lot less grace.

Taking the rat out of the bag, I tucked it into the little pouch under my seat, where I kept a spare inner tube, glad it fit. Now what to do with the bag? It was a nice compact paper bag with handles and the store's logo. A place like this would have a Dumpster around back. I clomped along the side of the store, skirting around a privacy fence until I reached the rear. A shed, or maybe a garage, was at the far end of the parking area. Weeds pushed up through cracks, and trash mixed with leaves hunkered in every corner. There was a Dumpster, all right, which smelled bad enough to knock a dog off a gut wagon. The odor of sour garbage turned my stomach.

As I walked, my toe hit a stone on the ground and I almost stumbled. When I looked down, the same black shapes I'd cleaned up this morning littered the ground. So Ed had real rats, and this was where he got the droppings. I threw my bag up and into the Dumpster. As I turned to go, my gaze traveled over the garage. The sliding doors sat half open, revealing a black car. *Ed's car. So he is here, after all.* Maybe he hadn't heard my knocking. *Oh, well.* I was going to let it go, at least for now. He'd deny staging the rats at my place even if I did talk to him.

After I hustled back to the front, I shivered as I straightened my bike from where I'd leaned it against a lamppost. A cloud hurried over the sun, turning the gorgeous day into a chilly fall afternoon. The sweat from my earlier ride chilled me, too. From out of the corner of my eye, I caught a movement from the store and glanced back at the door, but I saw no one.

On second thought, I figured, my ride home could wait one more minute. I leaned the bike back against the pole and pulled my phone out of the zippered pocket of my shirt; then I pressed the number for the

South Lick Police Department. I asked for Buck and waited until he came on the line.

"Heard about the rats. Too bad," he said. "I was hankering for a burger for lunch."

"They weren't real rats," I said. "I studied the pictures and they're all identical."

"You sure about that?"

"I am. Real rats wouldn't be sitting on a table with their heads all at the same angle, and their tails, too. The droppings were real, unfortunately. Listen, I'm over in Nashville, and I happened into a Halloween store."

"Glad you're getting your shoppin' done, Robbie. Listen, I'm kind of busy here."

"Wait a minute. They sold the identical rats as in the picture the health inspector sent me."

"Oh?"

Now his attention was on me again. "Yes, and the proprietor told me Ed Kowalski bought a couple dozen of them from her last week."

"Oh. Now that's pretty interesting."

"He's afraid of my competition," I ventured. "I'm sure he wants to have my restaurant shut down because my food's better than his."

"I will look into this."

"Can you tell the health inspector? Her number just goes to voice mail and says to call back during regular business hours. I'm at his store now and I saw droppings all around his Dumpster out back."

"I'll see what I can do."

"Thanks. I'm riding home now—"

"Riding what? You got a horse now?"

"No, my bicycle." *A horse? What century does this man live in?* "So I should be home in half an hour or so. I try not to answer my phone while I'm riding, in case you call."

"Got it. Ride safe, now."

I thanked him and disconnected. It was time for me to go home. With any luck, Graciela would have written to say Roberto was out of surgery and out of the woods.

Chapter 36

The magic of riding was doing its hat trick again. I'd been cycling about fifteen minutes, head down, pumping. It cleared out both the anger and the ice-cream calories. It was my own personal Zen zone, where all I was doing was this one thing. In the back of my brain, I knew I had a lot to deal with once I was home, but for now, the road was just the road. A Mary Chapin Carpenter song my mom used to play about a road being just a road came into my head and I sang into the wind, my legs going at the rhythm of the song.

I cut it off when an engine gunned behind me. I'd turned onto South Lick Road a few minutes earlier, a narrow way winding between wooded hills and marshes, with not a house in sight. Cars rarely traveled it, preferring the easier drive of Route 46. Slowing my pace, I glanced behind me. *Uh-oh.* A black sedan barreled toward me. *Ed's black sedan.* And I had a funny feeling he was after me. Where were those tourists when I needed them?

Now what? I could stop and pretend I was fixing my

tire. I could ditch the bike and run into the woods to the left, since it was all marsh on my right. I could ignore him and keep riding. I swore. If he decided to run me off the road again, like he did a week ago, was I better off as a moving target or a stationary one? The engine noise grew louder.

Right when I decided to ditch the bike and run, he roared up behind me. I instinctively veered right a second before he passed way too close. Gravel on the narrow shoulder scattered under my skidding wheels. I braked, fighting for control, and lost. The front wheel caught on a branch and stopped. The loss of momentum threw me over the handlebars. As I heard car brakes scream, I landed on my right shoulder, in a heap of legs and bike and dust. Or maybe that was me screaming.

The pain in my collarbone stabbed. As I pushed up to sitting with my good left arm, I grabbed a handful of gravel. I cradled the forearm of the one I couldn't move, keeping it close to my body. I'd seen a cycling friend break her collarbone and it wasn't pretty.

Hinges creaked, then Ed stood in front of me. He leaned down, setting his hands on his knees. "Oh, did you fall off your bike?" He faked concern, but his eyes gave him away.

"What do you think you're doing, running me down like that?" I bent my head back to see him. "The road's wide enough for both of us." The light behind him blinded me and I looked away.

"The sun was in my eyes. I didn't see you."

"Ed, the sun is that way." I pointed across the road behind him.

"What were you doing, snooping around the back of my store, anyway?" He straightened.

"I was looking for a trash can to throw something away in. What were you doing faking a rat invasion in my restaurant?" A wave of pain washed through me and I closed my eyes for a second. I could hear the car idling and the distant machine-gun rat-a-tat of a big woodpecker. When I opened my eyes again, his smug look had turned to a glare.

"Who says I did?" He squatted in front of me.

"The woman at the store in Nashville where you bought the plastic rats, for one. That was a nasty, cheap trick. You have your own restaurant and a loyal following. Why do you have to try to wreck mine?"

"Because you've been getting a little too close to the truth, that's why. Poking your nose in where it don't belong. Asking questions all over the place."

"What are you talking about?"

"I knowed it was only a matter of time before you figured out who killed that manipulative, blackmailing pig, Stella. And you're stealing my so-called loyal customers, too. Not to mention my best line cook."

Ed was the murderer. Stella had been blackmailing him, too. And I was here alone with him. I was in big trouble. I needed to make him think I hadn't suspected him. "I thought Roy killed Stella. The police do, too. After you left last night, I even found Roy in my apartment, hiding in a closet."

"That moron's too stupid to kill anybody. Unless it's by accident."

"I didn't steal your line cook, you know. Danna left of her own accord. And last night I saw why." A flash of pain as I moved a bit made me wonder if I was going to puke in front of him.

"Hey, it was just a little fun. She's too sensitive. They all are," he said.

"Why was Stella blackmailing you? Everybody knows you harass women."

He barked out a laugh. "That wasn't the goods she had on me. It was something a lot worse." He stood. He reached down and grabbed my left arm, pulling me to standing. At least he grabbed my good arm, but that removed support from the broken collarbone. As that arm fell limp to my side, another wave of pain almost knocked me out. He pulled a gun out of his waistband with his left hand.

A gun—the gun he shot Stella with. My heart had never beat so hard or so fast. My feet went numb and my gut was a block of ice. But I had to get out of this. I had a father to meet. And a business to run.

Pressing the gun against my temple, he said, "I'd rather shoot you right now." He laughed without a speck of humor.

"You don't want to do that, Ed." I gulped in as much air as my tense lungs could manage.

"I do want to, something fierce." He pressed it a little harder and his snicker was one of the scariest sounds I'd ever heard.

"You'll be in big trouble if you kill me." *Too,* I added to myself. "Lower your gun down, now." I couldn't believe it when he actually did.

"Instead of my killing you here, know what I'm going to do?"

I shook my head, terrified of the alternative, but relieved beyond belief the fatal metal no longer pressed into my skull.

"I'm going to watch you walk into that-there marsh and just keep on walking." He waved the gun toward the marsh at his left.

Oh, no, he isn't. "Don't be crazy, Ed. I'm sure we can

work this out." I was not going into the marsh. The air temperature was already dropping and I'd die of exposure, not to mention snapping turtles, leeches, and whatever else lurked in that murky weedy water. Give me a nice clean salty ocean any day.

"Nothin' to work out. You got too nosy. Now get the hell going." He let go of my arm and gave my back a push.

I managed to keep my balance and took only a single step. I turned back to face him, gauging the distance. I was only going to have one chance to get out of this mess.

"Watch out, though." He snorted as he waved the gun toward the marsh. "This here used to be a quarry way back when. And there's real quicksand in it, exactly like in all them B movies. It'd be such a crying shame if you got stuck. I don't think Lassie's alive anymore to run and get help for y—"

Ignoring my pain, in one move I threw the gravel into his eyes and kicked his kneecap with all the strength of my muscular biker's leg. He cried out and fell. I raced around the car and leapt into the open driver's side. I swore when the seat was too far back. No time to find the lever to move it. I scooched up until my foot hit the pedal and floored it. A shot shattered the back window as I drove. The driver's door waved madly, since I couldn't reach out to close it. I only possessed one usable hand, and that was clamped tight to the steering wheel.

Two more shots followed, but didn't hit me. I didn't look back. I took a sharp bend to the right, almost too fast. I had to fight the wheel for a minute, the knuckles on my left hand bleached white with the effort, but at least the momentum swung the door shut. I drove fast, another couple of minutes, just in case he decided to hop on my bike and give chase. I finally pulled to the side long enough to slide the seat up and put on my seat belt. I'd almost died just then. Meeting my end in a car crash, instead, would be really, really stupid. I took another second to pull out my phone and press 911. I put it on speaker and laid it on the seat next to me.

As I drove away, waiting for the dispatcher, I heard the rise and fall of a siren in the distance. The usually upsetting signal of an approaching emergency vehicle never sounded so good.

Chapter 37

Buck perched half his rear end on the far corner of my Emergency Department bed. Wearing a green print hospital johnny, scrub pants, and a pale blue sling, I sat propped up by the raised head of the bed and a bunch of pillows, with a couple of white blankets pulled up to my waist. I'd driven myself straight to the hospital in Bloomington, despite dispatch telling me to pull over and wait for an ambulance. I'd told them I'd get there faster on my own. And no way was I pulling over on South Lick Road, all by my lonesome. Once at the hospital, I'd tried to fight through the pain and convince the medical personnel not to cut off my expensive pink bike shirt. But when I came to, I saw it lying on a chair, the shoulder and sleeve slit open like the guts of a hog.

"Boy, howdy, I might oughta hire you," Buck said. Hire came out sounding like "har." "That was truly something—you disabling the suspect, like you did, and getting away alive."

I laughed from the slightly distant place of the

narcotically medicated. "Yeah, I'm joining the force, Buck. Not going to be able to flip many burgers like this." I frowned. That was true—how was I going to cook on Tuesday?

"Anywho, just wanted to let you know Mr. Edward Kowalski is all locked up and he's going to stay there. You don't have nothing to worry about."

"Good. Ed told me he killed Stella."

"I know. He's been charged with murder, false testimony to an officer, and a lot more." He grew somber. "We was on his trail. But it wadn't till Don come in today and confirmed your story, about Don seeing Ed driving up to Stella's right when Don was leaving on the day of the murder, that we put it all together."

I wrinkled my nose. "Was it only last night I overheard Don and Ed?" I whistled.

"Time flies when you're having fun." Buck smiled like he invented the phrase himself. "But I'll tell you, Ed wasn't having no fun when we hauled him in. He was squealing about how Stella was robbing him blind, threatening to tell the world that he mistreated his female employees if he didn't pay up. He was going on something fierce about how unfair it was and all."

"He said the same thing to me. It's true, he was all over the women who worked for him. That was why Danna left his place and came to work with me." I frowned. "I remembered what I wanted to tell you on Friday. Or one of those days. Ed told me about the pen being found. But you kept that secret, didn't you?"

"Yup. No way he'd know that unless he planted it there himself. Which I'm guessing he did. Too bad

DNA takes so darn long to process or we'd knowed it by now."

"Did Ed get far on my bike?" I had, of course, first told dispatch about Ed's attack and the approximate location.

Buck threw his head back and laughed. "You kidding me? That man was huffing and puffing. He's not one to get out and exercise much, in case you weren't aware."

"I hope my cycle's okay. You have it, right?"

"All safe and sound at the station. I wanted to leave it outside your back door, but Wanda said not to. She said it was expensive and we needed to secure it for you."

Wanda knows about bikes? Huh. Might have to explore that with her. I gazed lazily around the bay, then it hit me. *This is the same hospital Roberto was brought to,* I thought as my eyelids drifted down.

"And we got a head start on Kowalski, even before you called the second time."

Oh, right. Buck is still here. I forced myself to open my eyes again.

"Wanda saw him tear out of town, so after she checked in at the station and got the okay, she followed him." He rubbed the top of his head until his hair stood up. "One more thing you might want to know. After we took Roy for trespassing last night? He also confessed to shooting at you in the alleyway."

"Why, though?" I shifted in bed. When I got a dull stab in my shoulder for my efforts, I truly regretted the move. At least the pain was a dull one.

"He's just not all right in the head." He shook his head.

"I guess." I grimaced. "What time is it, anyway?" The room held more electronic devices than a modern kitchen, and not a one included a digital clock. With the Percocet circulating in my bloodstream, I'd happily lost track of time. But my stomach was growling; and through my haze I remembered Abe was supposed to be picking me up for dinner.

Adele walked in and announced, "Time for you to go home. Doc out there says you're cleared for takeoff."

I smiled and held out my good arm. "That's the best thing I've heard all day."

She slid past Buck and hugged my unslinged side. "Sure glad you're alive and kicking, Roberta. So to speak." She grinned.

"Our self-defense class came in handy," I said.

"I heard. So proud of you."

"Thanks. But, really, what time is it?"

Adele checked her phone. "Six-ten."

"Oh, man."

"What?"

"Can you find my phone? I left it in my shirt, but maybe they put it in that bag there." I pointed to a white plastic bag hanging from a cabinet handle. "No, wait. I don't think I have his number." I slumped, which made my shoulder hurt again.

"Whose number?" Buck asked. "Shermer's?"

"No, although I need to call him, too. Abe O'Neill's. I was supposed to go out to dinner with him tonight." At the narrowed eyes on Buck's face, I added real quick, "As friends. Just dinner, Buck."

He poked his own phone, then he extended it to me. "Want to talk to him?"

Adele shook her head. "No, she does not." She looked at me and said, "This girl's going home. You tell Abe what happened and that he's welcome to call tomorrow to see how she is."

Tears filled my eyes as I gazed at Adele. "Thank you." Going home was going to be heaven.

Chapter 38

I sat longwise on my couch the next day, with nothing to do but watch the sun play through the leaves and stroke a sleeping Birdy on my lap. I'd awoken from my own midmorning sleep a little while earlier, still propped up by pillows, since that was the only way I could get comfortable. Adele had taken superb care of me, bringing me water and food and the all-important pain pills. She'd reminded me to call Jim last night before she spent the night on this very couch, and this morning she set me up with a phone, a book, a TV clicker, and water before going off to do her chores. None of which I'd used, except the water.

Adele now bustled in, smelling of fresh air. "There," she said. "Sheep are all tended to and Samuel said he'll take the end-of-day shift so I don't have to go back again. I'm good here until the morning." She held up a plastic bag. "Found this outside the back door."

I frowned. "Is it suspicious?"

"I very much doubt that. Here's the card that was on top." She handed me a sealed greeting card, with *Robbie, Pancake Queen* written on the front.

After I ripped it open and read the message, I looked up with as much of a smile as I could muster. "Apparently, that's lunch. Abe made soup." He'd also wished me speedy healing and said he was going to demand a rain check on dinner out. *A man who could make homemade soup? Nice.*

Adele smiled. She took the bag into the kitchen.

I took a long sip from the bendy straw in the glass of ice water. "Hey, Adele?" I called.

After she popped her head back in, I said, "Can you get me my laptop? I'm so worried about Roberto. The last message I got from his daughter was that he was going into surgery for an amputation. It seems like a week ago, but I think it was yesterday. Or maybe Saturday?"

She came back in a minute with the computer. "Why don't you let me check for you? I have two hands."

I gave her the password and watched as she scrolled through my messages. My heart was a piece of cold lead. What if he hadn't survived? Or if they'd found the infection was too widespread?

"Here's one." Adele looked up. "Want I should open it?" At my nod she clicked, and then looked up with a big old grin. "Somebody named Graciela says he's recovering well. That he's going to be just fine."

I slid my eyes shut, the hot moisture under my lids matching my thick throat. I heard her snap the laptop shut and felt her hand stroke my hair.

"I'll be in the kitchen, honey. And in a couple months, I'm thinking you might be going to Italy for Christmas. You keep that in mind, now."

A tear slid onto my cheek, but I smiled. As I drifted

into sleep, I pictured wandering around the Leaning Tower of Pisa with my dad.

I awoke with a start when Adele called out, "Company." I wiped the corner of my mouth and said "Umph" as I pushed myself to sit up straighter, rubbing my tongue over fuzzy teeth.

Adele appeared a moment later, followed by Corrine and Danna. Danna carried a huge arrangement of fresh fruit. Slices of pineapple and melon cut into flower shapes stuck up on skewers, along with intact strawberries, grapes, and more—all of it arranged like flowers.

"Hope we're not bothering you," Corrine said.

"Not at all. I'm dressed. Sort of, if sweats and a robe count." I gestured to them with my good arm. As I moved to get a little more comfortable, I winced, and Adele pointed to the pill bottle on the table. Birdy leapt off my lap and streaked for the door.

"Time for another dose," Adele said.

I complied by downing two more pills with the rest of the water. Meanwhile, Danna set the fruit on the coffee table. She high-fived my good hand, then she sank to sitting cross-legged on the floor in one fluid move.

"You showed Ed," she said with a grin. "I am *so* glad that man isn't going to bother me anymore, or any other girls."

Corrine slid into the rocker, crossing her legs. It was the first time I'd ever seen her wear pants, although she wasn't exactly slumming, since they were perfectly tailored, black, and likely silk. If the woman even owned a pair of jeans, you could bet they were a designer label.

"The man's a criminal, through and through."

"Mom, you used to go shooting with him." Danna frowned. "You had no idea?"

"No." Corrine shook her head, then tossed back her hair. She picked an imaginary piece of lint off her slacks.

I laughed. "For a while I wondered if you'd bumped off Stella yourself." *Oops, that isn't very nice. Must be the drug talking.*

"Oh, it surely crossed my mind once or twice, let me tell you." Corrine laughed out loud. "People have been saying for years I killed Danna's father, too. It was an accident, pure and simple."

"Roy told me Stella was blackmailing you about it," I said.

"That pathetic man needs to have his mouth washed out with soap. Pure fabrication."

"Roy may be pathetic, but I sure hope he gets some help." I frowned again. "Danna, how am I going to manage in the restaurant with only one arm?"

She opened her mouth to speak, but Adele beat her to it. "Don't you worry about a thing, hon. Danna's got Samuel, Phil, and me, and we've all got your back. The show will go on until you're able to return to work."

"Yeah," Danna said, straightening her back. "You can sit on a raised platform and direct traffic. 'Bacon here! Biscuit there!'" she mimicked with a smile.

Another knock sounded at the back. Adele left and returned carrying a huge flower arrangement. Mostly yellow-and-red alstroemeria, it also included sprigs of white daisies, along with the ubiquitous baby's breath and ferny greens. She plucked the little card out of its holder and handed it to me.

"From Jim," I said after I read it. I didn't add that

he'd signed it: *Love from the frigid north. Your far from frigid admirer.*

"They're beautiful. Here?" Adele set them on the bookshelf across the room.

I smiled, nodding. Birdy moseyed back in, consented to a few strokes from Danna, then jumped back up on my lap. As I stroked his smooth, warm back and he chirped his satisfaction, my eyelids drifted shut. I thought it would be okay to rest for just a minute, now my world was set right again.

RECIPES

Cheesy Biscuits
(With thanks to *The Tassajara Bread Book*
for inspiration)

Ingredients:
 1 c whole wheat flour, plus extra for kneading
 1 c unbleached white flour
 1 T baking powder
 ½ t salt
 ½ c butter, cut in half-inch cubes
 2 eggs
 ½ c milk
 1 c grated pepper jack or sharp cheddar cheese

Directions:
Preheat oven to 450 degrees Fahrenheit. Mix the dry ingredients.

Cut butter into the flour mix, until mostly pea-sized pieces. Make a well in the middle and add the eggs and milk, mixing with a fork in the well. Add the cheese and stir all with a fork, until liquid and cheese are just blended with the flour. Do not overmix.

Sprinkle some flour on a flat surface and on the dough. Scrape the dough out of the bowl onto the surface, rubbing flour around the inside of the bowl until clean.

Lightly knead the dough until it comes together.

Flour a rolling pin. Roll the dough to a half-inch thickness. Fold in thirds. Roll, fold, and repeat several times.

Cut with a 2-inch biscuit cutter or drinking glass and position on a baking sheet. You don't need more than half an inch in between.

Bake for about ten minutes or until risen and golden brown on top.

Serve warm with miso or meat gravy, apple butter, or honey.

Miso Gravy

Ingredients:
    2 T miso
    2 T water
    2 T butter
    ¼ c flour
    3 c vegetable broth
    1 T tamari
    1 T nutritional yeast
    ¼ t black pepper
    1 t cornstarch, as needed

Directions:
    Combine the miso in the water and whisk until the miso is dissolved.

    In a large skillet, melt the butter over medium-low heat and whisk in the flour. Add the miso, vegetable broth, nutritional yeast, tamari, and pepper.

    Allow to cook until thickened, stirring frequently. Add the cornstarch, if needed, to make the gravy even thicker.

Whole Wheat Banana Walnut Pancakes
[Serves 4–6]

Ingredients:
  2 c whole wheat flour
  1 T baking powder
  1 t salt
  1 T brown sugar
  3 eggs
  2 c milk or buttermilk (of any fat content)
  ¼ c oil
  ½ c finely chopped walnuts
  2 bananas, thinly sliced
  Butter for cooking
  Good maple syrup
  Plain or vanilla yogurt, or sour cream

Directions:
  Preheat a wide skillet or griddle to medium.

  Mix the dry ingredients together. Beat the eggs, then add the milk and oil. Stir in the dry ingredients and beat until smooth. Fold in the walnuts and bananas.

  Melt one T butter in the pan and spread it evenly.

  Form pancakes of the size you like and cook until bubbles form and pop. Flip the cakes and cook until done. Serve with warm syrup and top with yogurt or sour cream.

Philostrate's Kahlúa Brownies

Ingredients:
  1½ c flour
  ½ t baking powder
  ½ t salt
  ⅔ c butter
  3 (1 oz. each) unsweetened chocolate squares
  3 eggs
  2 c sugar
  ¾ c Kahlúa
  1 c semisweet chocolate bits

Directions:
  Melt butter and chocolate in microwaveable dish. Pour ¼ c Kahlúa into a liqueur glass and sip. Beat eggs with sugar.

  Stir in chocolate mixture and ¼ c Kahlúa. Add dry ingredients and stir until mixed.

  Turn into greased 9 x 13 pan. Bake at 350 degrees for 30 minutes or until a toothpick comes out clean.

  While warm, brush with ¼ c Kahlúa mixed with semisweet chocolate bits. Cut when cooled.

Turn the page for an excerpt
from Maddie Day's next book,

GRILLED FOR MURDER

Coming soon!

Chapter 1

What had I been thinking, agreeing to cater a welcome-home party in my country store and restaurant tonight? I'd been working since six this morning serving up breakfast and lunch to wave after wave of hungry customers on the Saturday after Thanksgiving. I sank into a chair as the antique clock chimed. At least two o'clock was only half an hour until closing time, and just three people remained, lingering over their gourmet hamburgers. Two of them played a game of chess on the painted tabletop and the third read a newspaper, just the kind of scene I'd envisioned when I'd bought this old country store and opened Pans 'N Pancakes.

I gazed at the gleaming counters, the shelves full of antique cookware, the pickle barrel, proud that I'd accomplished most of the renovation carpentry myself. My mom had wanted to be sure her daughter would always have a trade, a trade that came in handy when I'd bought the run-down place in scenic Brown County, Indiana, last winter. Now that Turkey Day was over, I needed to get decorated for Christmas, but that could wait until tomorrow. After I got through this darn party. Oh, well. It was income, and my bank account could always use more of that.

I glanced up when the bell on the door jangled. Sue Berry bustled in with her daughter Paula, the hosts of tonight's shindig for Sue's other daughter. I waved them over to my table.

"Everything all set for tonight, hon?" Sue asked. She plopped down across from me, her short cap of bottle blond hair a little disarranged.

"I think so. Have a seat, Paula," I said to the daughter, a woman in her thirties.

"Thanks, Robbie. I think I'll stand. My back's kind of bothering me." Paula nestled her other hand in the small of her back, her pregnant belly pushing out a black knit shirt under her open coat. She wore her dark hair pulled back in a messy knot and her face was devoid of makeup, letting the high color of a woman carrying a child shine through, but also showing the dark splotches under her eyes.

"Three months to go. I sure can't wait to be a grandmother," Sue said in a bright voice, beaming up at Paula and then turning back to me. "So the cupcakes are all ordered, and Glen and Max will bring the drinks over a little early. I'm just as thrilled as punch we can do this for our dear Erica."

Sue's other daughter, Erica, had moved back to South Lick, our little town nestled in the hills of southern Indiana, a month earlier, and her parents were throwing a welcome back party for her at Pans 'N Pancakes. Erica's late husband had been my boyfriend's twin brother, so I could hardly say no. I wasn't quite sure why they'd waited a month to welcome her back, but I was happy they'd chosen me to cater it in the store.

"I'll have a veggie platter and a couple of dips out," I said. "I've made up a pasta salad and a coleslaw, as we discussed. I have the mini-sliders ready to go, and a couple dozen hand pizzas ready in the freezer. I'll pop those in the oven during the party so they can be served hot."

"What's a hand pizza?" Paula asked. "Shaped like a hand, with fingers?"

I laughed. "They're just small. Like the size of a hand. Maybe I should call them single-serving pizzas."

"It don't matter what you call them, they are going to be so yummy," Sue said. Her blue eyes sparkled behind a bit too much eye makeup.

"The mini-sliders sound interesting." Paula cocked her head. "Just like your lunch menu, but smaller, right?"

I nodded. Both women had been customers over the last month and a half since I'd opened. "Beef, turkey, and black bean. And my friend Phil is going to tend bar."

"Oh, good, so the guys can relax and enjoy themselves." Sue nodded her approval. "Hey, Robbie, you ever think about entering the log cabin competition?"

"The what? I mean, I'm a carpenter, but I have my hands full with this building."

Paula grinned. "Mom means gingerbread log cabins, right?"

Sue nodded and smiled. "It's so gol' dang cute. Everybody makes log cabins out of gingerbread and other edible stuff. They judge it over at the Brown County Inn."

"You could make a cabin of a country store and enter it," Paula said. "I bet you'd win a prize and all."

"If I have time, I'll look into it. It would be good publicity, I suppose." It did sound like fun, but when could I fit baking and decorating a log cabin into my schedule? Monday, my day off, was the only possibility.

The door jangled again and a frowning broad-shouldered man strode in. "There you are," he said, spying Paula.

Paula twisted her wedding band around and around. "Max, I told you I was going out with Mom."

"Max, honey, come meet Robbie." Sue gestured to him.

After Max approached the table, Sue said, "Robbie Jordan, this is Paula's husband, Max Holzhauser. Max, Robbie."

He extended a big, meaty hand. "Nice to meet you, Robbie." He barely got the glower off his face, which featured a jutting Neanderthal brow and heavy eye-brows now pulled together in the middle. His thick hair, tucked behind his ears, brushed his collar.

I shook his hand. "Likewise. Sit down?" What was he so mad about?

"Can't. Let's go, Paula." He took hold of Paula's upper arm. She wasn't much taller than my own five foot four. He was not only over six feet tall, he was also stocky and heavy boned.

Paula pried his hand off, twisting out of his grasp. "I'm doing errands with my mother, Max. I'll be home in time to get ready for the party." She pressed her lips together and her jaw worked.

"Have it your own way, then." He cracked his knuckles. "You always do."

One of my chess-playing customers looked up and

frowned at the disturbance. I watched Max leave, hearing the door close with more force than necessary, and glanced at Paula. Sue had taken one of her daughter's hands in both of hers and was stroking it.

"Things will work out, sugar," Sue murmured as the bell on the door continued to jangle. "He'll get a hold on that temper of his, bless his heart. You'll see."

The timer on the oven dinged just after the wall clock chimed eight. We were an hour into the party and it was in full swing. I hurried over to draw out the last pan of pizzas. I slid them onto a tray, the cheese bubbling in tan spots, the aroma of fresh crust almost too alluring. I sliced each pizza into quarters and carried them to the food table. I wiped my hands down my blue-and-white store apron, which featured our logo of a cast-iron griddle held by a grinning stack of pancakes, and surveyed the now-packed room. Late this afternoon Phil and I had pushed the tables to the sides and stacked half the chairs in a corner to leave room for mingling.

Near the banner reading "Welcome Back to South Lick, Erica!" a small group of men, including Max, Sue's husband Glen, and my green-eyed Jim, clustered with beers in hand. Paula, now made up and in a green dress that didn't try to disguise her baby bump, sat talking with Tanya Porter, an attractive local jewelry maker who owned a gift shop in town. Phil stood behind the bar table chatting with Sue. Other townspeople, some of whom I'd met, many I hadn't, chatted in small groups, with a few women browsing the shelves of cookware. Country music played from a couple of small speakers someone had set up next to an iPad, and the buzz of conversation over the tunes was loud.

The only person missing was the guest of honor, Erica. She was more than an hour late. I picked up an empty slider platter and headed back to the open kitchen area, smothering a yawn before drawing another pan of sliders out of the warmer. I'd made little rolls for buns, precooked the patties, and assembled the tiny burgers shortly before the party started. All I had to do now was serve them. Then maybe I could sit down for a few minutes.

As I set the platter of sliders on the food table, Tanya walked up to me.

"I really like all your cookware, Robbie." Her full lips curved into a smile that lit up her face, and her almond-shaped eyes crinkled at the edges.

"Thanks. I do, too. Half of it was already here when I bought the store, and I've acquired the rest."

"Don't you just love thinking about who cooked with it when it was new?" she asked, gazing at the far wall.

"Exactly."

"Do you have time for me to ask you a quick question about one piece?"

"Sure." We moved across the room together. Tanya, four or five inches taller than me, especially in heels, walked with a fluid motion, like an athlete might. Her light-brown hair fell in graceful waves below her shoulders.

She pointed with an elegant finger that ended in the perfect white tip of a French manicure. "What's that round thing with the two long handles?"

"That's a sandwich press." It featured two slightly convex cast iron disks joined by a hinge, and two long handles that extended out. "After you insert, say a cheese sandwich, between the disks, you clamp the press shut and then hold it over a gas flame or even a campfire to toast the sandwich. It makes the best grilled cheese in the world."

"And it's beautiful, too, isn't it?"

"Sure is. Browse as much as you want. The pieces for sale have tags on them."

"Thanks." She moved on down to the shelf area.

I turned back to the party and made my rounds, picking up empty dishes, tidying the food display. I paused when I passed a smiling Jim Shermer, my new boyfriend and my former real-estate lawyer. I knew he wanted more than the occasional date, but I was so busy with the store and restaurant, and he with his practice, we usually only managed Sunday nights together, since Pans 'N Pancakes was closed on Mondays.

"Everything looks great. And tastes even better," he said, smoothing an errant black curl off my forehead.

He looked more delicious than any food I could make, with those emerald eyes, curly red hair that he wore a bit long and shaggy, and his trim physique. Tonight he wore a deep blue shirt with well-cut black pants, but I could get lusty for him even when he was in an old T-shirt and ragged jeans.

"Thanks. It seems to be going pretty well, doesn't it?" I smiled back at him.

"Except that Erica isn't here." He frowned. "I wonder what's keeping her?"

"It's not a surprise party, is it? Sue never said anything about that."

"No, I don't think it's supposed to be a surprise. Oh, well. Erica has always been a bit, shall we say, dramatic." He pulled his mouth. "She probably wants to make a grand entrance."

I saw Sue glance at the phone in her hand and touch it a few times with her index finger.

"Gol' dang, she's almost here!" Sue announced with a big smile. "Get ready, y'all."

Sure enough, it wasn't two minutes later when the bell jangled and a woman who had to be Erica pushed in, shedding a puffy white thigh-length coat as she walked. She wore a snug red dress that crossed over in the front and nowhere near covered her cleavage. She was closer in height to her tiny mother than to Paula, and her spiky blond hair and light coloring were more like Sue's, too. Through the door behind her emerged Abe O'Neill, a handsome guy who worked for the local electric company whom I'd met earlier in the fall. He set a case shaped like a banjo on the floor as the talking fell to a hush.

Erica left Abe at the door and swanned over to her mother on four-inch red heels. She gave Sue a hug and then waved to the room.

"Hi, everybody," she called out. "Thanks so much for all this."

Her father, a man in his sixties whose dark hair was shot through with silver, raised his beer. "Welcome back, sweetheart."

A chorus of "welcome back" echoed throughout the room. Next to me, Jim raised his bottle of Cutter's Half Court IPA. "Welcome back, Rickie."

Erica turned her head sharply, then tilted her head in a seductive pose when she saw who had said it. She clicked on her heels over to where we stood and slid her arm through Jim's.

"Oh, Jimmy. You're the only person besides Jonny who can call me that." She pursed her lips in a pout.

"And he's gone." She stroked his arm with her other hand and cast luminous blue eyes up at him.

A shadow passed over Jim's face as he carefully detached from Erica's arm. Jon, his twin, had killed himself in Chicago a year ago. Jim had told me how hard it had been for him, and still was, to lose his twin, and to suicide, too. "I'm sorry. I wasn't thinking. I'll call you Erica from now on."

"No, I want you to call me Rickie. Please?"

Jim cleared his throat. "Have you met my girlfriend, Robbie Jordan? This is her restaurant and country store." He slung his arm along my shoulders, giving my arm a squeeze, a comforting gesture given how Erica had just been acting.

Erica narrowed her eyes and studied me before flashing a big smile. She held out her hand. "His girlfriend? Well, isn't that a surprise? I was hoping to come back here and claim Jimmy for my own."

"Nice to meet you, Erica. Welcome back." I forced a smile and glanced at Jim, who looked distinctly uncomfortable.

"Isn't this a cute place you've got here," Erica said. "It was a real dump last time I lived in town."

"Robbie did all the renovation work herself, too." Jim's smile at me was genuine.

"Imagine that. You're so talented," she said in a voice oozing insincerity.

"I'll be bringing out some hot sliders in a minute, and the pizzas over there are probably still warm, if you're hungry. Now if you'll excuse me, I'll let you two have some time to catch up." I cast a quick look at Jim before heading to the kitchen area, and if that wasn't a panicked expression on his face, I don't know what is. Well, he was a big boy. He could handle his former sister-in-law. Or not. I sure wasn't going to get in the middle.

It was nine o'clock before I finally got a chance to take off my apron and sit down near my desk in the far corner. When Sue had made the arrangements for the party, she'd also made it clear she hoped I would join them when I could, that I should consider myself part of the family and not just the caterer. So I'd worn my black swingy dress with the cap sleeves and my low black boots. A multicolored chunky necklace brightened up the dress. And even though I had to wear my thick, curly Italian hair pulled back when I was working, I'd pinned a hot pink artificial flower in it for a party touch.

A group of guys over near the door, including Abe, laughed at some joke, and several couples danced in the middle of the space. Erica flitted from group to group, a bottle of beer in her hand. By the smiles and hugs, people seemed genuinely glad to have her back in town. I let the party flow around me, glad to hold a plastic cup of white wine and get off my feet. It had been a long day, but I loved seeing the place full. Part of my dream in restoring the store and adding the restaurant had been to make it a community gathering place. Just like this.

A tune that sounded like west coast swing came on and Jim strolled up, his eyes sparkling. "May I have the pleasure of this dance?"

We'd gone dancing at a local roadhouse on our very first date, the one that unfortunately ended in news of a murder in town. We shared a love of dance, although my experience was mostly freestyle, while he knew steps to all different kinds of dances, from swing to contra to international folk dancing. He'd told me that was how he stayed fit, by going dancing every chance he got.

I grabbed one more sip of wine, then said, "Why not?"

I extended my hand and let him pull me up and lead me to where others were shaking their booties. He was a good half foot taller than me, and it felt just perfect to lay my hand on his shoulder and have him take my other hand in his. He waited until the song started a new phrase, then led me through the steps. I tried to stay loose and follow, not my strong suit, but we'd gone dancing several more times in recent weeks and I was starting to get the hang of it. He'd told me about staying in the box, about imaging a rectangle that defined our moves. It helped. Next to us, Phil twirled the woman he was dancing with, and then bent her down in a dip. He caught my eye and grinned, then straightened and waltzed away.

The music changed to a slower tune. Jim pulled me in close, and the feel of his warm, smooth shirt under my cheek, his head bent down over mine, was heavenly. But after only a minute in paradise, a woman's shouts broke the bubble. I pulled away from Jim. Erica and Tanya stood a couple of yards away facing each other.

"You're lying." Erica pointed a red lacquered finger-nail at Tanya's face. "I didn't do any such thing."

The room quieted, with only the music continuing. Glen Berry rushed to his daughter's side. "Now what's going on here?" He looked from one woman to the other, the silver at the temples of his close-shorn dark hair catching the light.

Tanya set her hands on her hips, nostrils flaring in

her golden-skinned face, earrings mixing gold and silver flashing in the light. "She's been stealing from me. She said she wanted to learn how to make jewelry. But all she wanted to do was own it."

"It's not true and you can't prove it." Erica glared at Tanya. "Why'd you come here, anyway? So you could party with a thief? Get some free food and drink?"

"I was giving you the benefit of the doubt. But that bracelet?" Tanya pointed to an intricate hoop of silver twisted with other metals on Erica's wrist. "It's missing from the store."

Erica snorted. "My late husband gave me that. I wouldn't steal your precious stock. It's not very well made, anyway."

Tanya took a step toward Erica. Glen stepped between them and pushed out both hands. "Now wait a chicken-picking minute, girls. Y'all don't need to fight about this."

"You're right," Tanya spit out. "Larceny is a matter for the police." She grabbed her bag from the table and rushed toward the door. She tore her coat from the coat tree and, with a fierce jangle of the bell, was gone at the same time as the coat tree swayed and crashed to the ground.

I looked at a frowning Jim and shook my head, then hurried to the coat tree, arriving at the same time as Abe. He set it back to standing, while I gathered up a couple of coats that had fallen. I dusted them off, one by one, and handed them to him.

"Thanks. That was quite a scene."

"I'll say. Erica has never held back from drama, that's for sure." He hung up the last coat.

"Did you bring her here?" Earlier in the fall Abe had asked me out to dinner, but with my accident and all, we'd never gotten to it. Anyway, I was seeing Jim. And it looked like maybe Abe was going out with Erica.

He laughed the delightful rolling laugh I remembered. "No way. I just happened to arrive at the same time she did. But we used to go out. Long time ago."

"How have you been lately?"

"I'm good. Keeping busy." He stuck his hands in the pockets of his jeans, which he wore with a white Oxford shirt and a gray blazer. It was a nice look, at least on him.

"Still playing banjo?" I gestured at the case, which he had set behind the coat tree.

"You bet. Might still drag it out tonight if inspiration strikes." He flashed me his big smile, that same dimple creasing his right cheek, his brown eyes smiling, too.

"I'd love to hear you play."

"Could happen. Hey, sorry we never got that dinner in. I know you're, um, hanging out with Shermer, but if an evening ever frees up, you give me a call, okay?"

"Okay. Right now I think I'd better get back to cleaning up the food table." I headed for the decimated dinner array, but paused at the drinks table.

"How's it going, Phil?" I asked. A couple of bottles of bourbon had made an appearance on the table, and neither was full, by the looks of it.

"Not bad, not bad at all." His dark face was aglow and he beamed his wide smile that always reminded me of President Obama's. "I'm keeping an eye on a couple of folks, though. Might need a little backup from the owner at some point." He raised his eyebrows and pointed his gaze toward Max.

"He's overindulging?"

"Getting a little sloppy. Ms. Berry told me to take

my job seriously, so I am." He gestured at the bottles of whiskey. "But with this stuff, we could have quite a few overindulgers."

"And Sue said it's okay to have the whiskey?"

He shrugged, and winked one of his startlingly blue eyes. "It was her husband who brought them. So I guess it is."

"Now," a man's voice said from a few tables away. I looked in that direction. Max stood in front of where Paula sat talking to a couple of women. "It's time to go." His deep voice carried to Phil and me.

Paula shook her head. "I'm having fun, Max. I'm staying."

"You need to come home with me. I'm concerned about our baby." He reached down and grabbed her wrist, pulling upward.

"Max." Now Paula raised her voice. She swatted at his hand with her free one. "Let go. It's my sister's party and I'm not leaving. The baby is fine."

Max drew his mouth down and looked like he might erupt. "Get your own ride home, then." He let go of her wrist and stalked toward the door.

Erica waylaid him halfway there. "Hey, big guy." She set one hand on her hip and laid the other hand flat on his chest. She gazed up at him, a little smile curving her lips. "You be nice to my big sister now, hear? She just wants to have a little fun before she becomes a mama."

"You, too, huh?" Max's face hardened. "Get out of my way, Erica." He lifted her hand off his chest. "I'm just thinking about her health, but I guess I'm the only one who is."

"Now, now, big Max. We all love Paulie, you know that." Erica still smiled but her voice turned as steely as my best knife. "And we love you, too. I don't want to be seeing you guys argue."

Max glared down at her. Without speaking he turned and left the store.

Whew. Erica sashayed back to the fold while I tried to remember what I'd been doing before that eruption.

"Oh, Robbie, hon," Sue called from the table where she sat, waving her hand. "Can you take and bring out them cupcakes?"

Shoot, of course. The dessert. I should never have taken off my apron.

"Coming right up," I said. I hurried to throw on a clean apron, and rushed through consolidating the rest of the food at one end of the table. I spread a clean cloth on the other half, headed for the walk-in cooler, and carried out the big box of cupcakes from the local bakery. After I opened the box and slid the foil-topped cardboard tray onto the table, I set a stack of small plates and napkins next to the dessert. The cupcakes were decorated with tiny versions of the town's landmark Jupiter gazebo, once the site of a famous sulfur spring and spa, thus the town's name. When I'd moved here, I'd found a name with the word "lick" in it slightly vulgar, but I'd learned it was like a salt lick—it just meant salts had been part of the mineral springs.

"Dessert, anyone?" I called out in my best outdoor voice. I stood back and watched people flock to the table. What was dinner without some sugar to top it off, especially when people were drinking.

Erica and Jim approached together. She picked up a cupcake and peeled back the paper with those red fingernails in four slow, seductive movements, watching Jim as she did. She took a bite, then ran her tongue around her lips. Jim glanced at me and rolled his eyes before grabbing a cupcake and turning away from her. I turned away, too. I had pans to wash.